FATAL EXPOSURE

THE CAPITOL TO LOWCOUNTRY SERIES | BOOK ONE

"She believed timing was everything in photography — until being in the right place at the wrong moment put the President's assassin squarely in her frame. Bergwerf brings insider knowledge to a story where power, attraction, and timing collide." - Mary Alice Monroe, New York Times Bestselling Author of Where the Rivers Merge

BARB BERGWERF

Published by Green Ferns Publishing House
6181 Chadderton Cir.
Myrtle Beach, South Carolina 29579

Edited by Lisa Borne Graves
Cover art and design by Mibl Art

Printed in the United States of America

FIRST EDITION
Paperback ISBN: 979-8-9996047-1-2

Fiction: Southern Fiction
Fiction: Political Thriller
Fiction:

Prologue

Now that I'm older and wiser, I think about what happened years ago when I was a young brash photographer for *The Washington Post*. Those memories still have the power to make my head spin. By chance, I was part of the two of the biggest political stories of the Twentieth Century.

The truth of these historic events, and my involvement, has never been made public.

I've been quiet.

For twenty-eight years, I've had my job, and much more, especially a wonderful relationship that brings me joy. I'm happy. But now, almost everyone else involved is gone. The few of us left may be relieved to finally have the story told.

Looking back, we did the right thing. After all these years, I am left to marvel how one decision, one minor event—missing a bus, being early, or lifting a camera and clicking at just the right moment—can change the trajectory of your whole life.

Of the country. Perhaps the world. Even destiny.

Chapter One

"Ladies and gentlemen, this is your captain speaking. Our flight today to Tehran will be four and a half hours. A bit of a tailwind may get us there ahead of schedule. Sit back, relax, and on behalf of the whole crew, thank you for flying Trans World Airlines."

For a week, I had been enjoying London with my college friend, Mary. Now, I sat staring out the window, biting my nails, and wondering how hard this assignment might be for a woman in an Arab country. I was trying to figure out how I was going to manage photographing the OPEC ministers' meeting in Tehran. *The Washington Post* had sent a team to cover the story, but the photographer, Ed Flynn, had a heart attack soon after arriving.

Many thoughts went through my head: *How was Ed doing? Would I even be admitted into the meeting hall? Should I wear a scarf?* It was 1969, *for goodness sake,* but propriety was at war with freedom—across the world. Since I was already in London, they sent me, a rookie, because I could get there on time for the meeting. *How hard could it be?* Take a few pictures of guys in Muslim thobes sitting around a table. *Simple.*

Six weeks ago, I was an intern learning my way around the photo desk at *The Post*. All I had to do was develop the rolls of film without screwing anything up and try to be accepted by the other staff of photographers. There were no females in the photo department, and being twenty-one years old, almost six-foot tall, and decked out in a mini skirt, I created quite a stir when I'd first walked into the office.

The photo staff had a lot in common; they were all middle-aged men. They had learned their craft, courtesy of the US government, while serving in the military. Nothing like slogging through the rice paddies of Vietnam. They were a tight-knit group. They did not like change and were quite a "boys only" club.

When they were done with their assignments, they dropped off their film and headed across the street to a little dive called Jimmy's. I learned quickly how to develop their film, print the negatives, and then run back and forth to Jimmy's to bond with the gritty photo staff over more than a few shared beers. But I was still a rookie, and I would have to prove to them I was capable of the position I'd been given.

And now, in about five hours, I would be expected to perform like an experienced news photographer.

Once we were on the ground, I made my way to the Hilton only to learn the hotel was fully booked. I pulled out my credentials, but it made no difference. I was not going to sleep in the Hilton that night. My only recourse was to hunt for my reporter and hope he had an idea. The hotel bar seemed like a good idea. Surely the press would be holed up there until the meeting began.

Oops, no bar in an Arab country. My next try was the hotel restaurant. *Good guess.* The hotel restaurant was filled with a bunch of

Westerners having lunch. I spotted a table where a group of men appeared to be American.

"Excuse me, I'm looking for Dave Johnson."

"Here," a skinny bald guy answered.

"Hi, I'm Kate Miller. *The Post* sent me here to shoot the meeting." I tried to sound nonchalant.

He gave me a look from head to toe. "I thought I knew the whole photo desk. How did I miss you?"

"I guess you don't spend much time in the darkroom."

Dave chuckled. "No offense, but our photo staff's average age is probably fifty. How old are you? Twenty? How long have you been on staff?"

"Twenty-one. I started a couple of months ago as a summer intern."

"Intern! How the hell did you end up here? Do not tell me this is the first assignment you've ever done."

"Actually, this is my *second* official assignment."

"Oh my God, do you have any idea what you're doing?" Dave stared at me.

"Well since Ed's flat on his back in the hospital with a heart attack, there was not enough time to get someone here from DC." I was trying to be calm, look confident, and keep my voice down. "I was in London when I called Scott Flesch, my photo editor, and he told me about Ed." I shrugged. "It's me or nothing."

"I hope you brought your Kodak Instamatic with you?" he scoffed.

"No, Dave, no Instamatic, but I did bring my Nikon." It was my turn to scoff. I had been dismissed because I was young and female.

Dave offered a small apologetic smile. "We'll get through this. Sorry about being so hard on you, Kate. I've got my hands full. Sit down. Have you had any lunch?" He scooted his chair over to make room for me.

"I had lunch on the plane, but listen, there is a problem. I can't get a room in the hotel."

"Did you tell them you were with *The Post*?" he asked.

"Yes, but they wouldn't budge."

"Not a problem. I've got the key to Ed's room. He's gonna be in the hospital for at least another day, and then he's flying directly back to Washington." He reached into his pants pocket and pulled out two hotel keys.

"Hey Dave," one of the other guys at the table shouted just loud enough for the entire room to look my way. "What's your wife going to think, bringing this pretty young thing on a business trip?"

I delivered an icy stare.

"Guys, meet Kate Miller. She's with *The Post*. Here to pinch hit for Ed Flynn." He turned to me. "You better go down to the ballroom and get your credentials for the meeting. Your Post press pass won't get you in the room."

Adrenalin shot through the jet lag. "Okay, thanks for letting me know."

The thought of me being turned away at the door for my first big assignment sent me scurrying.

At the entrance to the Grand Ballroom, I was promptly stopped and sent to security. *Here we go.* I knocked on the door of a room to the right of the concierge desk.

"It's open," a male voice shouted from the other side of the door.

I was met by a short man with a full beard, wearing Arab attire.

"Hi, is this where I pick up my press credentials?"

"Yes, this would be the place," he said in heavily accented English. "But you are too late. You should have picked up your boss's tags yesterday."

My boss's tags? Of course, that was what they always assumed. I was fuming on the inside. *Two could play that sexist card.*

I delivered what I hoped was a charming smile. "I am the photographer. I just flew in from London and didn't know I was going to cover this meeting until today."

"I do not really care where you have flown in from. You are too late. Also, your newspaper should have known that there are no women in this meeting."

"I have press credentials from *The Washington Post,* and I expect to be treated as a professional," I said, hoping he didn't see my knees knocking together.

"I *am* treating you as a professional. You are a day late. We will not establish any more passes for tonight's opening meeting. Period ... end of discussion." He stood up with both hands leaning on the table.

"If that's your final word on this matter, I'll have my publisher get in touch with your superior." I barked and stormed out of the room.

I stomped across the lobby and pounded on the elevator button. I was failing at my first solo job. And to make matters worse, it was because I was a woman. Tears threatened when the elevator arrived, but they would not make me cry.

I made it back in Ed's room where I started swearing a blue streak. When I calmed down, I sat on the end of the bed, trying to come up with a game plan. I wasn't going to give in this easily. I noticed Ed's camera bag next to mine on the floor. Desperate, I looked through it. My breath caught. Inside were his press credentials tucked inside his passport. A smile slid across my face as I took them out.

The press pass was a large, laminated tag clipped to an elastic lanyard. It was worn around the neck and flipped up whenever an ID was needed. Luckily, this one didn't have Ed's picture on it, but it did have his name typed in one-inch letters. Changing the name on the pass was impossible, since it was laminated. I looked at the clock; I had less than an hour before the meeting started.

Then an idea came to me. I checked his passport. Ed was five feet, eleven inches tall. Close enough to my height. He was heavier, but that wouldn't be much of a problem if I could find a belt. I hurried to his luggage. Hunting through his clothes, I turned up a pair of deep brown gabardine pants and a cardigan sweater. Drab clothing, nothing trendy—*no surprise there. All of Ed's shopping started and ended at the doors of Sears.* I had a white oxford cloth shirt. *So far so good.* I was sort of flat-chested, which was a bonus in this situation. But my sling back Pappagallos shoes wouldn't work. Luckily, Ed had a pair of brown-laced shoes that were size nines—*again, close enough.* Adding a camera or two, my camera case would hide any feminine curves.

Mascara and eyeliner were another matter. I scrubbed my face, but my hair was still a problem. It was short, but the style was too girly. I checked Ed's dop kit and found Brylcream. Thinking of the ad "A little dab will do ya," I decided that a *big* dab would do me.

It could work. I checked my image in the mirror. I needed a bit more camouflage. I fished Ed's spare glasses out and tried them on. They were readers, so I could make them work. Ed, like most of his generation, almost always wore a hat. That was the final addition to the outfit. Donning all of my equipment, I stood in front of the full-length mirror. *Not bad.*

I had no choice but to muster up my courage and get the show on the road. Besides, photographers were never noticed. They stand around for long periods of boredom, punctuated by a few minutes of frenzy.

I put everything back in place and set my luggage neatly by the door. I shoved the key in my hip pocket and headed downstairs. I was ready, as ready as I could be … dressed up as a fifty year old man. God only knows what they would do to me if I got caught.

One step at a time though. Once I made contact with Dave, at least he would be able to come to my aid before they dragged me out of the room. That thought sent shivers through my whole body.

When the elevator door opened to the lobby, I was in a sea of white-robed men with a few "Gucci" types mixed in. Stationed at the open double doors to the Grand Ballroom were four huge guys looking suspiciously like bouncers. Two of them were watching the crowd in general, and the other two were checking passes as a group of Western press waited together.

No one paid me any notice as I joined the group. The security guy waved all of us in, and I quickly disappeared into the crowd. I had been holding my breath the whole time, so I took a couple of deep breaths to hopefully bring some color back to my face.

The room itself was quite grand. A dark-burgundy carpet with a scrolled gold and navy border covered part of the marble floor. The walls were a rich, silk pattern, mostly a medium burgundy. Hanging from the ceiling were four enormous crystal chandeliers, each one probably costing ten years of an average person's annual salary. TV cameras were set up, but this meeting was not going to be sent out live. TV coverage would be completely controlled by our host, the Shah.

I spotted Dave talking to two men who were too well dressed to be with the press. He finished his interview, slipping his notebook into his coat pocket.

"Hi Dave," I said in a muffled voice.

He did a double take, and when he realized it was me, his face went pale.

"Oh my God," he muttered. "What in the name of heaven are you trying to do?"

"Shh, keep your voice down please. They wouldn't give me press credentials, and I couldn't think of anything else."

"Couldn't think of anything else to do! Are you out of your mind?"

"Relax. So far, so good. I got through the doors. No one is going to be looking at me once this thing starts."

"When you get arrested, do me a favor. Don't tell them I know you. I really do not want to spend any time in the jails here."

"Thanks for the vote of confidence," I said, giving him a dirty look. "What do you need me to shoot?"

"Once you get your shots, get out of here. Get what you need and then disappear. Got it?" he said, getting more steamed every second.

"Okay, but you still haven't told me who to shoot." Now, I was getting annoyed.

"Get head shots of each oil minister. I'm not sure of their exact names, so start at the top of the table and work your way around," he said, pointing toward the table across the room. "Once you get all of those individual guys, get an overall shot of the whole table. Something dramatic that could be used five columns wide. If they make any big decisions, this will run on the front of the business section on Sunday," he added.

"Okay, I think I can handle it."

"Don't mess around. Just get the shots, and then get the hell out of here."

The meeting started, and I did my best working around the room. I was right about the photographers not being noticed. Everyone was too busy to care about what was going on around them. The guy who made the comment at the lunch table gave me a strange look, but I stared through him.

After about a half-hour, I had what I needed. Dave was staring a hole through me and jerking his head in the direction of the door. I nodded and left the room. I was strolling down the hall when the door to my left banged open. One of the "Gucci" types stormed out. Not more than ten steps behind him was one of the oil ministers that I had just photographed. I didn't know his name, but I knew he was important. Everyone in the hall had turned to look at him when he'd entered the room.

I followed them, not knowing what to expect, but it had to be more interesting than what I had just photographed. They took a left and hustled through glass double doors out onto a veranda. They were arguing. Instincts flared. Something was going on. I quietly pushed the doors open and ducked behind a pillar, close enough to see and hear. Except they weren't speaking English.

I didn't know what was going on but, on instinct, raised my camera to shoot a couple of frames. The men were really having at it. The oil minister was shouting and poking the "Gucci" guy in the chest.

I depressed the shutter just as the "Gucci" guy pulled a knife from his waistband. He flicked open the blade and shoved it in under the oil minister's sternum, twisting the blade toward his heart. The minister went down like a rock.

It happened so fast. I was stunned. My feet felt like they were stuck in concrete. My Nikon's motor drive kept taking pictures. But the motor drive is noisy. I had banged off at least ten shots when the guy with the knife turned and looked my way.

My heart stopped. I had better get the hell out of there.

I raced back through the double glass doors, not sure where to go once inside. If I went back into the meeting, I might get trapped.

I slowed to a fast walk while I rewound my film, removed it from my cameras, and shoved the cassettes into a pocket.

The lobby was almost empty. Everyone was still in the Grand Ballroom discussing how the Arabs were going to stick it to the West over the next few months.

There were mirrors on either side of the elevator doors, so I could see if I was being followed. "Gucci" guy came through the lobby in a hurry. As the elevator doors slid open, I jumped in before the people in the car could get out. They were annoyed by the pushy foreigner, but I ignored their looks and made it to the back of the car.

When the doors slid open on my floor, I peeked out to check the hallway. I jogged to my room, slammed the door behind me, double locked it, and leaned against it with my eye plastered to the peephole, my heart pounding. There was no one in the hall.

With a rugged sigh, I dumped my stuff on the bed. *What the hell had I gotten myself into?* My hands were shaking. I needed to calm down and figure out what to do next. *Dave.* I had to try to get in touch with him.

The phone rang. I nearly jumped a foot in the air. Staring at the phone, I paused with my hand hovering over the receiver. It had to be Dave, but I couldn't take the chance. I let it ring as I stripped off Ed's clothes and washed the Brylcreem out of my hair. I searched my suitcase looking for something a photographer wouldn't be caught dead in.

I pulled out a pastel floral-patterned Diane von Furstenberg wrap dress and swapped the everyday bra for a push-up underwire. I donned a pair of dark mesh pantyhose, my sling-back Pappagallos, and reapplied my cosmetics. When I was done, I looked like I was ready for a hot date.

My only goal was getting my film back to *The Post*. I knew what I had was news. *No*, what I had was an exclusive that could end up on the front page of newspapers all over the world.

Chapter Two

"Dave, I've got to talk with you."

He turned to look at me, and his face revealed his shock at my changed appearance. "I like this outfit a lot better than your last one."

"Dave ..."

"Did you hear what happened?" he interrupted. "The Saudi oil minister was murdered right outside the hotel. No one has a clue what happened, and they're not telling us anything."

"Dave, shut up for a minute." I muttered through clenched teeth.

"No need to get huffy." He gave me a blank look.

"I saw the whole thing happen."

Dave's gaze sharpened. "What are you talking about?"

"I saw the *killing*." I blurted out, looking around to see if anyone overheard our conversation. I broke out in a cold sweat.

"What?" Dave turned pale. He scanned the room thinking the same thing.

"Let's get out of here." He took me by the arm and maneuvered me out into the lobby.

"There are a million security types all over this place," I said.

"The guy who killed him must be long gone," Dave added.

I leaned closer to his ear. "Actually, the guy who killed him is standing right there," I said nodding toward the "Gucci" guy.

"Shit," Dave said, turning away from the killer. There was a crush of people trying to get to their rooms, so Dave led me to the front door of the hotel. Security at the door was checking everyone trying to leave, so we smiled as they stopped us to ask the "who, what, and where" questions. Since we didn't have any luggage, Dave assured them that he was in the meeting, while I was *resting* in his room. He even gave them a little wink. They let us pass.

Once we were outside and out of earshot, he pulled me aside. We found an isolated spot tucked behind a hedge.

"Start at the beginning," Dave said, sitting me down on a bench.

I told him the short version of what I had seen.

"Did you get the actual murder on film?" he asked, incredulous.

"Yes. At least, I think I did. Dave, as far as I know, I've got ten shots of two guys arguing and one guy ending up dead in a pool of blood."

"Where is the film?" Dave looked around as he asked.

I patted my chest. "It's in a safe place. Which is more than I can say for us. What are we going to do?" I asked.

We could have gone directly to the U.S. Embassy, but the photos would have been confiscated. We both wanted to get the pictures out of Tehran. We could deal with the authorities once we were safely back in the States. Thoughts darted between our gazes without words before we verbally agreed to a plan.

Dave hailed a cab, and we slid in. "To the airport," he said to the driver. Then he turned to me and said, "Do you have your passport and everything else you'll need?"

I nodded, feeling better once the cab was moving. "I have got everything. Well, maybe I should have more money. I have my ticket and about $200 tops." He was all business. His voice was low and terse. He fished $200 out of his wallet and handed it to me. "Once we get to the airport, we need to get you on *any* plane going west."

Chapter Three

I fell asleep before the plane's wheels were off the tarmac. The next thing I knew, the plane was coming in along the Potomac River. It banked left and dropped down to land at Washington National. I was off and out of the airport in a flash. I was so damn happy to be back in Washington. At first, I couldn't find my car, but when I realized I'd landed at a different terminal, I was off and running. I finally spotted my blue Mustang and breathed a sigh of relief.

My luck held, and I arrived at *The Washington Post* in good time. I gave everyone a smile and met the usual disgruntled greetings.

Scott looked up with a huge smile on his face as I made my way over to his desk.

"Hi, great to see you." He jumped up to give me a big hug.

I stood there with my arms pinned to my sides, waiting for him to let me go. That got everyone's attention. Hugs were not the normal greeting for our gritty bunch.

"Boy, it is great to see you, too," I answered wryly. There was so much riding on the next couple of hours. I was confident in what I had shot, but at the same time, scared that something might go wrong when developing the film.

"Art Williams, the business editor, wanted to know the minute you walked in. I'll ring his secretary and tell him you're here." Scott grabbed his phone and turned back to me. "You'd better get started with the film. The sooner we see what you've got, the better," he added.

I nodded and took the film out of my bag. My mouth went dry. I had to concentrate on the job at hand, so I pushed my way through the darkroom revolving door.

Stan was working on a couple of his prints and looked up from the enlarger.

"Heh! Kiddo, how are you doing? Did you get everything you needed?"

I swallowed. "I hope so. I'm a bit nervous." I gave him a pained smile.

"Wait, and let Scott run the film for you. Then, if something happens, it will be on his head," Stan said with a laugh.

"No. I'll do it, no problem." I blew out a stream of air. If I screwed this up, my life as a photographer would be over before it got started. I had loaded film spools for developing a hundred times. Most of it I had done for the other photographers on staff, so I was used to some pressure. But this film would be the most important photos I would ever take, at least I hoped. It had been stressful but also a real adrenalin rush. What's the old saying ... "A picture is worth a thousand words" that can change the world.

My hands were wet with a nervous cold sweat. I dried them and tried to calm down before starting the developing process. I told myself it would just be another photo. That was all.

Outside the darkroom, Scott was at his desk talking to a distinguished looking man.

"The negs look good. The images are sharp." I smiled at the other guy in greeting. Seeing the images on film brought back the horrible scene of seeing a human being slumped to the ground with his blood covering his clothing. I was in over my head, and I didn't have time to think. I reacted. The fight or flight response kicked in. The fight part was over for me. The flight part set in. I was running for my life.

"This is Art Williams. He's anxious to see what you have got." Scott motioned to Art.

"What do the negatives look like?" he asked. "How long will it take to get prints?"

A calm came over me. I knew I had the images and short of the darkroom blowing up, I was okay. "The film is drying now. Everything looks good, the images are sharp and the exposure is spot on." I replied in a professional tone. "I should be able to print some of them in about ten minutes."

"The paper has already run with the story put out by the Shah," Mr. Williams said, using his fingers to make quotation marks. "Let's see if your shots give us something else to run with."

Scott and Art followed me into the darkroom. I retrieved the negatives from the drying cabinet and took a quick look as I handed them to Scott. He held the strip of negatives to the light. He looked at me and then back at the strip of negatives. "You've hit a home run here. You kept your cool and got the job done. No one on the staff could have done better. Kate, these are going to rock the news cycle for the next few days!"

I tried to keep my cool, but I couldn't help but smile. "Thanks Scott. I really appreciate the opportunity I've been given."

"You'll need to print the whole sequence, but for now, hit the high spots." Scott gave me a pat on the shoulder. "Nice job, I'm proud of you."

Chapter Four

The top floor of *The Washington Post*. I'd never met anyone who went to the top floor. The room was formal with dark wood paneling and framed front pages of *The Post* lining the walls. The history of the 20th century was represented there.

As I looked at each one, it hit me that no matter how impressive the banner headlines were, it was the photos that were imprinted in your memory. I wanted to be a part of all that.

The USS Arizona billowing smoke in Pearl Harbor. Lyndon Johnson being sworn in as President, while a solemn Jackie Kennedy looked on. A Black musician, with tears running down his face in Warm Springs, Georgia, when FDR died. So much history is remembered through photographs.

School children fifty years from now might be studying Pearl Harbor or the Kennedy assassination. The pages and pages written about the subject would be there, but I'm guessing it will be the photos that will capture their imagination. Being a part of that would be a dream come true.

"Excuse me, may I help you?" a tall, efficient-looking secretary asked. I had the feeling she had been trying to get my attention for some time.

"This is a wonderful room," I said.

"Well, thank you. I'm sure that Mrs. Graham will be happy to hear that," she said perfunctorily. "Are you here for the meeting?"

I nodded, looking around for a friendly face. I spotted Scott sticking his head out of the conference room. My photos were going to be the talk of the town and my future, hopefully. It was a done deal. I'd come a long way from delivering the other guys' photos to the copy desk. Here, I was at a table with the real power brokers in this town.

I recognized some of the people in the room. A few were from the newsroom and were easy to pick out with no suit coats and rolled up sleeves. The rest of the men wore suits and were most likely attorneys.

"We're waiting for upper management," Scott said. "I guess they aren't sure which way to go with this." He leaned over me to whisper.

Scott and I both looked up at the door in time to see a very distinguished woman and two executive types swoop into the room. Mrs. Graham, the legendary owner of *The Post*, had a timeless elegance and knew the effect she had on everyone around her. She took the chair at the head of the table.

"Good afternoon, ladies and gentlemen," she said, looking straight at me. "It seems you have some interesting pictures for us. Miss Miller, is it?"

"Yes ma'am. Kate Miller." I smiled.

"Kate," she said, making a point of saying my name. "We're glad you are safely back. I'm not sure any of us know the whole story, so perhaps you should start at the beginning."

I looked around the table. Everyone in the room had to be at least twice my age. Any cockiness that I might have possessed with the photo staff downstairs vanished. I was twenty-one years old, just out of college, and a mere intern standing in front of some of the most influential people in Washington. To make matters even worse, they were all waiting for me. I took a breath and began to speak.

When I finished the whole story, you could have heard a pin drop. It's not often you see that many people with white knuckles and their mouths hanging open.

"Kate, you certainly had an interesting time for yourself," Mrs. Graham said. "Perhaps you should share your pictures with us." She pointed at the envelope I was holding.

I rose and walked to where Mrs. Graham was seated. Without a word, I opened the folder, took the photos out, and spread them in front of her. Everyone gathered closer for a better look. I heard the gist of their comments from "Oh shit" to "Great shot." The photos made a huge impression.

When everyone returned to their seats, Mrs. Graham placed both hands on the table.

"This must run on the front page of the Sunday paper. Talk over any problems. I'll be calling the State Department to tell them what we have and try to explain how we got here." She rose, then added, "You have some decisions to make. I'll leave you to them." Everyone watched her leave in silence, then went back to looking at my photos. They were all talking at once until one of the senior men took over the meeting. Scott leaned over to whisper, "That's Ben Bradlee, Managing Editor of *The Post*."

"Well Miss Miller," Bradlee said. "I think we have our hands full for the time being. Why don't you go back to your office, and we'll let you know what's ahead for you. Scott, make sure Kate is taken care of. She will need to be put on staff full-time."

My heart skipped a beat, and I almost started to cry. Scott nodded and gave me a smile. I wanted to run up and plant a big kiss on everyone in the room, but instead politely thanked the boss and turned to leave. Once the elevator doors closed, I jumped up and down and yelled "*Yes*," over and over.

Everyone already seemed to know the basics and were all applauding as I stood in the open doorway and bowed at the waist, exaggerating every movement. I wanted this moment to last as long as possible. In between the cheers and catcalls, there were lots of shouted questions. I held my hands over my head to quiet the crowd and began to laugh.

"Thank you. Thank you very much," I beamed.

I was now a full-time employee of *The Washington Post*.

Scott was right behind me. He pointed to the chair next to his desk and we both sat down. "Kate, they're trying to figure out how to handle your photos. There are all sorts of legal problems that might pop up once they're printed. You were a witness to a murder. Add to that, who committed the murder, and it is a real problem. The last thing that we want is to have you dragged back to Tehran."

"Tehran! There is no way I'm going back there," I sputtered.

"Relax. Let's not put the cart before the horse. What they are thinking of doing is printing the picture without a photo credit and then hiding behind the cannot reveal our sources' line. Once the picture is printed the heat should be on the Shah and the killer." I sat there speechless, staring at Scott. You could work a lifetime and not come up with this kind of success.

"Are you telling me I've got *the shot* of 1969, and I'm not going to get credit for it?" I asked, trying to stay calm.

"Kate, you have got to understand, they are trying to shield you. If the photos have your name under them, we can't hide behind not revealing our source. They could try to get you to testify about what you saw. The paper has no real way to protect you. No matter how this went down, the Shah is still in a bucket of shit. After all, it was probably one of his relatives who did the dirty deed. They may go out of their way to discredit you. I can't tell you what to do, but if I were in your spot, I'd be thrilled to have *The Post* backing me."

Chapter Five

The Washington Post ran six of my photos. The best and most graphic were on the front page and five columns wide, which meant the entire width of the page. Dave wrote the story, at least as much as we knew.

To say they caused a stir was an understatement. Almost every newspaper in the world carried my photos over the next couple of days. *The Post* kept their promise and protected me completely. A few days after the pictures were printed, "Mr. Gucci" was arrested and following that, not a word had been heard since. The Shah didn't have to answer to anyone, and the West wasn't really interested in more than the price of gasoline. Since there was no trial, they didn't really care about who took the pictures.

The Post ended up winning a Pulitzer Prize for the photos. Mrs. Graham called me into her office and gave me a pep talk about my future. I had an opportunity that no other woman had ever had, and I better not screw it up. Well, those weren't her exact words, but they got the point across.

I settled in as a photographer at *The Post.*

I had a daily routine. I had to be at the office at noon, and I finished at 8:00 p.m. I was the low '*man*' on the totem pole. I didn't have to run errands or make coffee, but I did my share of cleaning up the darkroom and even developing film if the staff was running late.

My fellow photographers seemed to accept me—well, sort of. We all worked independently, so the only person I would see daily was Scott. The fact that I had actually gotten the shots in Tehran gave me some bragging rights which I never used. As Stan, one of the old-timers on the staff said, "Let your pictures do the talking."

My life changed drastically. Now that I had a steady job, I could afford a real apartment. Mary was back from London and thrilled to be able to help me organize a place to live. I glossed over how I had ended up being put on staff, and she didn't ask. She was always the organized one in school. *Hell, she even kept a list of the stains on her laundry.* It took her less than a day to put together a list of possible rentals. I had been sharing a townhouse in Georgetown, and the area was perfect for me. Close to friends and close to work. The place we agreed on was a hundred-year-old three story house that had been divided into apartments. It was short on space but long on appeal, since it was in Georgetown, one of the oldest neighborhoods in Washington. The Georgetown streets were narrow, tree lined, and the houses mostly red brick. Aside from the charm, I liked it because there was a cross section of people. Your neighbors could be college students, Senators, or anyone in between.

Being the first female photographer for *The Post* had its difficulties though. I wanted to be one of the guys and did enough drinking at Jimmy's to qualify. The challenge was the editorial desk. They were delighted to be able to send a "respectable" young woman out on important assignments, rather than any of the old-timers. There was nothing that I could do but hope for something more interesting than Daughters of the American Revolution tea parties. I was a star when I began at *The Post*, but that wore thin very quickly. You are only as good as your last photo.

Weeks turned into months, and every job except for sports was either on the Hill or at the White House. I never dreamed I would be on a first name basis with the President's Press Secretary.

Then on one very slow Tuesday morning, while I was sitting in the darkroom with my feet up, Scott came through the door.

"Kate, I've been looking for you."

I groaned. "The Redskins' game went into overtime, and I didn't get out of here until after midnight. What do you need?"

"I need you to cover a meeting on the Hill."

I grimaced.

"Don't make faces at me. Someone has to do it, and you're on deck." Scott added.

"Okay." I said, reaching for the photo assignment sheet. "You have got to be kidding. A Congressional Wives Luncheon? What exactly is newsworthy about this crap?"

"Kate, our job is not to reason why." He gave me a huge grin and escaped to the darkroom before I could protest.

Stan was working on some prints and looked up from his enlarger. "At least you got to cover the Skins last night. Hey kid, not every job is chicken a la king. In fact, most are chicken-shit."

The luncheon was in the large reception area of the Vice President's ceremonial office, just off the floor of the Senate. My job was to snap "Mrs. Congressman" receiving her plaque, or whatever they were going to give her. I found a spot against the wall and tried to blend in with the wallpaper. I noticed someone moving in to stand next to me. I was prepared to make some smart remark, but my words caught in my throat. The man was tall. Cute. *Very* cute.

Blue eyes, sandy-brown curly hair that seemed to have a mind of its own, he had a body that filled out his preppy clothes enough to be interesting. His clothing marked him as a Southerner—khaki trousers, penny loafers, powder blue shirt, and a navy blazer.

"Hi." His smile lit up his face. "What kind of camera do you use?"

"A Nikon. Do you take photos?" I wanted to reach up and brush the lock of hair from his eye.

"When I get a chance. I used to do a lot of photography when I was in college," he laughed, "but that was quite a while ago."

I wondered how long ago that was. *Was he even thirty?* His boyish features made it hard to pin down an age.

"I'm Jim Rayford. I work here. What's your name?" he added, offering me his hand. His accent dripped with Southern charm.

"Kate Miller. I'm with *The Post*," I offered a half smile trying to look cool while his hand was still holding mine. I sneaked a look at his left hand and saw no ring.

"Pleased to make your acquaintance, Miss Miller." I studied Mr. Rayford out of the corner of my eyes. I guessed that he was an aide to one of the congressmen, or maybe to the Vice President. He fit right in with this political crowd. It was also my job to study faces, and his expression revealed he would rather be any place but here.

He narrowed his eyes in scrutiny. "Wait. *You're* a photographer with *The Post*?"

"Yep."

"I didn't think they had female photographers."

"They do now. I'm the first."

The glimmer in his eyes revealed he was impressed.

I shrugged as I indicated my camera. "My boss ordered me here. What's your excuse?" I whispered, covering my mouth with my hand.

"Me too!" he laughed. The ladies nearest to us turned to give him a dirty look at the interruption.

"Are you important or just so charming that those ladies can't resist you?" I whispered.

"I'm definitely not important, but I'd like to think I'm a bit charming." He *was* so charming that I almost giggled like a schoolgirl.

I was also a rookie in the dating department. The guys in college were eager to make conquests. I didn't care about the games they played. A friend at school told me that when I found the love of my life, I'd know it by just talking to him. And for the first time, glancing at Jim, I wondered if that were true.

The Vice President had called one lady forward to receive her award. Duty called. I hustled forward to get my shot. If their picture wasn't in the paper, the whole thing was a failure. I took a few more just to be sure. I nodded to the Vice President indicating I got the photo, then said thanks as I backed away from the podium. Turning to make my escape from the room, I looked over at the wall where my "Southern hunk" had been standing. He was gone.

"Shit!" I muttered under my breath. Two women gave me a dirty look. I gave them a small smile, grabbed my gear, and hustled out of the room into the hall. To my surprise, Jim Rayford was holding the elevator door for me.

"Can I offer you a lift? No pun intended," he asked.

"How can I refuse?" The operator immediately asked what floor we wanted.

"Can I buy you a cup of coffee or something?" he asked.

I was touched that he seemed shy. "I don't drink coffee, but a beer would sure hit the spot."

His eyes sparked with appreciation. "Great. There's a little dive a block from here. Okay with you?" He asked, but didn't wait for an answer.

As we walked out of the Capitol, he offered to carry my camera bag. *There's that Southern charm again.*

"Christ, this is heavy," he blurted out. "How do you manage this for an entire day?"

"Oh, you get used to it. I love all of my equipment and my job, so I never even think about it."

"How long have you been with *The Post?*"

"A little less than a year. I started out as an intern, but ..." I paused, not able to go into the Middle Eastern event. "Everything fell into place, and they put me on full time."

"You must be good. You're the first female photographer I've ever had the pleasure to meet. Especially for *The Post.*"

I looked into his "baby blues" and smiled back. Inside I was turning to Jell-O. We walked around the back of the Library of Congress and to the little dive he had promised.

"So, do you come here often?" I asked.

"A little run down for your taste?" he teased.

"Nope. It's just my kind of place."

"I'm not that much of a drinker, but I have come over here for a quick lunch and to talk with a colleague. Too many interested ears in the Capitol dining rooms."

The place was dark. It was the kind of joint that had no atmosphere, and if the lights had been bright, you probably wouldn't want to sit down much less eat anything.

"So how long have you been working in DC?" I asked, sliding into a corner booth.

"Six years."

"Ah, the term of a Senator," I joked.

"Close. I'm in the House of Representatives. South Carolina."

I took a moment to digest that. I *had* thought he was some sort of aide.

Seeing my surprise, he asked. "Is that a problem?"

I shook my head.

"Too good looking?" he teased with an adorable grin.

"No. Too young looking," I fired back.

Jim set my heavy bag on the bench, then slid in the booth across from me.

"But that's all a bit boring." He set his forearms on the table, and I felt the power of his gaze. "Did you always want to be a journalist?"

I was caught off guard by his intense interest in me. The men I ended up with were younger, self-centered, and interested in their own egos while making a conquest.

"No," I replied, intrigued and willing to go to the next step of divulging personal information. "I came to DC to study government and international affairs. The photography thing sort of came out of nowhere." I smiled at the memory. "Like being struck by lightning. I bought a camera and never looked back." I looked at my hands, empty now without a camera. "The problem for me was how to go from a shiny new degree in government to a job at a newspaper. This was the first time I thought about how important connections were, especially in Washington."

"That's true," he said with a self-deprecating laugh.

"The father of one of my sorority sisters was the city editor at *The Post*. It was sort of standard procedure for anyone staying in DC for the summer to work there. Instead of running errands, making coffee, and the typical intern stuff, I headed for the darkroom. For the first week I did what photographers do—observe. I saw that the photo staff went to a bar across the street from the paper called Jimmy's while their film was being processed. They'd come back from an assignment, usually late for their deadline, and toss their film at the lab guys. I quickly became an unofficial lab guy and learned all the darkroom procedures."

"That's pretty gutsy."

I shrugged. *It was.* "I admit that at first, I was a nervous wreck trying to load the film onto a spool. The first few times I tried, I was ringing wet by the time the film was safely in the developing can. But after a few times, it becomes automatic." I looked up at Jim. "Any kid can develop film. The problem is that I was a woman."

Jim was smiling at me.

"I'm talking too much, aren't I?"

"No, not at all. Going from a summer intern to being on staff seems like a huge jump."

"Right," I said, hesitating at how much to divulge. "It's a long way from delivering photos to the copy desk and actually taking photos for a newspaper. Almost every day, I would ask one of the photographers if I could tag along. The answer was always the same. They would just laugh!" I looked up to seeing Jim laugh at this as well.

"Every journey starts with a single step." He said, raising an index finger.

I smiled and nodded in agreement. "One day, the Metro editor was looking for someone to shoot a 'Super Girl Scout'. I answered the phone and was trying not to chuckle as I promised to send whoever was on deck. Stan Wallach was in line for the next assignment.

Stan is the kind of guy who only wants to shoot urban disasters. The more carnage and mayhem the better. I could not wait to tell him he was off to Virginia in the middle of rush hour to take a picture of a Girl Scout."

Jim chuckled, and his eyes sparkled in anticipation of the story.

I was pleased to see his interest and added relish to the story. "Stan had been in Jimmy's for a couple of hours. I delivered the news in a serious voice. All the other guys were just about falling off their stools, laughing. The thought of Stan having to take directions from some little old den mother was hysterical. I thought the entire staff was going to follow him to Virginia." I paused to see Jim slumped back in the booth with his arms folded across chest, chuckling.

"What happened?" Jim asked.

"Well, Stan chomped down on his cigar, grabbed me by the elbow, and pronounced me his assistant photographer. To make a long story short, it took us forever to find that scout. When we finally did, Stan didn't even get out of the car. He shoved a camera in my hand and told me to 'knock'm dead kid.'"

"And you did?"

I shrugged my shoulders. "I did alright. Didn't cut anyone's head off and managed to create the feeling of a million boxes of cookies with only a few props. So, that began my career as a news photographer. From that point on, I was one of the boys. I never took up smoking cigars, but a beer or two at Jimmy's was a daily ritual." I leaned back and could tell Jim was enjoying my adventures.

"Over the next few weeks, I was relegated to the darkroom. Stan and the other guys took me along on a few jobs. I really enjoyed the baseball assignments. Baseball was an easy sport to shoot, and the players were my age and cute. Several pictures printed in the sports pages were actually mine, even if Stan's photo credit was printed below them. Things really changed when the editor of the women's page called and asked for me by name. The paper was going to cover a Daughters of the American Revolution luncheon, and she wanted me to cover the event."

"I guess the cookie picture made quite an impression on her," said Jim.

I laughed. "Actually, I think the idea of sending any of our cigar-chomping staff to the DAR tea party was too big of an ask. The next step in my career path was at hand. If I were going to represent *The Post*, I would need a press pass. And there it was in black and white: **Kate Miller, Photographer, Washington Post.**" I looked up at Jim. "Quite a moment."

"I bet."

"On my first official assignment, I was terrified that I would screw it up. I must have checked my equipment twenty times, loaded the film in my Nikon, and rechecked it over and over. I had enough equipment to shoot a major riot. You know how it is, if I missed the moment, I'd be toast without Stan to shield me. I was on my own. Luckily, the ladies of the DAR were a placid bunch with flowery dresses, white gloves and a hat on every head." Jim laughed out loud. "They were happy to see me at their luncheon, but not as happy as I was to see one of my sorority sisters, Mary, who was there with her mom.

"Mrs. Davidson was a proud card-carrying member, and I think her ancestors even came over on the Mayflower. Mary and I huddled in the corner and organized a plan. I got my shots that were too boring to mention. By the end, I had enough pictures to put out a special issue devoted to the DAR in the 20th Century. I drove back to the office with a huge grin on my face. Unless I screwed up loading the film in my camera, I had to have the shot I needed. Once back at the office, everything went without a hitch. I was proud as a peacock handing *four* proof sheets to the copy editor. He looked up at me as if I was a total idiot." I laughed at myself. "They would print *one* picture of one old lady handing a book to another old lady. The next day I rolled out of bed in time to catch my copy of *The Post*. There it was on page 21, Metro section, lower right corner, photo by 'Bate Miller.'"

"What?" Jim blurted out.

"Yep. My first official assignment, and I didn't type my name correctly for the photo credit."

"No!" Jim was listening to every word. It was as if I was talking to a close friend.

"I've been doing all the talking."

"No, not at all, I'm envious of that kind of passion."

"Your turn," I said, picking up my beer.

Jim paused, set down his, and looked at me again. "I came to DC to make a difference. But ..."

I saw the flicker of sadness across his face and leaned in. "But ..."

He shrugged. His short laugh sounded bitter. "I really like doing the work of a legislator, *but* I hate the politics of running for office every two years. It seems all I do is spend my time raising money for the next election."

"You said you're from South Carolina?" I said, remembering his comment from our walk to the bar.

"Yep, a Republican born and raised." He gave me a slight bow.

I said nothing.

"I'm guessing you're not?"

I shook my head. "I'm nonpolitical. My parents are Democrats, but it didn't really stick with me."

His smile was enigmatic. "Let's get back to photography."

Despite the surroundings, the hour had gone by in a flash. We talked like people who had known each other all their lives, about everything—sports, politics, and photography. No rancor, no agenda. Just give and take, the kind of conversation that was rare in my experience. I bolted upright when I spotted the clock behind the bar.

"Oh, no, look at the time!"

He glanced at his watch. "It's about 3:15, are you late?"

"Not yet." I began scooting to the edge of the booth. "But I'd better get going."

"Damn, where did the time go?" He said, throwing some money on the table.

We hustled back to the Capitol.

"Kate. Can I call you?"

I almost sighed in relief.

"I'd like that," I answered. I pulled a receipt from my purse, dug deeper, found a pen, and wrote my office phone number and name, then handed it to him.

He laughed. "Got it." Then his smile fell, and his gaze intensified. "It's been a pleasure to meet you, Kate, not Bate Miller."

"Me, too." I turned to walk away with totally mixed emotions. *How could I let this guy get away so easily? What if he didn't call?* I couldn't take that chance. After about ten steps, I turned to see if he was still there watching me. He had not moved an inch. That really threw me off a beat.

"Hey, I was thinking. Would you like to go to a Redskins game?" I asked.

"That would be great. Can you get tickets?"

"I cover it almost every week. The Skins play the Bears on Sunday. Call me." I turned and waved at the same time.

Reluctantly, I made my way back to work. When I turned in my photos the copy editor mumbled something about it not being another "prize" winner.

I tilted my head and assertively told her that it might be the most important picture I would ever take. I gave her a huge smile.

She gave me a blank look and waved me away.

Chapter Six

The next day started out like any other, sitting in the newsroom reading *Time Magazine*. I came across an article about the emerging "New South." Normally I'd skip this, but Congressman Jim Rayford was still on my mind. I flipped to the second page. My heart skipped a beat. There on the bottom corner was congressman and Mrs. James Rayford, smiling with a Southern plantation in the background. I looked closer. The woman in the picture was the same person I had photographed with the Vice President. I felt the heat rise to my face. *Jim Rayford was married.*

"That scumbag!" I shouted. Everyone within twenty feet looked up. I lifted my hand in a signal of apology, then quickly went to the darkroom before I let out a string of four-letter words.

"What the hell are you on about?"

I swung around to see Stan standing in a dark corner working on his film. I swallowed, *busted*. In the dark, small space, the story tumbled out like a confession.

"I met this very neat guy yesterday on the Hill," I muttered.

"So?"

"So ... he was really attractive. And interesting. And we stopped for a beer." I sighed. "And I really thought we hit it off."

"To repeat myself ... so?"

"The son of a bitch is married."

"You think that's big news in this city? Married guys hitting on political groupies?"

I shook my head, glad for the dark. "I didn't see this one coming. We walked over to a bar on the Hill and sat talking for a good hour. It was great, perfect, and now I find out he's married."

"What's the big deal? Did he hit on you?" Stan was starting to enjoy the conversation.

I huffed out a bitter laugh. "Yes. No. God damn it. I hit on him. I asked him to go to a Redskins game with me."

"Stand him up," Stan concluded and went back to his film.

"Shit, I can't believe I'm so dumb." I tossed the magazine into a trashcan and left in a huff. As I returned to the newsroom, Scott looked up from his desk.

"Kate, there's a call for you on line two."

"Who is it?"

"How the hell am I supposed to know ... do I look like your secretary?"

"Sorry, Scott, I didn't mean to snap at you." I moved over to an empty desk and picked up the phone.

"Kate Miller" I answered, pulling a chair up to the desk.

"Hi, it's Jim."

Several things crossed my mind, but I was speechless.

"Kate, are you there?"

"Yes" I answered in a cool voice.

"Have I caught you at a bad time? I can call back later."

No, it's not a bad time, I wanted to scream, but nothing came out.

"Are we still on for the game? I've been thinking about it. Should I bring a camera, just to look like I belong?"

"Do you think your wife will mind, or maybe she doesn't like football?" I slammed down the receiver and leaned back into the chair fuming. I'm not sure who I was more upset with, him, or me. *Damn him.* I never planned ahead, but this one had really felt right. This one really hurt.

Chapter Seven

I had the next day off, and then the only job I had on Sunday was the football game. I got to the game about a minute before kickoff. The day was as cloudy and gray as my mood. By the end of the first half the Bears were ahead of the Redskins, and it looked as if it was going to rain buckets any minute.

By the second half kickoff, the rain began. I had no choice but to stick it out. The game was too close to blow off, and I really didn't have much that would thrill the sports desk.

The third quarter was almost over, and the field was a mess. I was soaked and tried to keep my camera dry. Both teams had given up throwing the ball and were content to grind it out on the ground. I maneuvered close to the sideline for the big play. It was second and six, and the play was coming right at me. I had to get the shot and get out of the way before I got flattened. Normally, the guys will try to avoid the photographers. They aren't really worried about hitting a person. After all, they are covered with all sorts of pads. What they don't want to do is to run into five pounds of metal, camera, and lens. I was backpeddling like mad, still snapping off frames of film, when I bumped into someone. The play stopped short of me by just a foot, but I went sprawling on top of the guy behind me.

"God damn, son of a bitch," I growled, hustling to my feet to make sure I hadn't damaged my camera. Once up, I spun around to give the guy who was in my way a piece of my mind. Flat on his ass was *the* "Honorable" Jim Rayford. He looked miserable, wet, and muddy, and I couldn't help but laugh.

"I don't see what's so funny," he said, a puppy dog look on his rather wet face. He started to get up but slipped on the mud again.

"Good. You're right where you belong." I smirked.

He looked up, confused, and maybe hurt. "Give me a hand. Please?"

I turned and began to walk away. A few paces away, someone grabbed my arm. I spun around to see him, as drenched as I was, covered in mud.

"What are you doing here?" I snapped, jerking my arm out of his grip.

Jim wiped the water from his face, contrite. "I came to apologize."

"I don't really think there is anything to say, Jim. You're a rat. Or did I misunderstand something?"

"I'm sorry. I didn't intend to mislead you."

"Oh, really? I don't recall you telling me, in that hour-long conversation, that you were married."

Jim closed his eyes tight for a second. Opening them, he asked, "Can we get out of this rain and sit somewhere and talk please?"

"I'm not sure we have anything to talk about, and I have to get my photos back to the paper as soon as possible."

"Could I ride with you to the paper?"

He looked like a soaked puppy. "Do you know how pitiful you look?" I pointed at his dripping khaki pants and London Fog raincoat. "I really don't need all that mud in my car."

"Boy, I am a mess. I think I'm going to have to throw all this stuff away. You're right to worry about your car."

I sighed. "Follow me." I walked over to the team bench and scooped up a bunch of towels the refs used to keep the ball dry.

We hustled off the field and back toward the parking lot.

"I'm still not convinced that we have anything to talk about. You are married. At least that's the way it looked in *Time Magazine*."

He exhaled heavily. "Kate, I am so sorry."

I rolled my eyes.

"Give me a break. Did you mean to forget about your wife? The woman I photographed?" I stopped facing him. "Please, don't make things worse by insulting my intelligence."

"That's not what I mean. Listen, we can't really talk here," he said, looking around at the security guards who were getting a little too interested in our conversation.

"Okay, let's get out of here." I agreed, just wanting to get the conversation over with. I handed him some towels. We walked quickly to my car and rode back to the office in a thick, heavy silence. We were both chilled to the bone and my heater wasn't fast at warming up the frigid car. By the time we turned the corner and pulled into *The Post* parking lot, my heart was as frozen as I was. I looked over to see Jim slumped in his seat, staring at his hands. He looked defeated and vulnerable. *And cute, damn him*. I didn't see any way this story was going to have a happy ending.

"We're here," I said brusquely. When he didn't move, I said, "You can't stay out here. You'll freeze." I jumped out and motioned for him to follow me.

He looked up from the car. "I can't go in there. What if someone sees me?"

"Don't flatter yourself. There's hardly anyone here on weekends, and they won't give a rat's ass who you are. Besides, I think the mud is a quite good disguise."

"OK, and thanks. I *am* freezing."

He followed me into the building. We hustled to the photo desk and dumped our wet coats. Only a few people were there meeting their deadlines. No one even saw us arrive. Jim followed me into the darkroom. I could see he was intrigued. This whole scene was new to him, so he was both impressed and interested.

"Sit there and don't touch anything," I pointed to a chair behind a small desk. "I have to run my film."

"Run your film?" he repeated with a blank look on his face.

"Yeah, develop the negatives so I can see what I've got." This was my turf, where I felt in control. I needed that now.

"Hey, this place is something. Do you know how to use all this stuff?" Jim motioned to all the darkroom equipment.

"Of course, it's really not that hard." I went to work finishing my rolls. After they were hanging in the drying cabinet, I walked back into the main part of the darkroom. Jim was sitting behind a desk, arms folded across his chest, deep in thought.

"A couple minutes more and we can look at the negatives," I said, all business.

"I hope I didn't screw up anything, getting in your way. You didn't get hurt when you fell, did you?" He looked concerned.

"Maybe my pride, but that's about all."

"Kate—"

I raised my finger in front of his mouth to cut him short.

"Not now, Jim. I must get this done, and I really don't need to be thinking of anything else but these pictures. The negatives should be dry now. I'll go grab them and take a look." I moved quickly away. Standing that close, just a few inches apart, seemed dangerous.

I grabbed the negatives and moved over to one of the enlargers. Once you worked with film for a while, one can just look at negatives and know whether they were going to be usable. I fed the first strip into a holder and then the holder into the head of the enlarger. I flipped a switch on the wall that put the room into complete darkness and then a second later, three small red bulbs came on.

"Jim," I called out. "Give your eyes a few seconds to adjust to the light, and then come over here and take a look." My need to concentrate on my work dulled my anger at him.

"Damn, this is really dark." He said, drawing closer.

"You get used to it. Some of the guys actually sit in here and read the newspaper." With the light from the enlarger I could see each of my negatives projected on the paper easel. Granted, everything was backward. Black was clear and white looked black, but I could still see if the image was in focus and what kind of action I had captured. Jim was standing just off my elbow leaning in to see what I was looking at.

"I can't really tell what I'm seeing," he said, turning to look directly into my eyes. His face couldn't have been more than six inches from mine. Our eyes met.

I looked away. "It's not hard to figure out. It just takes a bit of practice." I grabbed a pencil to use as a pointer.

"Look here ... Jorgensen is getting rid of the ball, and this guy is going to cream him."

"Oh yeah, now I see it. Great shot."

I felt his body close to mine as he studied the negative. He was taking this entire process very seriously. I shook my head to focus on my work. I turned off the enlarger, slipped the photo paper into the easel, and exposed the paper to print my first photo. Beside me, Jim whistled softly. I was enjoying showing off for him.

"Will this one make it into the paper"? he asked.

I couldn't help but smile. "God only knows," I laughed. "What actually gets used depends on the editor and the space available. I try to give them more than enough to keep them happy. I like covering football, and I don't want to take any chances."

"What if you get back here and you don't have anything good?"

"Bite your tongue!"

"Sorry, I'm sure that would never happen to you." He smiled.

"Let me put it this way ... it would only happen once. Not everyone is thrilled having a woman on the staff. Truth is, some would be delighted to see me fall on my ass."

"Too bad they missed tonight."

"Very funny. Let's get this stuff done. Lord knows I don't want to be late."

"Sorry, I'll keep my mouth shut and let you do your thing. Do you want me to stop looking over your shoulder?"

"No," I said too quickly. "You're fine." I could feel the smile on his face without looking.

I printed the pictures and had them finished in plenty of time to make my deadline. I decided that a couple of the shots were too average to submit, and I tossed them into the trashcan as we left the darkroom.

"What are you doing?" Jim asked, rather surprised to see me throw the prints away.

"I have enough, and those aren't the greatest," I answered.

"Don't throw them out. Can I have them?" he asked, reaching back and grabbing them out of the trash.

"Sure, if you really want them."

Walking back into the newsroom brought us both back to reality. "Wait here a bit while I drop these off."

Jim stood by our coats while I delivered my shots to the sports desk. It took about ten minutes to do the captions. When I returned, I could tell Jim was beginning to feel awkward.

"Okay, let's get out of here," I said, grabbing my coat.

We made our way through the newsroom to the elevator without anyone noticing us. Once we were safely outside the building, Jim turned to face me.

"Do you think I'll be able to get a taxi this late?" Jim asked, looking around the empty streets.

I shrugged. "Where exactly do you live?"

"I have an apartment north of Georgetown, just off Wisconsin."

I paused. "Okay, I guess I can give you a lift. I'm in Georgetown, just north of M Street."

We walked out to the car, each of us deep in our own thoughts.

He paused as he closed the car door. "Kate, I never meant to deceive you."

I blew out some air. "Jim, was I wrong or were you flirting with me at the reception?" Just the thought of it made me mad all over again. I pulled into traffic and headed to Georgetown.

"It wasn't like that," he paused. Then said, "Well, yes, I guess it was."

"So, just to be clear, your wife was receiving some damn award, and you were there to pick up chicks!" We didn't say another word until we pulled up in front of Jim's apartment building. Staring out the windshield, I waited for him to exit. He didn't.

"I know that I haven't handled things well. I was going to explain my situation the next time I saw you," he said, looking me straight in the eye.

"It's really late, and I'm beat. I would like to get home and get some sleep. I'm not sure there is anything more to talk about."

"I would really like the chance to explain myself."

"It's late." I countered.

"I know. Could I buy you breakfast tomorrow?"

"Won't the little woman miss you sitting across from her at the breakfast table?"

"I deserve that," he grimaced. "Please let me buy you breakfast and tell you my whole story. Hear me out, and then you can tell me to go to hell."

"You're not going to give up, are you?"

"Nope." He ventured a smile. "Please. Just coffee. How about Martin's in Georgetown? It's on Wisconsin, just north of—"

"I know where it is." I was hoping I wouldn't regret this. "I don't mean to harp, but won't your wife miss you?"

"She's in South Carolina. She left right after getting her plaque. She doesn't like Washington much. Or me, for that matter."

"If you tell me 'she doesn't understand me' I'll scream."

"No, the truth is she totally understands me," he said, jumping out of the car. He leaned down with both hands on the car door. "Like I said, she just doesn't like me much."

"Fine," I said. "Breakfast." I looked down at my steering wheel and shook my head.

His expression shifted to relief. I saw something flicker in his blue eyes. "Drive carefully. I'll see you at Martin's at 8:30?"

I nodded and started to pull away from the curb. I checked my rear-view mirror. Jim was still standing there watching me leave.

Chapter Eight

I made it to my apartment and spent miserable hours tossing and turning while listening to two little voices in my head. One telling me to get rid of this jerk, he's married, and the other one reminding me how he treated me ... the attraction was clearly there, but it was more than that. *After an hour of conversation, I felt like I had known him forever.* Then the first voice would chime in. *He's not only a married man, but a congressman to boot.* I put my hand to my forehead, thinking *I am in trouble.*

I tossed and turned all night, checking the clock about four times an hour just to finally fall asleep in time for the alarm to explode in my ear. It took me a few seconds to remember what was ahead of me. I groaned and put the pillow over my head. I wrestled with my decision. It took a half-hour to accept that my conflicted mood wasn't going away.

I showered and dressed in a black turtleneck and my tightest jeans. Who was I kidding, I *wanted* this guy to fall head over heels in love with me. A glance in the mirror confirmed the jeans and sweater looked good. The shadows under my eyes were another story. I looked as if I'd been up all night on the losing side of a catfight.

Martin's was a short distance from my apartment. As I walked, I worked out different scenarios. I could go in and get a table, but maybe that wasn't such a good idea? *What if he didn't show up? I could wait outside, but was that too obvious?* Luckily, the decision was taken out of my hands. Jim and I came around the corner at the same time and almost knocked each other over right in front of Martin's door.

"Hey, you're right on time." Jim greeted me with a smile.

"Good morning," I answered, trying to be cool.

"Let's go in and get a table. I love this place, and it should be empty. Everyone should be at work by now." Jim held the door open, and I stepped in front of him.

Martin's was an old Washington tradition. No more than a bar with tables and booths finishing the room. In addition to that dark wood paneling and Tiffany type lamps hanging over every table, it was a political watering hole. Several booths had plaques naming politicians and Washington power brokers who spent time there. That included one booth that honored *Washington Post* owner Katherine Graham, which made me do a double take. They basically hadn't changed anything in fifty years, including the waiters. With the smells of last night's beer and cigarettes, it didn't seem like a place for breakfast.

Jim steered me to a booth farthest from the bar. There were people already at the bar *drinking*.

The balding waiter came to our booth and almost threw the menus at us. "What can I get you to drink?" he asked.

Jim ordered coffee and looked over at me.

"I'd like a glass of milk, please." I answered, giving him an insincere smile.

The waiter turned and walked back through the kitchen's swinging doors without saying a word.

"This place is full of charm, isn't it?"

"It grows on you," Jim answered. "Doesn't matter whether you're the King of England or a cab driver, they'll treat you equally bad!"

We both laughed.

Neither of us knew where to begin. Jim looked at the guys at the bar, who were discussing the football game. They had a copy of *The Post* and were showing the bartender something on the sports page. Jim leaned across the table as if to tell me a secret.

"Do you think they're looking at one of your photos?" he asked with boyish enthusiasm.

God, he was irresistible. "Maybe," I answered, looking at the bar and listening to their conversation. The bartender commented that Jorgensen was getting too old for the game. "They must be looking at the shot of Sonny getting creamed. Maybe they'll let you see the sports section when they're done with it," I teased.

"Good idea," he said, turning to the bar. "Hey guys, could I see the paper when you're done?"

The stranger nodded and brought it over to us as he was leaving the bar.

"Thanks," Jim said and immediately started turning the pages. He stopped and pointed to three pictures. "Damn, is this great or what?" Jim looked up from the paper and smiled.

After a while, you get used to seeing your pictures in the paper. I'd almost forgotten how excited I was the first time one of mine was in print. Jim brought that feeling all back to me.

"Let's see what they used," I said, reaching across the table for the sports section. The waiter came back to the table with our drinks, and we ordered. Jim studied my pictures, told me how great I was, and what a neat job I had. It's hard not to like a guy who makes such a fuss about you. Just the fact that he was more interested in me than talking about himself was delightful. We'd been in the restaurant for almost an hour and had not come close to talking about the reason for our meeting.

Jim, finally, pushed his untouched plate to one side and clasped his hands on the table in front of him. "Kate, I know I owe you an explanation. So where do I start?"

I stayed silent and waited.

Jim took a breath. "I met Angela at a party in college. She didn't seem to be a very motivated student, but she was fun and always up for a party. We started dating and one thing led to another. One night, after a wild frat party, we ended up in the back seat of her car." Jim sat staring at his hands. "To make a long story short, she got pregnant. Her father, who was one of my dad's law partners, had a long talk with me. A month later, we were married. I was to finish school and go on to law school. I really didn't have the balls to do anything but comply with our fathers' plans." He paused. "Angela lost the baby."

Jim looked up at me, his expression pained. "It was terrible. Everyone was heartbroken. By then, I really cared for Angela, and more to the point, I felt responsible. We were suffering as a family. After a period of mourning, we both moved on. I finished law school and went to work at the family law firm. Angela spent all her time with her 'horsey' friends. She traveled to horse events all over the country while I worked at the law firm. She had one trainer that was always with her. I suspected something was going on, but honestly it was a relief. What started in the back seat of a Chevy ended not with a bang, but with a silent mutual disdain. I knew I was lucky being out of school with a cushy job dumped in my lap. Our lives were set." He looked up to see my reaction. I was listening but not feeling very sympathetic.

He continued. "One of the law partners was a member of the House of Representatives. That set my life on its present course. I helped him with legislative problems, and honestly, I loved it. Everything about it seemed so important. Then the world really turned upside down. The congressman died of a stroke. The 'movers and shakers' in the party knew I was doing most of the work for the district. These guys were the power brokers for the party and in South Carolina, that means everything. Hell, Angela's dad was the chair of the South Carolina Republican Party."

My brows rose, but I said nothing.

"They asked me to run, and I jumped at the chance. It was a slam dunk." Jim smiled, remembering how his life had evolved. "I loved everything about being in Congress. Angela, on the other hand, hated Washington and stayed at her parent's horse farm in Columbia most of the time. Whenever she did come to see me, all she did was complain. We argued." He shook his head. "She hated my apartment so much, she even started staying at a hotel. We drifted apart. Our lives were separate. I spent almost every waking hour at work, while Angela played at being the congressman's wife. To be fair, she was good at it. She took part in all the social stuff and had a talent for getting attention. She seemed to get off on acting as the congressman's wife more than being a wife."

The waiter came by every fifteen minutes to ask if we needed anything. We both mumbled, "No thank you." I kept staring at Jim, while most of the time he sat staring at the table. At first, I thought he couldn't look at me because the whole story was bull. Then I realized he was embarrassed because he felt that everything was his fault.

"I've been content," he shook his head. "No, that's too strong a word. I've *endured* my situation until the day we bumped into each other on the Hill." He looked up at me, his eyes appealing. "I ran into this amazing woman. She's intelligent, funny, independent, and completely comfortable with who she is."

I could feel the heat rise on my face and tried not to smile.

"Not to mention a great smile. After spending an hour with you, I realized what my life could be and what I was missing. Kate, I know this all sounds lame. That I've been acting like a schoolboy. Let me level with you. Cards on the table. I can't divorce my wife, and I want to see you."

I laughed shortly. "Damn, Jim. You're not offering me much," I said, shaking my head and reaching for my purse. "Look, I've enjoyed the few hours we've spent together. I feel like I've known you forever. But I don't want to get involved with a married man. I know how this story ends. I'd fall head over heels in love, and you'd be off posing for magazine spreads in Southern Hospitality with Angela."

The waiter returned and with a smirk, handed us the lunch menu. The ice was broken, and we both laughed. Jim asked for the bill and quickly paid up. The waiters didn't thank us, or say come back soon, but at least they sort of smiled as we left.

Outside, we stood at the door for an awkward moment. I looked at the traffic.

"Are you going to work now?" he asked.

"I'm not expected until one or so."

"Can I walk you to your car?"

I shook my head. "I live about two blocks from here."

"Oh? Where?"

I hesitated. "Over on 33rd and Prospect."

"I know where that is. Prospect runs right into one of my favorite restaurants. Do you ever go to the 1789?" he asked.

"I've never been upstairs, only the bar in the basement." I answered. "It's sort of a college hangout ... pizza and beer." After Jim's serious heartfelt conversation, we were talking about mundane things, avoiding the tough topic we'd left at the restaurant. I wanted to believe every word, but there were still doubts I had to face.

"I'll walk you home." Jim said.

Not sure if this was a good idea, we took off. I put my hands in my pockets against the chill as we matched our pace. As we turned the corner at N St. and walked west toward my apartment we both noticed the marquee at the Georgetown Theatre. *Butch Cassidy and the Sundance Kid* was playing.

"That's supposed to be a good film," Jim said, nodding at the theatre.

"I haven't seen it, but Paul Newman's always good," I replied. I *had* already seen it, but I thought I knew where Jim was going with the conversation, and I wanted him to get there quickly without any roadblocks.

"Why don't we go see it?"

"Now? I don't think they're open yet."

"No tonight, Okay?" He smiled.

"You're kidding, right?" I smiled.

He shook his head.

"Would this be like a date then?" I asked.

"Hey, if you'd feel more comfortable paying your own way ..." he shrugged. "But it would be against the Southerners Code of Conduct to allow that to happen." He smiled.

I hesitated. This was my decision point. Yes or no. I licked my lips and went for a delay tactic. "I'd like to see it but, I'm on call at the paper, so I won't know if I can make it until later today."

"Fair enough."

"I can find my way the rest of the way. I'll say goodbye here," I said.

Jim hesitated, taking in my words and their meaning. He nodded, lips tight.

I turned to face him. "I appreciate how difficult it was for you at the restaurant, and to be honest, I don't know how I feel about this, and I have no idea where this is all going."

"For now, Kate, let's say it's going to the movies and maybe out for a pizza, okay?"

I shifted my purse. "Okay." After a pause I asked, "How will I get in touch with you to let you know if I can go?" He reached into his back pocket, took out a beaten-up old wallet, and pulled out a business card.

"It has my office number on it. Just call and say you're with *The Post*, they'll put you right through."

So, there we were. I tucked his card in my jeans pocket and promised to call at about five to let him know if I could make the movie. By now, we were both feeling more than awkward. A handshake seemed stupid; a kiss was out of the question, so I took the coward's way out and waved quickly and walked away. This time, I didn't look back.

With each step I took, my mind battled the pros and cons while my heart skipped happily. I wanted to believe his story and believe him. He wanted us to have a chance. And God help me, so did I. I would never regret trying, but there would be a lifetime of wondering what might have been. By the time I reached my apartment, I knew I was not going to miss this date.

***

When I walked into the office, Stan and Scott were sitting in the newsroom talking about the new cameras we were getting. I walked to where they were and dropped into the extra chair next to Scott's desk.

"Well, you look like the cat that swallowed the canary," he said.

"Why, do I have feathers on my chin?" I answered smugly.

"Here are your assignment sheets." Scott handed us three sheets of paper each, got up from his desk and left us to look over our assignments.

"You look too happy. What's up?" Stan asked, eyeing me with more than a bit of suspicion.

"I've got a date tonight. I have to be out of here by six at the latest." I quickly looked over the papers. There was nothing too exciting; in fact, it was going to be a downright boring day. The last assignment on the list was at the Library of Congress. They were opening a new exhibit for their Gutenberg Bible. Today was going to be a snap. Easy, boring, and best of all quick.

"Who are you going out with?" Stan asked, breaking into my thoughts.

"Oh ... no one you know. Just a guy I met a while back."

"Not the married guy?" Stan gave me a stern look. I fiddled with my assignment sheets, avoiding eye contact. When I didn't answer right away, Stan said, "Kate, it's not that guy you met on the Hill last week, is it?"

"What if it is?" I asked, not really wanting an answer. Stan noticed my mood and didn't ask another question. He just moved toward the darkroom door. "Okay, babe, your call. If you ever want any advice, don't come to me." He peered into my eyes. "Seriously, kid, be careful, Okay?"

"Thanks Stan, I will." I gave him a weak smile.

Even though the jobs were quick, the day dragged by. After the Bible exhibit, I hustled back to the office to develop my film. I wanted to get it processed and leave the office before I was assigned something else. I turned in my shots to the copy desk and called Jim at his office. I had already checked the show times.

"Congressman Rayford's office, may I help you?" A sweet southern voice answered the phone.

"This is Miss Miller with *The Washington Post* calling the congressman," I said trying to sound very official, drumming my fingers on the desk impatiently.

"Is the congressman expecting you Miss ... Miller, is it?"

"Yes, he is," I was feeling guilty, and therefore defensive. "The congressman is expecting my call. Could you please put me through? I have limited time."

"One moment please." She clicked off, and I was ready to hang up when Jim came on the line.

"Kate, sorry you had to wait. The young lady who normally answers the phone is running an errand. Did she give you a hard time?"

"No," I lied. "How is your day going?"

"I was afraid you would change your mind."

"I have to admit, waiting for you to come to the phone, I thought about it."

"Well, I'm glad you hung in there. I'll make sure it doesn't happen again. I picked up a paper at lunch. Funny, now when I look at *The Post*, I check out the photo credits on each picture. Anyway, the movie starts at 7:00 and 9:30. What do you think?"

"Let's make it 7:00. I have an early morning tomorrow." I lied. I wanted to give myself an out in case this date didn't go well.

"Fine. Should I pick you up?" he asked.

"I'll meet you in front of the show."

"Okay, see you there."

I put down the receiver and let my hand rest on the phone, feeling a moment's panic. I couldn't see a mature man being satisfied with holding hands and a kiss on the cheek at the end of the evening. I wanted to believe I was in control of the situation, but I was going out with him *because* I wanted something to happen.

He was good looking, smart, sensitive, sexy, and most of all, interested in me. That's a winning combination, except for the *slight* problem of his wife.

Chapter Nine

I made it home in plenty of time. I showered and brushed my teeth. I wanted to call Mary and tell her what was going on, but was afraid. What would I say? What would she say? Mary was traditional, and I didn't think she would approve of the married man part. But she would love that he was a Republican. I shook my head. It was not the time to be flippant. After a short call, Mary's reaction was very measured. She realized how serious I was and how serious this situation was. She told me to be careful and remember what I was doing would impact several lives ... including breaking up a marriage. I assured her that all those things were running through my mind, and I would be careful.

The movie theater was only a ten-minute walk from my apartment. I left a few minutes late because I wanted him standing there when I crossed the street in front of the show. As I approached, I could see him buying tickets at the box office. I was so nervous I didn't check traffic, and a VW camper almost ran me down. A few rude words were exchanged, but the driver was in no mood to stick around when a DC police officer walked over.

"Kate, is that you?" he asked.

"Hey, Officer Gaines, how're you doing?" I answered.

"If you're not going to cross at the light, at least look both ways," he admonished. He looked over his shoulder at Jim who was crossing the street to see what was happening. "Hot date?" His lips eased into a knowing smile.

"Just a friend," I answered. "How are things going with the DCPD?"

"Not bad. I'm taking the sergeants exam next month. It might mean I'll have to leave Georgetown, but it's more money."

"Kate, are you okay? Officer, is anything wrong?" Jim asked as he joined us in the street.

"No sir, everything's fine. I'm just educating this young lady on the jaywalking laws in our city. What say we get out of the street, and you folks go and enjoy the movie." He nodded toward the show.

"Thanks, and good luck on your test. I know you'll do great," I said, giving him a thumbs up and a smile. Jim took me by the elbow.

"Do you know that guy?" Jim asked, watching the officer walk away.

"Yeah, his beat is my neighborhood. At first, he gave me tickets if I didn't park legally. Once he knew that I worked at *The Post*, he started to cut me some slack. It also didn't hurt to give him some homemade cookies every once in a while. We have to support our men in blue." I smiled.

"We'd better hurry or we'll miss the beginning of the film." Jim said.

The Georgetown Theatre was small and vintage 1930's and hadn't been kept up that well.

Since it was a weeknight, the show was less than a quarter full. We found seats near the middle just as the movie started. I'm not sure either of us really watched it. I spent most of my time watching Jim watch the movie. More than once, we locked eyes and gave each other a sheepish embarrassed smile and looked back at the screen. I was relieved when the film ended in a blaze of gunfire. The theatre emptied out quickly, leaving us sitting there enjoying the closeness ... shoulders touching.

"Are you hungry?" Jim asked.

"Starving. You?"

"Yes ma'am, how about the bar at the '1789?'" He asked. "It's still early, and it's a nice night to walk."

"That sounds fine."

We walked out of the theater and Jim immediately took my arm as we crossed Wisconsin. Once we were across the street, he still had his hand on my elbow. It seemed weird, but nice. For the first block, we just made small talk about the film. We agreed on everything ... In fact, we were finishing each other's sentences. Once we got near Georgetown University, there were students everywhere.

"What a neat place to go to school," Jim said.

"Where did you go?" I asked.

"College of Charleston. How about you?"

"George Washington. The city may be the same, but this neighborhood is a lot more fun. What did you major in?"

"I majored in having fun first and foremost," Jim replied. "Secondly, History."

"So, why law school after that?"

"My Dad was a lawyer, and it was always a given that I would follow in his footsteps. You? Why international affairs?"

"Just about the same. Fun first, of course."

We had become so involved with our conversation that we almost missed the turn to the pub.

"This is the corner, isn't it? I buy a lot of clothes at this shop," he said pointing to the Georgetown Shop.

"No surprise there, preppy." I said teasing.

"Don't you like my clothes?" he said looking down at his khakis and Weejuns.

"I like your outfit but it's a bit conservative." I laughed.

"Hey, I'd love to wear jeans to work, but somehow I don't think my colleagues would approve."

"I'm just kidding ... you fit right in here. You could be a student or maybe a professor," I said, trying to mend fences.

We dropped the conversation about Weejuns and quickly made it to the entrance to the basement of the "1789" called The Tombs. I stepped in front of Jim to go down the stairs first, and he pointed at my shoes.

"Hey, aren't those Weejuns?" he teased.

"Yeah, they're great shoes." I laughed.

He put his hands on my shoulders and gave them a friendly squeeze. The place was nearly full of typical college kids. Why study when you can be with friends and have a few beers?

A small empty table next to the fireplace beckoned. The place wasn't loud, just a low chatter. The entire room was full of rowing memorabilia. The Tombs was a campus tradition. The waiters were all seniors at Georgetown, and it was considered an honor to work there.

"This is a neat place. Did you come here when you were in school?" Jim asked, looking around.

"Often."

"What's the story on the long table with those microphones hanging from the ceiling?"

"They have a tradition here. There's a singing group called The Chimes. They're a men's group that sings and drinks here four or five times during a school year. The tradition goes back to when they first opened. I covered one of their shows a few months ago. Alumni are invited to join in. I'm not sure if they do more singing or drinking. It was fun, and this place is always packed when they're here."

"Sounds great. Students never understand how much fun college is until they get thrown into the real world." Jim said, sounding a bit sad.

We ordered beer and pizza and spent time comparing notes on our college experiences. After the pizza and a couple of beers, I had both a warm, fuzzy and scary feeling at the same time. Jim spent this morning staring into his eggs and bacon. Tonight, he was looking me straight in the eye. He was clearly into me. The problem was, I was just as into him. He reached across the table and held my hand.

"We'd better get the check. You've got an early day tomorrow," he said, rubbing his thumb over the top of my hand.

I caught the message and my mind stalled. "I do ... right, I do." He promptly paid the bill, and he took my hand.

We walked up the stairs and out of the bar.

"Which way?" he asked.

My heart started beating harder. "This way," I said, indicating east.

I knew where we were headed. Guys might think they are the instigator when it comes to sex, but most women are in control of that important first serious sexual experience. Not a grope in the back seat of a Chevy. The time when a woman decides to lose her virginity. When we girls talked about it in college, we laughed that guys thought it was their idea because the girls had it all planned out. I think many of them just wanted to get it out of the way. Some used it as a means to make the relationship long lasting or even permanent.

But now, here I was, confronted by an adult male with far more experience than me and for the first time I was feeling very insecure. A big part of that was because he was married. His heartfelt story at the restaurant this morning was sincere—I hoped.

When we reached the gate to my garden, I was confused. I took my hand from his and crossed my arms.

Jim spoke first.

"Katie, I've had a great time. Can we do this again?"

The decision was mine to make. I looked behind me at my apartment door and made a decision. I took a deep breath. He called me Katie, making me feel close to him, making me feel so many things. "Jim, this is going too fast. I'm not sure I'm being very sensible. Wait. I know I'm *not* being sensible." I looked into his eyes. "I'm not ready."

"Don't say another word. I want it to be perfect. So, let's say goodnight and both of us can spend a restless night thinking about it. Okay?"

He didn't wait for an answer. He pulled me close, looking into my eyes as if he were searching my soul. He slowly brought his lips to mine and gently kissed me.

Not too long, but more than a friendly peck. Testing. Tasting.

I put my arms around his neck and moved my half-open mouth over his, inviting a much more serious meeting of our bodies. I was totally gone, about to invite him in, and to start tearing off his clothes. As if Jim could read my mind, as he pulled away from me.

"You better go in before I ... I'll call you tomorrow. Oh ..." He patted his pocket. "I don't have your home phone number."

The chilly night air revived us as we exchanged numbers. He kissed me one more time, soft and lingering.

"Goodnight," I said, then turned and went up the steps to my front door. Jim waited until I opened my door and was safely inside. I looked back just before I closed the door and smiled. He smiled back and walked down toward M Street to catch a cab.

I put my hands on my head, my heart beating wildly. If his kisses spun my head like this, I wondered what more would do to me. I'd had sex before, but nothing memorable. I brought my fingers to my lips, closing my eyes, still feeling his lips on mine. I was tempted to take a shower but decided not to waste the feeling. I undressed and was in bed in a flash ... hugging a pillow. Jim was right, there was no way I was going to get any sleep.

I'd been in bed for about five minutes when the phone rang. I nearly jumped out of my skin. I was tempted to not answer but decided I'd better in case it was my office.

"Hello," I said tentatively.

"Hi, it's me." Jim said. "I just wanted to tell you again what a great time I had tonight."

"Me, too." There was silence on both sides of the phone. Neither of us knew exactly what to say, but we didn't want to hang up the phone. We both started to laugh, which broke the tension.

I spoke first. "Where are you? You can't possibly be home yet."

"No, I'm at a phone booth down the block by the cleaners."

"Jim, are you out of your mind?" I laughed.

"No, for the first time in a long time, I'm seeing things quite clearly."

"Are you coming back?" When there was no answer, I asked, "Jim are you still there?" The phone wasn't cut off, but there was no one on the other end.

I hung up, then realized what was happening. I jumped out of bed and reached for a robe when the doorbell rang. I raced downstairs and opened the door without looking to see who was there. I already knew. Jim had me in his arms before I could even pretend to protest. I never got the robe on and my ratty sorority T-shirt may not have been very seductive, but it seemed to do the trick.

We were all lips tasting and hands groping. I helped Jim out of his coat, sweater, and pants. My apartment was small, and I didn't have a lot of furniture. We tumbled onto the sofa, Jim on top of me. He smoothed my hair from my face and met my eyes.

"Katie, do you want me to st—"

"Don't stop," I answered, almost breathless.

In a rush, Jim worked my T-shirt off, and I helped him get out of his shorts.

"Katie, it's been a long time since I've done this. I feel clumsy ..."

"No," I laughed. "You are just right."

***

"Kate, I'm sorry that it didn't last very long. It's been a long time since I've done this."

"You've got to be kidding. I think my insides have turned completely into jello. No one has ever made me—"

He devoured my mouth in a kiss before I could finish.

We lay on the sofa like two pretzels twisted together until the chilly air on our sweaty skin stirred us.

"I'm freezing. Let's go up to bed." I gently disentangled my arms and legs and slipped back into my shirt as Jim watched. I think he was as amazed by the experience as I was. I started to climb the spiral staircase that led to my bedroom, stopped, and turned to see if Jim was following me. "You coming?"

"I think I should go ..." he said halfheartedly, looking up at me.

"You didn't do anything to which I wasn't a willing partner. Come upstairs and at least take a shower before you go." I added as a tease, "Don't beat yourself up ... You'll do better next time."

"You really know how to hurt a guy." He couldn't help smiling.

A few moments later, I could hear him making his way up the wrought iron spiral staircase.

"Damn, how do you deal with this stupid staircase?"

"Sorry, can't hear you, I'm in the shower," I teased.

"Are you sure you want me to stay?"

"Yes, I am," I said, sticking my head out of the bathroom door with my hair wrapped in a towel.

"Boy, that was quick."

"There are extra towels on the bar. Want me to scrub your back?" I smiled.

"No, you better not. I've already embarrassed myself enough for one night." He grimaced.

Jim went into the bathroom while I threw off my towel and climbed into my double bed. I was exhausted both physically and mentally. I slipped the blanket over my breasts and wondered how I got here. The whole night was more than I could get my mind around. My lids felt heavy with the weight of my decision. In a minute, I was sound asleep.

But soon, I stirred a little when Jim cuddled in behind me. He put his arm around my waist and pulled me into his body. It wasn't long before I could feel he was ready for round two.

"Shhhh ... don't move. Let me do everything," he whispered.

I couldn't have moved if I had wanted to. The next hour was the most amazing time of my life. I had no idea something could feel that good.

Afterward, Jim reached down and scooped up the blanket that had fallen on the floor and covered us. I rolled over and fell into the best sleep of my life.

Chapter Ten

I never heard Jim get up or leave the next morning and was relieved. I was unprepared for the entire experience. No amount of Harold Robbins books or chats with my friends could have prepared me for what I had experienced. I showered and dressed for work, trying not to think about it. The problem was, I couldn't tell anyone what had happened. Hell, I wasn't even sure I wanted to talk to Jim about it.

I grabbed something out of the fridge and was almost out the door, when I saw a note Jim had left. I picked it up and read it out loud. "Good morning, last night was amazing." I had been holding my breath. "I have a meeting in Williamsburg and have to be out of town for two days. I'll call you tonight. I can't wait to see you again." I smiled at myself and shoved the note into my coat pocket.

That night I got home a bit after nine, and I tried to tell myself that I didn't expect him to call. I grabbed a bag of cookies and a glass of milk and had settled in bed to watch the news when the phone rang.

"Hello," I said, picking the phone up on the second ring. I was long past trying to play hard to get.

"Hi, it's me." Jim's voice warmed me.

"Hi, thanks for leaving the note."

"I didn't want to wake you; you looked far too comfortable."

"What time did you leave?" I asked.

"It was about 6:30 when I left your place. When I woke up, I realized my chief of staff, Bob, was picking me up at my apartment for a flight to Richmond this morning. I got there, and he was waiting in the car for me. You should have seen the look on his face when he saw me walking into the building instead of out." He laughed.

"What did you say to him?" I asked, sounding a bit worried.

"Nothing. Bob is my closest aide. He's also a friend. I told him to wait and that I'd be right down. Katie, I have to be here until Saturday. Can I see you on Sunday? Do you have to work?"

"I think I'm off on Sunday. The Redskins are out of town, and I don't think the paper is going to send anyone out for the game ..."

"Can we have dinner or something?" he asked.

Neither of us had mentioned what had happened last night. We chatted about how our day had gone when I heard a knock on Jim's door. He put the phone down, and I could hear him answering the door. His aide needed to talk to him about the next day's meeting.

"Katie, I have to hang up now. I might be tied up for some time, so I won't call you back if it's too late. We'll talk tomorrow ... okay?"

"Jim, I'm glad you called."

"Me too, goodnight," he said softly as he hung up the phone.

The next two days were back to business as usual. I tried putting Jim out of my mind, but I didn't succeed.

My assignments were average ... a small fire and the usual news stuff. I had to be in the office at noon on Saturday, so I had time to do a bit of house cleaning and pick up my laundry. I used a full-service laundry just down the street from my house.

I parked—illegally—in front and was just going to leave everything in my car while I ran in and picked up my cleaning. But there were four teenage boys eyeing my cute little convertible. They were far too interested in the car for me to leave my camera lying on the passenger seat. I grabbed it as I slid out.

The laundry was a small family-owned business. I chatted with the owner while keeping an eye on the kids. I noticed a dark sedan stopped across the street. The door opened and Senator Henry Baldwin, the senior senator from California, stepped out looking around furtively. I wouldn't have given it a second thought, except he looked out of place.

It was probably my imagination.

The senator walked into the garden of this seedy-looking Georgetown residence. He stopped and checked his surroundings again. It was unusual to see a US Senator visiting a ratty house that looked abandoned. Even the windows were covered with some sort of cloth. The small patch of lawn was overgrown with weeds and the path covered with windblown leaves and twigs.

My policy, for the most part, was if you expect the worst, you will never be disappointed. I thought I might be about to catch the senator in an extramarital tryst. It occurred to me that the idea was more than a bit hypocritical considering how I had spent the past couple of days. The possibility of catching this particular senator had a devilishly, delicious quality to it. Baldwin was an extreme right-wing type and saw communists everywhere. He also had been involved in a shady water deal in California. His development group had been trying to steal water from the Colorado River.

I went outdoors and had my Nikon off my shoulder as the senator walked up to the front door and reached for the bell. I swung my camera up to my eye, focused, and pushed the shutter. My motor drive shot four frames a second. The door opened and a man greeted the senator. He looked around, wary, and then they shook hands. I shot off a few more frames before the two disappeared into the house.

Lowering my camera, I watched the door for a minute or so. There was nothing more to see. I returned to the counter to see Mr. Chow waiting to hand me my things, with a perplexed look on his face.

"Oh, sorry to keep you waiting, just testing something on my camera," I mumbled.

"No problem, Miss Miller." He grinned.

I signed for my cleaning and quickly left the store. I had completely forgotten about the local delinquents and was happy to see that my car was still there and in one piece.

It was a beautiful fall day and driving with the top down was my special treat. I swung around behind the White House to the Ellipse—the park between the White House and the Washington Monument. There, I spotted a group of college kids flying kites, and I recognized the scene immediately. My sorority at George Washington University had a kite flying contest every fall. The new pledges made their own kites. Whenever I saw kites, it took me back to the time I was twelve and believed it was a miracle if I got a kite up in the air.

I decided to stop. If there were no big breaking news tomorrow, maybe I could get them in the newspaper. Even if they didn't make the first section, they might make the Metro section. It was worth a try. Some of the kites were really up there, several hundred feet off the ground.

I parked and hustled over to where they were standing. Just as I was going to introduce myself, someone on a bullhorn told the girls to pull down their kites. Apparently, the President was about to take off from the south lawn of the White House, and security was afraid the kites might interfere with Marine One. *Great.* I grinned. Now, it *was* newsworthy. I got a picture of two girls with their kites still in the air in the foreground, the Washington Monument in the background, and in between were two helicopters. It only took a few minutes to ID the students and I was on my way to the office.

The next morning, the kite flyers were on the front page with the headline, **Girls pull in their kites for the President**, complete with a short article describing how the kite was the symbol of the sorority. *They were going to love this.* I smiled, thinking, *right place, right time.*

That's really a simplification. I was an observer. The trick is to be able to have the instinct to see and be able to react. That means you have to be ready, know your equipment, and react before the moment is gone. I succeeded in Tehran big time. If I stuck to my instincts, I might just be able to do it again. Every job wasn't going to be a world shaking event, but the pressure to deliver was always there. Coming back to the office empty handed a few times, I would be out, and I'd become the precedent for why women don't belong.

I know I can do the job. In fact, my attitude was ... bring it on.

Chapter Eleven

Jim called and we arranged to meet at a little French café, Au Pied du Cochon, another one of Georgetown's oldest spots. I spent the rest of Sunday tidying up my house and was ready to go early. If I was apprehensive the last time we were going to meet, this time I was eager. I still found the whole experience overwhelming because our chemistry was off the charts, but I couldn't wait to see him again.

I got to the restaurant, and Jim was nowhere to be seen. I walked in and found two empty stools at the bar. I would have to talk to Jim about his choices ... it looked like it was a scene from a 1940s movie.

I ordered a beer and sat staring at the huge fish tank on the back bar. it. It was full of plants and the glass had a green algae coating. At first, I didn't think there was anything in it. It looked like the seaweed and algae had completely taken over the tank.

"See the turtles?" Jim said, leaning close to my ear.

"Hi, I didn't see you come in." I leaned into him. After seeing the senator this morning, I didn't want to become the target of anyone else's camera. "What turtles? Nothing could live in that mess."

"Just keep watching. I'll have a beer, please," Jim called to the bartender. "Have you been here long?"

"No, not really. I got here about five minutes ago. Is this another one of your favorite spots?" I asked.

"Don't you like it?" he asked, looking around. The waiter brought Jim his beer, and we both settled in to stare at the fish tank.

"I think you are wrong about the turtles," I teased.

"No, keep watching," he said. "There's one."

"Where? You're kidding," I laughed.

"Charlie, can you feed the turtles? This young lady doesn't believe anything can live in your swamp," Jim called to the bartender.

"You're on a first name basis with the bartender?"

"I don't cook. This place is on the way home, and they serve food at all hours. I love their onion soup if you must know." Jim said, leaning close enough to have our shoulders touching. The bartender walked by the tank and dropped in some pieces of cut shrimp. Three small green turtles charged the top of the tank and began to battle over the food.

"Look at the little critters go at it." Jim laughed.

"Hey, I'm really glad to see you," I whispered.

"Me too," he whispered back, and we both smiled. This was not going to be an easy relationship ... always being on guard when we were out in public. I told Jim about my run-in with the senator and my concerns for Jim's reputation. He didn't seem concerned but saw the irony in my attempt to nail the senator.

"Senator Baldwin is a real piece of work," he said. "He's looking for a place on the national ticket."

"Hopefully, it won't matter ... I don't really think the Republicans have a chance." Jim didn't respond, instead signaling to the waiter we were ready for our table.

Dinner lasted for hours. Jim talked about his meeting in Williamsburg. I listened, thinking things seemed backward. We had been incredibly intimate and now were talking about work. We were about to be the last people to leave the restaurant. Unlike the breakfast place, this place made us feel completely at home.

"I really like this place," I said as we waited for the bill. "Though I am a bit worried we might see turtle soup on the menu."

***

We walked back toward my townhouse arm in arm. Georgetown at night is magical. The houses go back to the late 1700s and early 1800s. The streetlights are gas as are most of the outdoor lights on the houses. Many of the streets are still cobblestone and you could just imagine carriages making their way down the narrow lanes. Except for the cars parked on the streets, you could be in the middle of the last century. We walked back to my apartment, but were in no hurry, taking the long way.

"Jim, this is all new to me," I said.

"What is?" Jim asked.

"You ... me, whatever it is that we're getting into," I answered.

"Katie, if you turned around and walked out of my life tonight, and these last few days were all I could have, I could die a happy man." He looked me directly in the eyes. "*But* ... I'm hoping for a lot more days and nights like this past week. The way I see it, things are only going to get better."

He stopped, took me in his arms, and looked at me.

"You should know. I've never done anything like the other night," he whispered. "I've led a sort of boring life, until then. What I'm feeling now is new, wonderful, and scary all at the same time."

I took that in and believed him. "Me either," I felt exposed, perhaps a little embarrassed, but better. We walked the rest of the way in silence.

We reached the front of my apartment and shuffled around. Neither of us knew what to do. I knew what *I* wanted to do, but Jim stopped me dead in my tracks.

"Katie, I really want to be with you tonight, but I want you to feel comfortable with what we're doing."

"Okay ..."

"Do you want to slow down a little?"

I stared into his eyes, warring with myself.

"Am I the only one doing the talking here?" he laughed.

"Jim, I agree. This is happening amazingly fast ... I want you to come in ... but maybe you shouldn't," I said, reaching up to touch his cheek with the back of my hand.

He took my hand and gently kissed it.

"Seeing the senator yesterday hit me. I've been thinking about our situation, and I feel more than a little hypocritical. I have a lot to think about."

"I understand. Are you saying you want to stop?"

I shook my head. And whispered no.

He blew out a stream of air. "I'm glad. So ... I have meetings the next two nights. Can we have dinner Wednesday?"

"That would be great ... I'll cook and we can stay in."

His brows rose. "Do you know how to cook?"

"No, but I'll learn by Wednesday," I said, trying to sound serious.

Chapter Twelve

Jim and I settled into a comfortable relationship. From that night on, we spent all of our free time together. Fall turned into winter, and I pretended not to mind when Jim had to go to South Carolina for the holidays. I flew home to Chicago to spend Christmas with my parents but only stayed two days. I never turned down any extra shifts at the paper. The other guys had families and were happy to have the time off. I was happy to see the New Year and hoped that life would get back to normal.

The New Year was also a presidential election year, which meant Jim had to stand for reelection in his South Carolina district. I really didn't fully understand the magnitude of the job, or the implications an election would have on our relationship. Jim had to win a primary in March. Once that was done, he could coast for a while. It was probably decades since a Democrat had won his district, but he needed to be in there as much as possible, which meant he had to fly home almost every weekend.

I learned that an election year changes everything in Washington, DC. All the politicians want to make sure their constituents know how hard they are working. At *The Post*, we were deluged with photo requests from the Hill and the White House. Jim and I spoke on the phone daily but were lucky if we got to spend two evenings a week together. I did my part to help Jim get reelected. Anytime I had an assignment that included him, he came out looking like a star. I would make sure Jim got shots he could use in his campaign. I was part of the political scene by virtue of my job, but I really wasn't paying much attention to the races. Most of my photographic jobs involved night work. I didn't mind; in fact, I welcomed it. Being busy helped to keep my mind off Jim.

Just before the South Carolina primary, the political picture started to shift. The senior Senator from California, Henry Baldwin, was making a big push for the Republican Presidential nomination.

I didn't think he had much of a chance. Senator Baldwin was too conservative for the top spot, but his name recognition could help the ticket win California, and that alone would get his name in the ring for the vice-presidential spot. *The Post* started to follow Baldwin with more than a passing interest. They were traditionally a liberal paper, and the thought of Baldwin on a national ticket had management on their toes. They decided to send a reporter and photographer to Columbia and Charleston to cover his campaign. South Carolina was conservative enough that he could possibly carry the state in the primary.

Scott dropped the information sheets on the desk where I was camping. "Kate, I've got a three-day assignment for you."

"Hi Scott, nice to see you too," I answered.

Scott was up to his eyeballs in political stuff and was in no mood to put up with my smart remarks. "You have a flight to Columbia in about three hours, so you better get your stuff together and get your ass to the airport."

I sat there looking over the assignment sheet without answering.

"Kate, are you listening to me? Your reporter is Dave Johnson. He'll meet you at the airport."

He was my buddy from Tehran. I would enjoy seeing him, but I didn't want to go to South Carolina where I'd run into Jim and his wife campaigning together. "I don't suppose I have any choice, do I?"

"Nope, Dave asked for you, end of story." He strolled off.

I grabbed my camera stuff, enough film for the trip, and hustled home to pack just enough to get me through three days of hot, muggy daytime rallies and probably some kind of political dinner at night.

There was one bright spot to the whole trip. I would be working with Dave. I made it to the airport with plenty of time to spare. He was nowhere in sight, so after I checked in, I headed to the nearest bar. Dave was camped out in a far corner reading the *New York Times*. I walked over and dumped my stuff on the empty chair.

"Dave, how are you?"

He jumped, at first startled, and then stood up to give me a big hug.

"Kate, great to see you. I'm glad you're coming to Columbia with me."

"Yep ... together again. Let's hope this time isn't as exciting as our first adventure." I laughed.

Dave moved his stuff, called the server over, and ordered another beer for himself and one for me.

"Dave, what do you think of Baldwin?" I asked.

"I don't really know too much about him, but what I do know, I don't like. He is a real hawk. I was covering a committee hearing, and it was obvious he thought the women members were not mentally equal to the men. If you asked him, he probably would tell you it was a dark day when women got the right to vote. Why?"

"I don't really like him much. He seems, I don't know, weird." I shrugged.

"What makes you say that? I know he's too conservative for me. I won't be voting for him, but I don't know about weird," Dave answered. "I don't think it really matters; he doesn't really have a chance even if he were to get on the Republican ticket. I can't see the Republicans winning no matter what." We sat chatting about nothing in particular and managed to down another round of beers before boarding our flight. We were to meet up with the Baldwin campaign in Columbia, the capital of South Carolina.

Our plane was late, and we had to go directly to a political dinner and fundraiser given by the governor and the Republican Party. Columbia really isn't a very big city. After we rented a car, we were able to find the hotel without much trouble. Dave gave our luggage to a bell boy, arranged for him to get our bags to our rooms, and collected our keys.

"The dinner we are supposed to cover is in the 'Fort Sumter' room. Can you believe it? Do you think they have an Appomattox room?"

"No, they probably don't celebrate their defeats," he said, giving me a bit of a dirty look, and handing me my room key.

"Just kidding, don't get serious on me now," I said, giving him a dirty look right back. "I hate these dinner things. There's nothing good to shoot."

"We're late so let's get going. At least we get a free meal out of the deal. I'm starved." He smiled.

We headed down to the ballroom where the dinner was being held. The nice thing about these events, they always have a table set up for the press right near the head table. They wouldn't want us to miss one word of the speeches. This was a fundraiser for Baldwin, and he was busy meeting the local political hacks. One of his aides would take someone up to the senator, he would put down his fried chicken long enough to pose for a picture, and drip with charm. It was also another one of those events filled with flowered dresses, white gloves, and cute little hats. Dave and I settled in and waited for something to happen. This had all the promise of being a very boring evening. The chairman of the state Republicans finally rose to introduce the senator, and I went up front to get ready. I quietly moved into place kneeling in front of the podium. Photographers basically get to go wherever they want. The trick is to not start sneezing or do anything else that will throw off the speaker.

The state chairman looked a bit nervous. He kept smiling and making eye contact with someone just over my shoulder. I shifted around to get a look. A raven haired "Scarlet O'Hara" type I'd seen once before in Washington was giving him her best supportive smile. I looked at the guy sitting next to her. It was Jim.

My heart skipped a beat. He looked me straight in the eye. I brought up my camera and snapped a couple of pictures in self-defense, then quickly turned back to the podium. I broke into a cold sweat and really hadn't been listening. As I turned to face the podium, the senator was standing and waving to the adoring crowd. I shot more than enough pictures during the senator's speech without hearing one word that he said. I wanted to turn around and look at

Jim but couldn't. My stomach was tied in a knot. I thought I was going to throw up.

Baldwin finished, and the crowd came to their feet to give him a hearty round of applause. Dave came closer to the head table. He had a few questions for the Senator and was too busy to see what I was doing. Jim was surrounded by a group of local "pols," and I didn't think he saw me leave the room.

I wanted to get as far away from the Sumter Room as possible. Once I was outside the building in the night air, I felt a lot better. At least I didn't think I was going to lose my dinner. I was leaning against a tree sorting out my feelings. I knew sooner or later I was going to run into Jim's wife. *She may have him legally, but at least I hoped I had his heart and mind.* That sounded so stupid I couldn't believe I was even thinking about it.

"Hi, seen any little turtles lately?" a voice came from over my shoulder.

"Jim, where are you?" I turned to look for him.

"Here," he said, stepping around the tree and ending up right in front of me.

"Do you think this is a good idea? What if someone sees us?" I said, looking around.

"Angela and her father went up to the senator's suite. I told them I had to talk to some of my campaign people, and I would see them later."

"Shouldn't you be with the senator?"

"Hey, are you trying to get rid of me?" Jim smiled seductively.

"No. God, I miss you. How long are you going to be here?"

"I'm going to Charleston tomorrow, and I'll be back in Washington right after the primary."

"Me too. I'm with Dave Johnson. He's probably with the Senator in his suite, too. Actually, I'd better find out. He might want me to get some shots."

He looked over his shoulder to scan the crowd. Then he looked at me again. "Where are you staying? Here I hope."

"You're not thinking ..."

"I sure am. I miss you so much, I ache," he whispered as a bunch of the dinner guests passed by. "Let's live dangerously. You go up and do your job. Just make sure the senator looks bad. Okay? Give me your key." Jim looked around. Luckily, it was really dark where we were standing. The large live oaks blocked all the light coming from the hotel patio.

"So much for being careful." I laughed. I dug my room key out of my pocket and gave it to him. As he took the key, he held my hand long enough to give it a gentle squeeze. I quickly pulled it away from him and looked around to see if anyone was interested in what we were doing.

"Jim, let's be smart here. Remember when I thought Senator Baldwin was having an affair? How many photographers and reporters do you think are down here?" I didn't wait for him to answer. "Let's get you reelected before anyone finds out about us."

"I see your point. I'll see a few people and then make my way to your room. Sounds exciting, doesn't it?"

"You're an idiot. Yes, it does sound exciting." I laughed.

I turned and walked back into the hotel without looking back at Jim. Once I was inside, I got the senator's suite number and a second key to my room. The senator was on the top floor, about as far away from my room as you could get. I shared the elevator with some of the senator's staff who totally ignored me. They were too busy talking about how well the dinner went, and how they felt they had a chance to carry South Carolina.

The door opened on the top floor, and we all poured into the hall. I just followed the crowd into the Calhoun Suite. The place was full, and they even had a piano player contributing elevator music to the scene. Dave was standing by the bar with a beer in his hand. I waved and made my way across the room.

"Hey, where have you been? The senator is going to give me ten minutes alone. It might be a good idea for you to get a few shots." Political chatter filled the room. Everyone seemed to think Baldwin was a winner and someone they wanted to hang out with.

"I was outside getting some air. Anything important happen?"

"No, not really, but I agree with you." Dave said.

"Agree about what?" I asked.

"The senator is weird. In fact, it is more than weird. He's downright scary," he whispered.

"What makes you say that?"

"Nothing you can put your finger on. I don't think he can win the presidential nomination. I don't know, it's like he's playing some sort of game, but he wouldn't be the first guy to be running for Vice President," he mumbled, watching the senator charm the locals.

Baldwin was holding court. Angela and her father were standing on either side of him, obviously enjoying the limelight. From the laughter, you would think the senator could have a second career as a stand-up comic.

"Who is the woman next to him?" Dave asked, leaning over and whispering in my ear.

"I think it's Angela Rayford. Her father is the guy on the other side of Baldwin."

"Rayford, the congressman's wife?"

"I think so. Her father is the state chairman."

"I wonder where the congressman is?"

"I don't think he likes Baldwin much. Their politics certainly aren't the same."

"Let's get in the senator's face and have this over with. Our flight leaves early. Oh, did I tell you? We're flying to Charleston on the senator's campaign plane. He's invited us to breakfast and from there, we'll leave for Charleston."

"What do rightwing reactionaries eat for breakfast these days?" I asked as we walked toward the senator.

"I'm sure something with grits," he said, moving across the room.

I followed behind, dreading the next ten minutes but looking forward to the next few hours. Just thinking about how absurd this whole scene was made me smile.

"Senator, do you think you'd have time now to give me a few minutes?" Dave asked, nodding to the adoring flock gathered around him.

"Mr. Johnson, glad you could make our little party. Who is this charming young lady?" he said, smiling at me. Giving me a long look from head to toe.

"Kate Miller, sir," I said, extending my hand.

"Miss Miller, a pleasure to meet you. You'll make sure to get my good side when you take my picture now, won't you?" he looked pleased with himself.

"Senator, I'll do my best." *Your good side would be a picture of your ass, you turkey.* I smiled all the while.

"Mr. Johnson, I would like you to meet our state chairman, Alex Bradford, and his lovely daughter, Angela Rayford," the Senator said, introducing us to Jim's wife and her father.

"Pleasure to meet you," Dave mumbled. He hated all this bullshit and could care less about the little niceties. He wanted to ask how many Black people they had in the party and a bunch of embarrassing questions, but he just smiled. "Mrs. Rayford, is the congressman with you this evening?" Dave asked.

"He's somewhere," she said, waving a hand. "He was at the dinner, but then he's more interested in talking to his staff than joining the senator."

I just smiled. The senator excused himself, giving Angela an overly friendly peck on the cheek as we followed him into the bedroom of his suite. He was making silly small talk about how charming southern women were. Dave and I just nodded, like those little dolls with bouncy heads. Dave started to ask him questions, and I unpacked my camera to get ready to shoot the senator.

Dave was serving up softball questions to this guy. I gave him a questioning look. He gave me a *mind your own business, don't you have some pictures to take*, look. I just smiled and worked my way around the room to get a good angle. I didn't want a lampshade growing out of the senator's head.

Baldwin was also doing some serving up. Platitudes were flying right and left. He managed to skate over every question while saying the right thing. He announced he was going to do well in this state and on and on.

Dave leaned close. "Have enough?"

I nodded. We thanked the senator for his time, and he reiterated his offer for breakfast and a ride to Charleston.

"We'll meet you in the restaurant at 8:00 tomorrow, Senator. What time do you expect to leave for Charleston?" Dave asked.

"That's the beauty of a private plane. It will leave when we get there." The senator laughed.

We joined in the merriment and quickly made our way out of the senator's bedroom. The party was still going strong. Angela's father had taken over the piano and was having a sing- along. Those Republicans sure knew how to party. Dave was still scratching down notes while we waited for the elevator.

"Kate, do you want to get a drink?" He asked, looking up from his notepad.

"No, I don't think so. Guess I'll turn in and rest up for round two with the senator. He really thinks he's a charmer, doesn't he?"

"Boy is that the truth," he said, stepping aside to let me on the elevator first.

I pushed my button and asked him what floor his room was on.

"Push lobby, will you? I think I'll go hang out in the bar and see if I can dig up any dirt on these good ole boys."

The car stopped at my floor, and I quickly stepped out giving Dave a little wave. "See you tomorrow in the restaurant at 8:00, right?" I asked, not really waiting for an answer. I wandered down the hall looking for my room. It must have been a two-block walk from the elevator. I hadn't told Jim I was going to get a second key, so it was going to be fun to see how he reacted when I opened the door. I slipped the key in as quietly as I could, smiling to myself. I opened the door and listened for any noise in the room. The TV was on, but that was about it. I walked into the main part of the room and was about to drop all of my camera equipment when I found Jim sound asleep on the bed. He jumped a little when I sat down next to him.

"Hi, I didn't hear you come in," he said, still half asleep.

"Hi, sorry it took so long. The senator was throwing quite a party. Jim, I met your wife and her father. They seemed to be very chummy with Baldwin."

"My father-in-law thinks he's hitching his wagon to a rising star," Jim said, stretching his arms over his head.

"Boy is that scary," I said, sitting on the edge of the bed next to Jim.

"Enough about politics, come here," Jim said, taking my hand and pulling me forward, until I was mostly on top of him. "It is so nice to see you. I've been miserable here."

I looked into his eyes and smiled.

"It's nice to see you, too," I agreed, leaning down to kiss his half-open lips. We laid there holding on to each other for dear life.

"It was very weird being introduced to your wife and her father." The moment I said it, I regretted it. *What a way to kill the mood*. I rolled away from Jim and sat on the edge of the bed.

Jim turned toward me, rubbing my back with his hand.

"What did you think?" He asked.

"About what?" I turned and asked.

"That's a fair enough question."

"You mean Angela?"

"I'm sorry. I'm sure it was very awkward for you."

"Oh no, not at all. Hello Mrs. Rayford. How're you doing? I've got your husband holed up in my hotel room." I crossed my arms. "Hell, yes it was uncomfortable. It's one thing knowing she exists. It's another to stand there making small talk."

"I'm sorry." Jim said dejectedly.

I blew out a plume of air. "Wait. Let's see ... What did I think? She's extremely attractive, but you're right. I don't think she likes you very much. She was much more interested in talking about the senator than talking about you. Dave asked her where you were, and she didn't seem to care." I paused, looking to change the subject.

"I'm thirsty. I'm going to order something from room service. How about some beers and a pizza?" I asked, not waiting for an answer.

Jim nodded vaguely, thinking about what I'd just said.

I called room service, and they promised to get a six pack and a pizza up to the room in 45 minutes or less.

"It's going to take three quarters of an hour." I turned and smiled. "Now what do you suppose we can do to fill up forty-five minutes?"

From then on, it was a race to see who could get out of their clothes the fastest. We'd been apart long enough to make this reunion a bit frantic. I'm not sure if it was because we hadn't had sex in a while, or that we were worried about the pizza delivery, but we'd finished making love in fifteen minutes. I climbed out of bed and put on Jim's shirt. It was long enough to cover all of the essentials.

"Why are men's shirts so long?" I asked, modeling his oxford cloth button-down.

"I'm not sure, but I like the way it looks on you. I would prefer it about six inches shorter though," he grinned.

We both jumped with the knock on the door.

"Just a second," I called out. I grabbed my wallet and walked over to the door. I turned just in time to see Jim roll off the far side of the bed and crash onto the floor.

I giggled, opening the door just enough to see the waiter standing there with the pizza and a brown bag.

"Hi, how much do I owe you?" I asked, as he handed me a bill. "Here's a $20 bill and keep the change," I said, taking the box and bag. I closed the door before he could say thank you as Jim's head popped up from the far side of the bed.

"Nice move, very smooth," I laughed. I took the pizza over to the bed and went into the bathroom to retrieve face towels to use as napkins. We managed to devour the pizza, and in no time had killed off most of the six-pack.

"Why were you at this dinner?" I asked.

"I could ask the same of you." he answered.

"Fair enough. The paper is interested in Baldwin," I answered, sitting cross-legged at the end of the bed while Jim sat propped up by pillows at the head. "All of a sudden, he seems to be a contender. I'm sure *The Post* isn't thrilled about it. Dave's angle is 'right-wing going mainstream, I think. How about you?"

"I really didn't have to be there, but I would like to get as much support from the state committee as possible. I could use their money and manpower, so it seemed like a good idea. And besides this was a big night for Alex, and my absence would have been noticed."

"Baldwin thinks he can carry the state," I said, more of a question than a statement. "I don't think so, but I could be wrong. If he does, he'll have a bit more influence at the convention. Even more important, he'll have two states waving his placards in front of the TV cameras. There's no question, in my mind, Scheffen has had a great career, first as Illinois governor and then in the Senate. He seems to be a real *man* of the people. The Republicans would be nuts if they didn't nominate him. Baldwin is just a bump in the road."

We sat talking about politics and finished the six-pack for at least another hour. It had to be past midnight, and I knew Jim had to leave or really get himself in hot water.

"When are you leaving for Charleston?" he asked.

"We're meeting Baldwin for breakfast, and we've been invited to fly with him to Charleston."

"Small world. Alex and I are flying with him also."

"How about your wife?" I asked, afraid to hear the answer.

"I'm not sure. I think she plans to drive down. She doesn't like flying much, especially in anything smaller than a Boeing 707. We haven't talked about it," Jim shrugged. The *we* part hurt a bit, and I think Jim realized it the moment he said it.

"Katie, I know how awkward this is for you. Before I met you, I was content with my life, but now nothing could be further from the truth. I can't do anything about it right now. Once the election is over and we're safely into the next session of the House, I will deal with Angela. Hopefully, she's as unhappy with our relationship as I am. Our marriage has been over for a long time. I just didn't realize it until I met you."

I just listened. I wanted to hear this, and yet I didn't want to push him. I was willing to keep everything the way it was. The thought of losing Jim was impossible to comprehend.

"Jim, I knew you were married, and I chose to be in this relationship. Does that mean I don't want more? I'd be a liar if I said that. I also know how much you love your job, and that it could be taken away from you. So, let's keep everything on an even keel for now. Let's get through the election and just live our lives. I'm happy with that for now. After the election is history and everything gets back to normal, then you can start thinking about our future. I'm not going anywhere."

"Thank you." He glanced at the clock. "Oh my God, do you know what time it is?" Jim asked.

"I have no idea," I said, looking at the small digital clock on the TV. "It's past two, you'd better get going."

"Yep, can I have my shirt back? It might make me a dead give-a-way to show up with only half of my clothes," he laughed.

I rolled toward Jim on the bed, and we kissed goodnight. I was tempted to take it a few steps further but thought better of it. I rolled back off the bed, unbuttoned his shirt, and tossed it back at him as I escaped to the bathroom.

"I'm going to take a shower. You better make your getaway before I change my mind and have my way with you."

Jim caught his shirt and laughed as he put it on and started looking for his pants and shoes. I started the shower and jumped in as soon as the water was hot. Jim quickly dressed and stuck his head though the bathroom doorway.

"I'm going. See you at breakfast. Sweet dreams," Jim called.

"See you in a few hours," I said, sticking my head out of the shower.

Jim left, and I was both happy and sad. Tomorrow was going to be a tough day. I'd never been anywhere in public in such close proximity to Jim. I wasn't sure how it was going to play out.

Chapter Thirteen

The phone next to my bed woke me from a dead sleep. I managed to knock the receiver off the table trying to answer it. "Hello," I mumbled.

"Good morning, this is your wake-up call. It's 7:00 o'clock." A perky voice chirped.

"I didn't ask for a wake-up call, did I?"

"No Ma'am Mr. Johnson set it up," the operator answered. "Ya'll have a nice day."

"Okay thanks." I put the phone down. I had a whole hour before I had to be downstairs. I didn't really feel like taking another shower. I decided to catch the local TV news and organize my hair. Might as well see how Baldwin played with the locals. He was the lead story right after the weather. I watched with some amusement as the local reporter fawned over the senator's visit.

"The senator's right. He might just carry this state," I mused. I dressed with the TV playing in the background, and I also got my camera gear ready. I should have asked Dave about today's schedule but figured I'd have time to take care of that over breakfast.

I was ready in plenty of time. I found the breakfast room the senator had arranged and also found a newsstand where I picked up a copy of *The Post*. Last night's happenings didn't make the paper. A little too provincial for *The Post*, I guess. I found a comfortable chair with a good view of the dining room. This hotel had chosen the Civil War for their entire décor. It was a bit weird. I couldn't imagine a German hotel decorating the lobby with pictures of dead WWII generals. Maybe they didn't want to admit that they lost the war. I sure wasn't going to be the one to tell them.

I started with the front page of *The Post* and methodically made my way through the paper. I read it cover to cover every day, wanting to see my pictures and everyone else's for that matter. Being part of the photo staff was sort of being part of a team. Maybe not a really friendly team, but most of the time, it was an "us against them" mentality.

Watching the door, I wasn't planning to move until I saw Dave. Everyone appeared all at once. The senator chatted with one of his aides. Just behind him was the Rayford contingent and behind them was Dave, looking a bit worried until he saw me waiting. Alex Bradford, his daughter Angela, and Jim all gave me a small nod as they passed. At least Jim and Mr. Bradford gave me a friendly smile. Angela was far more interested in catching up to the senator and jockeying for the best seat at the table.

"Good morning, Kate, Sleep well?" Dave walked up to me

"Yes, I was in bed almost immediately." I hid my smile.

"Time to go in and watch the show begin."

The two of us hung back and waited for all the political types to find a seat. We took what was left.

"We don't need anything for the paper until after the election Tuesday. I'm supposed to be getting background for a feature that will run about the time of the convention. I'm not sure what my angle will be yet. Go ahead and make him look as bad as you like. Consider yourself an assassin with a camera," he grinned. "But don't forget the piece can't be all negative, so you better get at least one shot of him kissing a baby or something."

"How about kissing the congressman's wife?" I said, watching the senator plant a big one on Angela.

Jim was already seated, reading the paper, oblivious to the whole scenario.

"Huh?" Dave asked, looking around to catch the tail end of the scene.

The breakfast went by quietly, and thank God, quickly. Jim and I made a game out of not looking at each other. The senator chatted with everyone, but he seemed mostly interested in Angela.

"Isn't the senator married?" I leaned over and whispered into Dave's ear.

"Yeah, he's been married for at least a dozen years to some Newport Beach socialite."

"He sure has taken a shine to Angela, hasn't he?"

"No more than you flirting with the congressman."

"What the hell," I sputtered.

Dave just smiled and gave me a sort of "who you are trying to kid" look. Everyone was finishing their coffee as the senator stood, smiling around the room, as if he were going to start a speech.

"Ladies and gentlemen, thanks for joining us for breakfast. Why don't we adjourn to the airport and head for Charleston?"

While we were at breakfast, the hotel staff had loaded our luggage into a couple of vans parked outside the front door. We made our way to a small bus. Much to my surprise, Angela joined us. She seemed in good spirits and made a point of telling everyone that she was going to be the hostess for the senator's reception in Charleston since his "poor" wife was stuck in California.

Once we were on the plane, I sat as far from the congressman and family as possible. I might not have sat near Jim, but that didn't mean I wouldn't watch him from behind my sunglasses. Dave spent most of the flight sitting across the aisle from Baldwin and taking notes. Jim kept his head down most of the flight reading several papers, one of which was *The Post*, which brought a small smile to my face. Angela spent most of the flight checking her makeup and listening to the senator's conversation.

When we landed, there was another bus waiting to take us to a downtown hotel. It only took us twenty minutes from the airport until we were in the historic section of the city. I was surprised how small Charleston was, considering all the history in the area. We were staying in a hotel General Lee had stayed in according to Angela. It reminded me of Georgetown. Sort of a Georgetown with palmetto trees. Dave and I thanked the senator for the ride and made our way to the hotel lobby to check in and see if there were any messages.

The next two days were a vacation for the two of us. The senator had a few things on his schedule, but for the most part, we were free to enjoy the city. We followed the senator around to very predictable and boring events. I didn't see Jim at any of them, which was actually a plus. This guy was too right wing for my liking. I was happy Jim wanted to stay away from him. I couldn't say as much for Angela. She showed up at *every* event. I was beginning to enjoy the show she put on. I guess what I really liked was her being away from Jim and his campaign. I was waiting for Dave to come down to the lobby when he walked up behind me.

"Kate, I was just on the phone with the office. They seem to think we should get back and start covering some real news."

"I don't really think I have got anything great to put with your article. At least election night might be a good photo op."

He paused, trying to decide what the best thing to do was.

"Okay, if you think you need to get more. I can't believe you don't have enough, but I'm not going to tell you how to do your job. I'll call them back and tell them we'll get the first flight out on Wednesday morning."

Jim and I hadn't talked since we left Columbia, but I caught him on the local news. He sounded confident and looked quite relaxed. We followed the senator around for the next two nights and ended up camping out in a hotel ballroom waiting for the primary results Tuesday night. There were no surprises. That was the best news that I could hear. Baldwin didn't carry the state, but he did come in a respectable second and seemed happy about it. All the other races went as expected. Jim won his primary handily and was headed for an easy fall reelection. I wanted to talk to Jim but knew that was out of the question. Dave and I made an early night of it. The senator gave a "rah-rah" speech to his adoring fans. Angela was at his side with tears welling up in her eyes.

The next morning Dave and I were booked on the first flight back to DC. Before leaving for the airport, I checked with the front desk to see if there were any messages for me. The desk clerk handed me an envelope with my name and room number on it. Just then, Dave appeared. He had a cab waiting outside and was in a hurry to get going. I shoved the envelope into my pocket before Dave could ask me about it.

We were running late, and the cab driver couldn't, or more likely wouldn't, guarantee we'd make our flight, but we made it to the airport with a good five minutes to spare. Dave paid for the cab, and I went ahead to the check-in. We ran through the airport, shouting apologies over our shoulders. We made it to the gate in time, but not without almost flattening three little old ladies and a couple of toddlers. I'm sure we reinforced the stereotype of the rude northerner.

When Dave went to use the facilities, I opened the envelope and read over the note quickly before I saw him coming back up the aisle. All it said was, **Everything's fine. I'll see you back in Washington.** I folded the note and tucked it into my bag as Dave and I settled in for the rest of the flight.

The great thing about a feature article for a photographer was that you didn't have to get your film back to the office for any kind of deadline. What wasn't used for Dave's feature would become file shots and could be used in the future, depending on how much influence the senator had.

Back in Washington, we went our separate ways. I wanted to get back to my house in Georgetown, drop my luggage off, and check to see if I still had a car. Turning the corner onto Prospect, my little Mustang was right where I left it. I quickly checked to see if it had all of its tires. *God, there were times I was such a pessimist.* The first thing I did, once I wrestled my gear through my front door, was to check my answering machine. I was happy to see the little red-light blinking. Jim had left three messages. Two were from his election headquarters. He sounded happy, and more than that, relieved. The third call was just a few hours ago. He had called the hotel and was told I had checked out. He would be staying in Charleston for the rest of the week and not return to DC until the next Monday. He promised to call later.

His re-election in the fall was just about a sure thing, but he still needed to spend every weekend in his district. That was really a blessing in disguise. I had been concentrating on my relationship with him and not working very hard on my job. I planned to spend every weekend with the photo staff, which gave me some quality time to bond. I think they missed having a "broad" to pick on. A few weekends with the typical urban mayhem brought me back to reality. Nothing like some good murders, robberies, and fires to hone your photo skills.

Chapter Fourteen

In April, the cherry blossoms around the Tidal Basin brought out the tourists in droves. The city would be rife with them all summer right through August when school started. If this city was hard to get around normally, it was murder when you were caught behind a Winnebago trying to find a place to park. August would also bring the National Conventions. *The Post* would send a lot of writers, but probably only one photographer. They could get all the "art" they needed using the Associated Press or United Press International. I certainly wasn't high in seniority and didn't look forward to watching the party faithful prance around in silly hats. I didn't get to see Jim more than a couple nights a week, but we managed to talk several times a day.

It was a slow Thursday, with all my assignments already in for the weekend paper. Congress would be out of session the beginning of next week, and Jim was going to South Carolina to take care of some political business and check in with his wife and her parents. My logical mind told me that there was no problem with this whole thing, but my gut was twisted in a knot. I was trying to be mature. The reality was, I was madly in love with a married man, and I could only be in part of his life. I accepted the reality, but I didn't have to like it.

I looked up from my desk to see Scott walking toward me.

"Don't you have some pictures to print?" he asked.

"Nope everything's done," I replied, looking rather smug.

"Go find something to do. I don't want to give the impression that the photo staff is underworked. By the way, you have a lot of overtime. If you don't use it, you'll lose it. Why don't you take tomorrow and the weekend off?" he added.

"Nah, I don't think so. The weather is supposed to be bad all weekend. I'd rather save it for another time."

"Your call, just an idea," he shrugged. "In any case, get your butt out of here. Go hide in the darkroom or something."

"Yes sir." I picked up my camera and headed for the darkroom. I spent the next half-hour working myself into a really bad mood. I was being selfish. I wanted to be with Jim, not sitting here waiting for some silly assignment. The darkroom phone rang on the second line, which meant it was someone from the paper or someone with close ties to the photo staff.

"Darkroom," I barked into the phone.

"Hi, Katie?" Jim answered.

The edginess melted from my voice the moment I heard his voice. "Hi, where are you calling from?"

"I'm on the House floor, well actually just off the floor. What are you doing?"

"Just sitting around working myself into a bad mood. You haven't left, and I already miss you."

"That's why I'm calling. I was planning to go next Tuesday but how about going with me for the weekend? We can drive down. You can come back when you need to, and I'll stay and get my work done. Sound good?"

"It sounds great, but how do we work it out? Got a spare room in the family homestead?" I asked, pointing out the obvious with a heaping dose of sarcasm.

"Wouldn't that be something?" he pondered. "I have a place at the beach. It was left to me by my grandfather. It's on an island near Charleston. My wife hates it. She was there once and has never been back."

"I love it already. I have to get time off from Scott. Can you call me right back?

"Sure, how much time do you need?" He asked.

"Give me five minutes, no make it three minutes."

He laughed as he hung up the phone. It took me about a minute to find Scott. He was standing at the Metro editor's desk on the other side of the newsroom.

"Scott, I've changed my mind," I called out to get his attention. He looked up as I walked over to him. "I'm going to take a couple of days off. I've got all my assignments in, so I'll see you Wednesday, okay?"

"Boy that sure was a change of heart." He looked confused. "I thought you said the weather was bad."

"It changed!" I smiled and waved as I made my way back to the darkroom. The phone rang just as I stepped through the door.

"Darkroom," I answered, picking it up on the second ring.

"All set?" Jim asked.

"Yep, when do we leave?"

"How long will it take you to pack some things?"

"Including the drive to my apartment, about forty-five minutes, why?"

"Well, I can leave from here. I have clothes at the beach, and I can have my aide bring some material for work when he comes down on Tuesday."

"It's almost noon now, do you want me to get my clothes and pick you up at your office?"

"Call me when you are leaving your house. I'll wait fifteen minutes and then walk over to the front of the Library of Congress and wait for you."

"Sounds good. How long of a drive is it?"

"Let's see. If I drive, it's eleven hours. If you drive, it will be about eight hours."

"Smart-ass. I'll see you within the hour." I laughed as I hung up the phone. I grabbed my cameras and quickly left the office. I made it to my apartment, packed, and was on my way to the Hill in less than a half-hour. I turned off my police scanner. I didn't want to take any chances. The White House could blow up, and all I wanted was to pick up Jim and get out of town.

When I pulled up across the street from the Library of Congress, Jim was sitting on the steps watching a gaggle of school children running up and down, driving their teachers crazy. I gave him a friendly beep on my horn, and he waved in recognition.

"Wow, that was fast. You have to stop speeding around here," he admonished me.

"Hey, it's one of the perks of being with the press." I grinned.

"Okay, but humor me. I'd like to get out of town in one piece," he said leaning over and giving me a friendly kiss on the cheek.

"You're the navigator. Buckle up."

We made it out of Washington without any hassle. I asked Jim about exactly where we were going, but he just kept putting me off.

"I want it to be a surprise. I know you'll love it. If I talk about it, you'll have a preconceived notion of the place. It's very small, and old, but it's my special place."

"That's good enough for me," I smiled.

We didn't really talk much on the way down, just small talk about my work and the latest gossip on the Hill. I was happy the latest gossip didn't include us. It took us seven hours to get to where we had to turn off of Interstate 95 onto I-26, which would take us directly to Charleston.

"Did you have a nice nap?" I asked.

Jim had fallen asleep just before we hit the North Carolina/Virginia border and slept all the way into South Carolina.

"Sorry about that. I didn't mean for you to do all of the driving."

"Well, I'm glad you slept. I think I made good time."

"I don't want to think about it. Do you want me to drive for the rest of the way?"

"That's probably a good idea. I'll pull off for gas, and then you can take over."

In a few minutes, we were back on the road.

"Okay, we have to be getting close by now, so are you going to tell me now? What's the name of the place we're going to?"

Jim gave me a teasing grin before he caved in. "It's called Isle of Palms. It's a small residential island. No big hotels or golf courses. People have used it as a summer getaway since before the turn of the century. My grandfather had a small house there. He used it mainly for fishing. One side of the island is tidal marsh, and the other side is the Atlantic Ocean. My grandmother didn't like it much. She liked being part of Charleston high society, so granddad kept it as a weekend fishing hideout. It wasn't a fancy place; in fact, there were bunk beds and no hot water. Grandma wanted no part of it. When I was a small kid, my dad would take me out there for the weekend. I didn't care that much about fishing, but I loved being on the ocean. I loved everything: the pelicans, crabs, everything. Especially the dolphins."

"Dolphins?" I piped in.

"Sure, I used to see dolphins almost every day. I don't get down here nearly enough these days, between Washington and other responsibilities."

"About those other responsibilities?" I gave him a cockeyed glance.

"Well, as I said before, Angela hates the beach. She doesn't want to mess her hair, and the heat makes her 'wilt' or so she says."

"Aren't you worried someone will see us who knows who is and who isn't your wife?" I asked seriously.

"It's out of season, and there won't be many people on the island yet. My little place is rather isolated. It would be hard to find if you didn't know where to look."

With that we stopped talking and in a few minutes, I felt my eyelids getting heavy as I drifted off.

I woke up when my car was bumping along a rutted gravel road. "Are you lost?" I asked sleepily.

"No, we're almost there. In fact, here we are!" he announced.

The lights of my Mustang shone on a rather weathered shack. No, that wasn't fair; cottage would be a better description. I could see Jim was thrilled to be there and was dying to show me his hideaway. We walked up the stairs that led to a deck that ran around the entire building. As we got to the front, I could hear and smell the ocean.

"Who put that there?" I laughed. No more than thirty yards from the deck was the ocean shimmering in the moonlight. The tide was on its way in, and row after row of small breakers were reflected in the moonlight.

"Like it?" Jim grinned, looking rather pleased with himself.

"Like it? I love it!" I grinned back. "I'm glad I brought my camera."

Jim gave me a quick peck on the cheek and moved to a screen door. "Come on, let me show you the rest of the place." He reached above the door and took a key that was hidden on top of the door frame.

"Nice security," I chided.

"No problem. We only have very short thieves around here. They couldn't possibly reach this. My neighbor over there keeps an eye on the place," Jim said, smiling and pointing to the left.

The inside of the house shouted *fishing*. There were rods, nets, and all sorts of gear stuffed in every corner. Jim could see me eyeing the room and began to fidget.

"I guess this place could use a little fixing up. Maybe you can help me with the decorating," he said, a bit embarrassed.

"No, it's perfect, if you're a fish!" I laughed. With that, he came flying across the room and grabbed me in a big bear hug. He spun the two of us around until we fell onto the overstuffed couch.

"Never criticize a man's fishing or his sexual ability," he tried to sound serious.

"I'm sure you're a great fisherman." I laughed.

"Damn straight, and even a better lover, right?"

"How am I supposed to know? I've never seen you fish, now have I?"

We rolled around on the couch, until Jim ended up on top of me. We both stopped moving, and I was looking up into his blue eyes. He closed his eyes and slowly brought his lips down on my half-open mouth. His kiss was slow and deliberate. He was definitely not thinking about fishing. I groaned, enjoying the moment when a loud banging noise came from the screened porch.

"Shit, what the hell was that!" I yelped.

Jim jumped off of me and moved toward the porch.

"Hey, who is it?" Jim snapped. He walked over to the door and started to laugh. "Doug, you old goat, how are you?" Jim reached for Doug's hand and greeted his friend.

"Jimmy, you should have told me you were coming down. I saw a light and was ready to crack some heads."

"Sorry, Doug, I didn't mean to scare you. I didn't plan this trip. It was a spur of the moment thing." Doug had stopped looking at Jim and was concentrating on me.

"Hi Doug, nice to meet you I'm Kate Miller," I said, jumping up off the couch, extending my hand.

"Miss Miller, my pleasure," he smiled. *There's that old southern charm again. God knows what he was thinking.*

Jim looked a bit uncomfortable, so I excused myself.

"Jim, where's the bathroom?"

"Oh, it's through that door," Jim answered. "I'll go get our things."

Jim walked out of the cottage with Doug while I inspected the bathroom facilities and bedroom. He was gone for quite a while, far longer than it would take to unload one suitcase and a camera bag. Doug seemed like a nice old guy. I assumed Jim was explaining who the hell I was.

The bedroom was cozier than the rest of the place. At least there were no stuffed fish on the walls. The room was a fair size. Along with the double bed, there were two chests of drawers and an oak desk. A bookcase was directly behind the desk containing an old beat-up set of Hardy Boys Mysteries. Tucked in between the books were at least a half dozen framed photos. Jim looked to be about twelve in one of the photos. I wished I'd known him as a young kid. Doug was in two of the photos. He and Jim were proudly displaying the fish they had caught. There was another older man in the pictures. It had to be his father. The family resemblance was striking. I was leaning over studying the photos when I heard Jim bang through the door with my luggage. I walked back into the main room to see what he was up to and to save my camera equipment.

"Need any help?"

"No, I think I can manage to drop these all by myself, thanks."

"What's the story with Doug?"

"Oh, he has been living here at the beach forever. He and my father were best friends. Probably more important than that, they were fishing buddies. My dad would come out here almost every weekend while I was growing up."

"I'll bet that thrilled your mother."

"No, she never seemed to care. She didn't like the beach much."

"How could she not like the ocean? It's gorgeous!"

"I guess like father, like son. We both seemed to pick the wrong women to marry. Let's open all the windows. The breeze off the ocean will cool this place down. I've been thinking about putting in air conditioning."

We moved from room to room and opened every window. The difference was almost immediate. I loved seeing where Jim had spent so much happy time. I wrapped my arms around myself, my face caressed by the soft scented breeze, and felt maybe I'd found one place I could share with Jim that was *ours*. Not a place of memories with Angela.

"Katie, I'm going to walk over to Doug's for a minute. He's going to lend us some food for breakfast, and I want to tell him a little bit more about you. Okay?" he asked, with a sweet look on his face.

"Sure, I'm going to take a bath and then start one of your books." I showed him the well- worn Hardy Boys Mystery.

"I'd forgotten they were here. I loved those books when I was a kid." He turned toward the screen door. "I won't be long."

"Okay."

I unpacked my things, which must have taken all of two minutes. A warm bath felt great, but it also completely relaxed me. The drive was exhausting. Any hope of getting into a book soon faded. I didn't get past the title page. On the top corner of the page, a young Jimmy Rayford had printed his name in pencil. I ran my finger over the letters trying to absorb some of Jim's past life.

I hadn't heard him come back from Doug's, but I felt him climb into bed and only half woke when he cuddled into me. We had gotten into the habit of falling asleep spooned up next to each other. The warmth of his body against my back lulled me into a deep sleep.

The next noise I heard was the sound of a rather persistent bird outside the window. He sure was a cheerful little devil. I reached over to wake Jim, but he wasn't there. I swung my legs over the side of the bed and made my way into the main room. The smell of bacon filled the room, but when I poked my head in the door, no Jim. I walked to the screened porch and could see him sitting on the top step of the stairs that led to the beach.

"Good morning," I called, walking over to the stairs.

"Hey, good morning, I thought you were going to sleep all day."

"Hardly, there was a bird outside the window singing up a storm. How long have you been up?"

"I've been up for hours. Remember, I slept most of yesterday while you did the driving. I watched the sun come up," he said pointing to the left.

"I'm really confused. I figured that we're facing east, we're facing more south, aren't we?"

"See that big ship?" Jim pointed. "It's on its way to Charleston. It's a few miles to the right." A huge container ship slowly slid past the beach in front of Jim's cottage.

"What a beautiful day. This place is perfect," I said, sitting down next to Jim on the steps. "Isn't it great?" He smiled. "It's before the summer season crowds, and even then, there aren't many people out here. I used to love coming here as a kid. I'd be out on the beach all day. My dad and Doug would be fishing on the other side of the island. Most of the time, I would stay here and swim or just walk on the beach, or sit on these steps and think."

"Jim, what did you tell Doug about us?"

"I told him you were someone very important to me, and that I wanted to share this with you."

"Oh." I couldn't get any other words out without Jim seeing the tears building up. I just took his hand in mine, and we sat there looking out at the ocean. He gave my hand a squeeze.

"Hey girl, you must be starving, how about some breakfast? I'll cook you a southern one. Plenty of grease!"

I laughed and followed him back into the cottage.

He had already cooked the bacon which supplied enough grease to finish off the eggs. We made two plates and returned to the deck to a small, weathered wooden table and benches. We sat on the one side facing the beach, eating in silence, and watching the pelicans skim over the waves. They almost touched the water as they moved in a line, first gliding, and then beating their wings almost in unison.

"How do they do that?" I asked incredulously.

"Fly?" Jim asked, puzzled.

"No, you goof. They look as if they are going to hit the waves with their wing tips and tumble in the water."

He smiled.

We finished breakfast and headed toward the beach. As we started down the path, we were greeted by a huge, wet, and sandy labrador retriever.

"Hey buddy, where did you come from?" Jim asked, leaning down to scratch his head. The lab rubbed his wet body against both of us.

He had a collar with tags, so it was easy to figure out. "His name is Sullivan, and he lives at 524 Carolina." I looked up at Jim.

"Well since we're planning to take a walk anyway, why don't we take this handsome guy home?" Jim gave Sullivan a scratch behind the ears. By then, he was sitting between us, looking at each of us as we chatted.

"I'll go grab something to use as a leash just in case he gets bored with us," Jim smiled. He came back from the house with one of his belts and a dish with water for our new friend. "Sully" appreciated the water, doing some serious tail wagging while lapping it up. Once he was finished, we set off down the beach path. The sky was getting darker and darker as we walked along.

"How far do we have to go? I think the rain is going to beat us." I pointed at the clouds rolling in.

"Not much farther. Let's take the 6th Avenue path," Jim said.

Sullivan seemed to know where we were going and took the lead from there. He pulled away and was trotting up the path.

"Well, our job is done," Jim laughed.

Chapter Fifteen

The next three days—and nights—were the best time of my life. We walked on the beach during the day, read books on the deck, shot photos of everything in sight, swam in the sea, and made love by the fireplace at night. Jim convinced me he could catch our dinner from the ocean. Luckily, there was a supermarket not too far from the cottage, so I knew we wouldn't starve. The nice folks from the Red and White Market and the ABC liquor store were the only people we saw all weekend, plus Doug. Jim invited him over for supper. Lucky for us, he brought fish he'd caught.

"The only reason you didn't catch any fish was the wrong choice of bait," Doug said in an obvious attempt to assuage Jim's pride.

"What bait should I have used?"

Doug scratched his head and said, "Well, sir. I can't divulge such information to a rookie."

We all laughed, and they spent the rest of the evening telling stories of Jim's childhood. The combination of the sun and the wine really knocked me out. I was sitting on the floor, leaning on Jim's knee almost asleep.

"Katie, why don't you go to bed? I'll be there in a few minutes."

I didn't argue. I walked over to Doug, leaned down and gave him a kiss on the cheek, and was in bed and sound asleep in five minutes. I don't know how long I had been asleep, when Jim came in and was leaning over me, whispering in my ear.

"Wake up, there's something you're going to want to see," he whispered.

I didn't move.

"Come on now, there's something on the beach you have to see."

I rolled over and looked up at him. I was still half asleep and didn't know what was going on.

"Jim, is there something wrong?"

"No, everything is great. Get up and throw on some clothes."

"Have I ever told you I'm not a morning person?"

"Yeah, more than once, I think?"

"Come here and give me a hug," I said, grabbing his hand and trying to pull him into bed. But instead, he pulled me out, pillow, blanket, and all.

"This better be good," I grumbled, tossing my pillow back on the bed and grabbing a pair of shorts and a T-shirt. I walked into the main room to find Jim standing there with my camera in his hand.

"Are you going to tell me what's going on?"

"Nope, not yet. Here, I think you're going to want this," he said, handing me my camera.

"Okay, buddy, this better be good. This is our last night here."

"I know. I think this will be a fantastic way to end our trip." Jim walked in front of me, holding the screen door open. There was a full moon and the deck, stairs, and path to the beach were easily visible without a flashlight. Jim walked quickly down the path.

I followed, half walking and half hopping, trying to pick the sand spurs out of the bottom of my foot that I'd collected on my way.

"Ow, these things are killing me," I yelped.

"Come on ... don't be a wimp."

"Wimp ... who are you calling a wimp?"

"Why didn't you put on your sandals?" He laughed.

As we climbed over the last dune that separated the cottage from the beach, I could see the moon shimmering off each line of waves making their way to the beach. The sea was gorgeous. The sky was clear, but with the moon so bright you could hardly see any stars at all.

"Come on, up this way," Jim called. He was walking quickly up the beach toward Doug's house. I followed in silence. Up ahead, I could make out a dark mound on the sand. We had walked about a hundred yards and by then, I could see that the "mound" was moving. "Oh my God!"

"Shhhh ..."

"Is that what I think it is?"

"Yep, it sure is. It's a loggerhead," Jim whispered, with a pleased smile on his face.

"How did you find him?" I picked up the pace.

"Her."

"What?" I turned, waiting for him to catch up.

"It's a she. She's coming in to lay eggs."

"This is unbelievable. It's like a dream come true," I whispered. "Do you have any idea how many Jacques Cousteau shows I've watched on TV?"

Jim just laughed, putting his arm around me, as we walked along the beach.

"Stay behind her. We don't want to disturb her. Once she finds a good spot and starts digging her hole and dropping eggs, she won't notice us."

We stopped and gave her plenty of room. The turtle was slowly making her way up into the dunes, stopping from time to time to rest.

"How far will she crawl before she starts to dig?" Any worry or pain from the sand spurs was forgotten as we made our way through the soft sand.

"I have no idea. They seem to look for just the right place. Sometimes they crawl all the way in and then just turn around and crawl back into the sea without laying a nest."

"This is the coolest thing I've ever seen. Thank you," I said. Tears welled up in my eyes.

"You're welcome," he answered. "It never gets old."

I noticed his eyes held water, too.

"Are we sentimental fools or what?" I asked.

"Sentimental yes, fools no," he answered. Jim was behind me with his arms around my waist and his head resting on my shoulder.

We stood and watched *our* sea turtle drag herself around the dune, looking for a safe place to lay her nest. She finally stopped moving and rested a few seconds before she started to dig. First, she used all four flippers to create a shallow pit that lowered her whole profile. Then she started to dig her nest, using her back flippers like scoops. She was measured, alternating back flippers digging a hole deep enough to hold her clutch of about 120 leathery eggs. She worked hard, stretching her back flippers, leaning back to get the depth she needed. She then started dropping eggs two or three at a time. They resembled ping pong balls. We moved in closer and sat on the sand to watch her every move.

"I can't believe I'm seeing this. Can I take some pictures?" I asked.

"Not with a flash."

I moved in to get the best angle I could. I wanted Jim in the background. I wanted him in the picture so you could compare him to the size of the turtle, and because I wanted him in every picture and every part of my life. The full moon gave me enough light. It wouldn't be a prize winner, but it would capture a memory that would last a lifetime.

There it was. I was madly in love with a married man, almost ten years older than I was, and with his seedy little cottage on this wonderful beach.

We sat in silence, except for the sound of the waves lapping on the shore, watching one of the true wonders of nature. The turtle finished laying and was using her back flippers to cover the nest. She shoved sand into the nest, covering the eggs. She packed it down and then using all four flippers, she flung sand around the whole area to disguise the location of the nest. She rested and then slowly turned back to the sea. I shot a few more frames as she dragged herself back into the ocean as the sun cut through the thin cloud layer on the horizon. We sat on the sand with our arms wrapped around our knees and watched until she was completely out of sight beneath the waves.

"That was great. I'm exhausted." I leaned into Jim, enjoying this magical moment. It had taken her almost an hour to finish laying the eggs.

We walked back to the cottage hand in hand, deep in our own thoughts. We were both keenly aware of what this long weekend had meant, and neither of us wanted it to end. At the bottom of the stairs, I put my hands around Jim's neck, turned to face him, and pulled him into my body, every inch of our bodies touching. I didn't move. It was as if I was holding on for dear life. I leaned away from Jim so I could see his face in the moonlight.

"This has been perfect. I could stay here forever."

Jim smiled down at me and held me as if we were one.

"Jim, I love you." It was the first time I had said it aloud.

"Katie, you have changed my life, my direction, and I don't want to spend a day without you in my life. I love you and want us to be sitting on the deck of this beach house when we're old and gray."

We rocked back and forth holding on for dear life.

Chapter Sixteen

If the last three days were the best time in my life, this day would rank up there as one of the worst. We both knew that our beach retreat had to end. Jim had appointments in Charleston and Columbia, including seeing his wife. I knew it was coming, but it didn't make it any easier. I stood on the deck watching the pelicans fly in formation toward Charleston.

"I can't believe how the time has flown by," I mumbled.

Jim took me in his arms and held me tight, rocking us back and forth.

"I know. I don't want to go, but I have to. So, do you," he said in a soft voice. "We'll get back here a lot, I promise." I knew he meant it, but he wasn't being realistic. Both of our jobs took up a lot of time.

"We'll make time to be here," he said, almost reading my mind.

We didn't talk much while we got ready to leave. Jim went over to Doug's with all the food from the fridge and to say goodbye. I kept walking around each room trying to memorize everything. As we left the cottage, Jim took the key off the table by the front door and locked it. He started to put the key back over the door and then stopped. He turned and handed it to me.

"You keep it. I think this place belongs to you as much as it belongs to me," he said, with a catch in his voice.

I took the key from his hand and shoved it into my jeans pocket. These couple of days had changed everything. I had been living for the moment, now I was longing for a future with this man. If I looked at him, tears would flow.

"I'll keep it safe for you," I whispered.

I drove him to the Charleston Airport, where he waited for his aide, Bob, who was flying down from Washington. After a rather formal goodbye, I was on the road to DC. *Welcome back to the real world.*

Our lives went back to a routine. Life was busy but uneventful. Both conventions came and went with only one surprise. The Republicans gave the vice-presidential spot to Senator Baldwin. He kept coming in second in the state primaries, and Scheffen really had no choice but to put him on the ticket. I was still optimistic the Democrats would carry the fall election, and the senator could go back to the senate and hopefully disappear. *Some hope.* The Democrats seemed to have an uncanny ability to screw up.

The last straw was when a group of diplomats got themselves kidnapped in Peru. No one gave two shits about Peru until then. It was a gift from heaven for the Republicans. Scheffen, and especially Baldwin, jumped all over the current administration which couldn't get them out, and we couldn't "nuke" Peru. Democrats were caught in the proverbial rock and a hard place. The American public is a forgiving lot, but not when it comes to a perceived weakness.

November came and went and so did the Democrats hope of winning the White House. Jim carried his district by a bigger margin than Scheffen and Baldwin carried South Carolina. The January inauguration kept me busy as the new Republican administration moved into the White House. Once all of that crap was behind us, I hoped we could just continue our lives. I was happy with what Jim and I had and was in no real hurry to take it to another level. I felt no need to push him. Angela was the one doing the pushing, not of Jim, but of her father and certainly Baldwin. She seemed to be near Baldwin all the time.

Angela was consistent and so was my life. I worked and spent what time I could with Jim. Life took on a wonderful pattern that made me happy and comfortable. Ever get the feeling things are going too well?

I was hanging out at my office and life took another surprising turn. The phone in the darkroom jolted me out of my comfy nap.

"Darkroom, Kate Miller," I said, trying to sound alert.

"Hi it's me," Jim answered.

"Hi, nice to hear your voice. Can we meet tonight for dinner?"

"I would love to, but a bunch of shit is happening all at once. The President has nominated my father-in-law to be the ambassador to France and even more earth shaking, Baldwin's wife was in a fatal car accident in California."

"Where's Angela?" I asked.

"I thought of that immediately," Jim mumbled.

"Sorry, very tacky of me. I suppose everyone will be heading out west for the funeral. Have you talked to Angela?" I asked.

"Not for a couple of days. She's been with her father in Columbia. He's very excited about the prospect of being sent to France. Angela not so much. She really doesn't want to be away from Baldwin. I guess everything is really going to be up in the air now. I can just imagine Angela not knowing which way to turn. She is good at doing the funeral thing, so I'd guess she will be on her way to California for sure. Then the ball is in Baldwin's court."

"I think I'll hide out here in the darkroom. Let me know how it all comes out," I said, half kidding.

Chapter Seventeen

M ost Sundays, I had only one assignment, the Washington Redskins. Jim loved coming with me, and I enjoyed seeing him work the game with me. This week he made it to Georgetown about a half hour before kickoff. We took my car, which had stickers to park right next to the stadium. I liked to be there on time but not a minute early. The last to get in was usually first out of the parking lot.

We drifted through the first quarter, and I had enough for the paper. I could see some of the guys on the sideline had brought their police scanners, and several others were huddled around one trying to listen over the crowd noise. We all had scanners. It was a way to get a jump on the news. If the police or fire departments were on the move, so were the photographers.

I moved closer to listen. Something had happened at the President's Prayer lunch that was being held on the Hill. From the chatter, I learned that shots were fired, and the President had been hit. The shooter had been grabbed by security. A couple of the photographers were heading to the Hill. I turned and jogged back to Jim. He was concentrating on the game and hadn't noticed I had gone.

"Something happened at the President's luncheon," I shouted.

Jim moved in closer to hear what I was saying.

"The President has been shot!"

Jim's face froze. "Let's get out of here. The police will be taking the shooter to the 23rd Precinct, which is really close to the stadium. Come on!"

We trotted past the bench and out the opening under the stands. My heart was beating double time. Time was of the essence.

"We'll probably beat anyone coming from the office," I said as we rushed out the exit. I had a really good working relationship with the police and hoped I'd run into someone I knew.

Jim and I were in front of the precinct in a matter of minutes. I wasn't sure I had made the right decision when we pulled up. There was no activity at all. Seems we'd beat the bad guy and the hordes of press that would follow. I pulled into a press spot and flipped down my visor so my press card was visible. Two police officers were just stepping out the front door of the building.

"Kate, how the heck did you get here so fast?" asked Officer Gaines, one of my buddies from Georgetown. "We just got the call not five minutes ago." The electricity of excitement and anxiety crackled in the air.

"We were at the Redskins game, and someone on the sidelines had a police radio. I have no idea exactly what's gone down," I said, giving him a questioning look.

"Katie, you've hit a home run today," Gaines said. He swallowed hard, "Someone shot the President. At the luncheon. I don't know what kind of shape Scheffen is in, but they got the shooter, and they're bringing him here."

I nodded, fully aware of what that meant.

Officer Gaines stepped closer, and his voice was low, "If you want to get a photo of this guy, walk through to the back garage door. They're going to drive him right into the building."

"Thanks, I appreciate it," I said fervently.

I glanced at Jim, who nodded. We jogged up the stairs and into the building. I looked over my shoulder. Jim was three steps behind me.

"Look like we belong here," I whispered. "Keep moving, and try not to make eye contact."

Jim nodded. We made our way down the hall. I nodded confidently to the few cops we passed. They nodded back. It didn't appear they'd been told yet that the President had been shot. *All the better for us.* Being one of the "guys" came in handy once again.

We hustled through to the back and got in position as the double garage door started to open. I handed my camera bag off to Jim and had my camera ready. The first car raced in and came to a sudden stop. I could see they had a guy in the back with a police officer on either side. The two cars that followed stopped just outside the door. Two officers jumped out to move the prisoner.

Lucky for me, I knew at least half of them. They looked surprised to see me but just smiled and offered a curt nod. The boxes of cookies I had brought occasionally were a big help. I lifted my camera to my eye and went to work. The man in handcuffs was in his late thirties, with dark short-cropped hair. He appeared to be about 6 feet Tall and sort of average looking, except for the fact that he had just shot the President of the United States. I banged off at least a dozen shots before they whisked him in to be processed into the system. I turned to Jim, who gave me a serious look and a wink.

"Let's get out of here," he whispered.

"Yep. I need to get these to the office. I can still make the deadline for tomorrow morning, and let's find out what exactly happened."

We walked quickly out the back door and around the building to where we had parked the car. Just as we made it to the front of the building, we heard a commotion. At least fifty people were jostling for position, including several from *The Post*. Stan was in front of the crowd.

"Hey, where have you been? They're bringing the shooter in any minute," he yelled over the noise. He gave Jim a questioning look.

I waved Stan over. "Stan, I've got some bad news for you. They brought him in the back door."

"It's all over?" His face fell, and he cursed.

"I've got it covered," I said with a smug smile.

"Damn girl, how did you manage that?" Stan asked with a painful look.

"Just lucky I guess." I shrugged.

"Lucky, my ass. You've got the knack for being in the right place at the right time. That's more than luck. That's a gift from the gods."

I saw the respect in his eyes, and it left me speechless.

"What are you waiting for?" asked Stan. "Get back to the office."

"Right. Are you coming?"

"I'll stay here. They might come out with a statement."

"Okay, see you back at the office." I turned to go, then stopped and looked over my shoulder.

"Stan? Thanks." I waved as Jim and I got into my car.

Once we were back in the car, Jim reached for the radio. We hadn't even driven twenty feet when we heard a harried reporter interviewing someone who had witnessed the shooting. The person spoke haltingly, in shock.

"It was terrible. The President was at a Sunday prayer event. Halfway through the luncheon, one of the waiters with a coffee pot in his hand walked right up to the President's table. He dropped the coffee pot and managed to get off two shots. At point blank range. All hell broke loose. The guy was wrestled to the ground by a swarm of Secret Service and some of the guests. I can't believe it."

This radio announcer wasn't saying anything about the President's condition, but it didn't sound good. I stopped driving. My car was in the middle of the street. Jim and I sat, stunned.

"I'd better get to the office," I said.

"Right. You'd better drop me off on the Hill. I have no idea what's happening there, but at least I can make some calls and talk to the party leadership." He raked his hand through his hair. "What the hell? The president has been shot. What do we do now? Go into special session?"

Jim stared blankly out the window.

I reached out to hold his hand. "I'll call your office and let you know what I find out."

I cut through the back streets and ended up at the Rayburn Building. Jim jumped out and gave me a somber wave as I pulled away.

Back at *The Post*, I went directly to the darkroom, quickly loaded my film, and set the timers for the developer. Despite my nervousness, my hands were quick and professional. It only took eight minutes before I was hanging the filmstrips up to dry. With that done, I went looking for my editor.

Everyone in the newsroom was crowded around the TVs waiting for an update. Both the city editor and my photo editor huddled together.

"Hey," I called out to them. "I got photos of the shooter!" Everyone turned around and stared at me.

"I caught up with him at the station. I think I'm the only one to get the guy, unless someone got him at the hotel."

Everyone started asking questions at once. "How? Where?"

"I was at the game and got to the precinct before the shooter. The cops kept everyone outside."

Scott's brow rose.

"I know a couple of the guys ... I was the only one around back when they brought him into the garage," I added trying to sound serious and not too cocky.

"Have you run the film?" Scott asked urgently, walking up to me.

"It's drying right now."

"Let's go see what you've got." Scott and I walked back into the darkroom with the sounds of TV news anchors coming from every direction. The president was in surgery. They were dealing with two profoundly serious gunshot wounds, and there was no news coming out of George Washington University Hospital so far.

Scott and I were hunched over the light box when the announcement came over the darkroom radio. My stomach was in a knot. This couldn't be happening again. It had only been six years. I had been sitting in class when the principal had come on the intercom and announced that President Kennedy had been assassinated. He had been so young. I had looked at my teacher and she sat there, tears running down her cheeks.

Innocence died that day. Today was a stark reminder of that.

The President of the United States died on the operating table at approximately 2:00 p.m.. Scott and I stopped looking at my film and stood speechless. Moments later, he was all business. He handed me my negatives. "Go print a picture of the President's assassin."

"Yes, sir."

The picture would have been unremarkable except for the historical implications. I finished my work, feeling numb inside. It had been hours since I had talked to Jim. I needed to hear his voice to somehow make sense of this disaster. I called the private number to his office, and his assistant picked up.

"Hi Bob, this is Kate. Can I talk to Jim?"

"Hi Kate. Isn't this all unbelievable?" He lowered his voice. "Angela just left. I think she's more concerned about the Vice President than she is about the President. What a waste of oxygen that woman is. Anyway, I'll put you through."

"Thanks Bob. Hang in there."

Chapter Eighteen

*T*he *Washington Post* carried my picture at the bottom of the front page with my photo credit. *How the times had changed.* I took no joy in that photo credit. I had been only doing my job. The sadness in the country was palpable. *The Post*, and every other media source, was busy around the clock. I ended up on the Hill the morning after the assassination. Everyone in the halls of the office building seemed to be on autopilot. I walked into Jim's office as his chief of staff, Bob, was sitting in the reception area. Bob had known about Jim and me for months, and I really considered him a friend.

"Bob, how are you doing?" I asked.

"Shocked is the best word to describe it. Jim is in his office. I think his wife has called him ten times so far. The last two calls came from the Baldwin office. Can you believe it? She wants to be there for the swearing in!" He shook his head. "She's making all sorts of sympathetic noises, but I think she's thrilled to be a heartbeat away from the presidency."

"I bet Jim is *thrilled* she's right in the middle of things," I replied as I knocked on Jim's door.

"Come in." Jim looked up from his desk and smiled as I entered the room.

"You look beat. Are you okay?" I flopped down on the oversized chair opposite his desk.

"What a night," he said, tossing *The Post* across the desk.

"Tell me about it. I really feel numb."

"Congrats on the photo. That's one for the history books."

I shrugged, feeling too depressed for glory. "Bob just told me about your wife and Senator Baldwin. She is a piece of work."

Jim nodded in agreement.

"They're swearing in Baldwin in a couple of hours at the Naval Observatory," I added.

"Well, I can tell you one thing, I'm not going to take part in any of it." Jim shook his head.

"Jim, Angela is going to help us out one way or another. Her attachment to you is more than a bit problematic for her now. Don't you think?" I asked, looking at him slumped in his chair.

"I have no idea what she is going to do. A lot will depend on the new President. If she thinks she can weasel her way into the White House, she will be gone in a shot. But don't be so sure Baldwin will want any part of her. It's one thing to have her nipping at his heels as Vice President, but he will be a bit too busy for her now is my guess. Don't you think?" Jim asked.

"I have no idea." We sat in silence for a moment, both of us deep in our own thoughts. "I'd better call my office and see where they want me to go."

I called Scott and he told me to hang tight. They had everything covered for the moment, so I gave him Jim's private office number and hung up. We sat staring at the TV, quiet, exhausted, and depressed. Jim was a junior member of the House, so he didn't fit into any congressional contingency plan. He wouldn't be called to go to the White House. On the other hand, I probably would be going and soon.

We passed the time watching TV. My picture of the unnamed assassin popped up on the screen every few minutes. TV stations were scrambling to come up with the appropriate footage of the President's life. They usually are prepared for this possibility, but this time, with such a young president, and his being in office for such a brief time, they were caught off guard. The only live footage right now was at the Naval Observatory with cars and people coming and going.

The first real sign of activity was a shot of the Supreme Court Chief Justice arriving. About fifteen minutes later, the live TV switched to the gardens behind the Vice President's residence. The media seemed to outnumber the invited guests. The Justice walked out carrying the Bible. Baldwin followed him and took his assigned spot. Jim and I leaned forward in unison, almost falling off our chairs when we saw Angela, not far behind, on the arm of her father.

"Can you believe that?" Jim muttered.

We sat there staring at the screen. There was nothing to say. I started to consider how all this would affect our lives. *Would Jim feel free to get away from Angela? Of course, more likely, Baldwin was going to dump her as a liability. Either way, we were going to have to be more careful.*

We sat in Jim's office, in a funk, for what seemed like hours. The TV announcers covered the swearing in and were waiting to see what the new President was going to do. The new President was a bit of an unknown. I personally hoped he was just a bit too conservative and not dangerous. How things were going to work out with Jim's wife was another issue.

"Jim, do you want to come home with me? We can fix something to eat and see what's going on. I don't have to be at work until tomorrow."

"No, I'd better not. I'm going to stay here and make some calls. There are going to be a lot of meetings over the next twenty-four hours, including coming up with a Vice President nomination. God this guy scares me. Who knows what he is going to do? We'd better find a 'middle of the road' person, not someone totally in his pocket."

I walked behind Jim and put my hands on his shoulders.

He covered my hands with his and gave them a gentle squeeze.

"Give me a call. I'll be at *The Post* first and then at home. Everything is so upside down I need to know where you are." I told him.

Jim turned my hand over and held it to his lips.

"I'll keep in touch," I said. "This is all so overwhelming. I want to curl up and sleep for a month, until this all works itself out." I gave his shoulders a squeeze, grabbed my camera bag, and left.

The streets were quiet, unusually quiet. Every day is a holiday in DC, but now the tourists must have been in their hotels watching TV. It was so strange to see empty sidewalks. There was virtually no traffic, and it took only minutes to get to *The Post*. As I got off the elevator to the editorial floor, I could see Scott at his desk, and he looked exhausted.

"How long have you been here?" I asked, dropping my camera bag on a chair.

"I was on the desk early. I am beat. As soon as we put the morning edition to bed, I'm out of here. Kate, you better hang out here for a while. Everyone else is out on the street."

"Okay, but I'd like to get home."

The phone started to ring. Scott held up one finger to cut me off while he grabbed it.

"Scott here ... yep ... okay. I'll send someone. Right." He put the phone down and looked my way. "Kate, you better get down to the precinct. They're going to move the shooter to a federal holding facility. I don't know if you will be able to get anything, but it's worth a try. He may look a bit different now that they've cleaned him up."

"Okay, I'll call in when I'm through." I turned to leave. "Do you want this for the morning edition?"

"You better bring it in—all depends on what they want upstairs." Scott shuffled the papers on his desk and continued. "Right now, the story is about the new President and getting him settled in the White House."

Getting to the precinct didn't take any time at all. I found a parking spot right out front, grabbed my camera, and bag. Pushing the heavy door open, I smiled recognizing the Sargent behind the front desk.

"Hey Mac ... How's the family?" I gave him a small wave.

"Kate, good to see you. The kids are great. John's at GW."

"Great, my alma mater. Hey Mac, are they moving the shooter soon?"

"He should come right by here in a couple of minutes. You've really got a nose for news, don't you girl?"

"Yep." I gave him a small laugh. "Thanks a lot, Mac. Great to see you." I moved into gear, shoved my camera bag under a desk, and got ready. I'd have only about fifteen seconds to get what I needed. They were going to move this guy as fast as possible and certainly were not going to stop to pose him for me. All the police stations in

DC were old and had bad lighting, so I had to be ready with a flash. Because of the recycling time of the flash, I would only have time to get off two or three shots.

There were noises from down the hall, and I spun around to see three uniforms coming my way in front of two detectives, one on either side of the man who had killed the President of the United States. As the uniforms got closer, they recognized me and separated. I smiled and clicked off my first shot. *Easy enough, but the guy was looking at the floor.* When he was six feet from me, I clicked my tongue. He lifted his head, looked me straight in the eye, and I took my second shot. Lowering my camera, I stared at him.

The detectives each had him by an elbow and moved past me in a hurry. I probably could have gotten one more frame, but I couldn't take my eyes off him. He was average looking and oddly familiar. My instincts tingled. Calling out thanks to the police officers, I hustled back to the office, got my prints run and up to the desk in no time at all.

Chapter Nineteen

The paper would run a six-column picture of the inauguration with Jim's wife in the background. On the bottom of the page would be my photo with a description of the move of the assassin to federal lockup. Before leaving the office for the day, I decided to give Jim one more call.

"Hi Kate," said Bob. "Jim's gone. He had a meeting with the Majority Leader, and then he said he was heading home. Said to tell you he would call you in the morning. He's exhausted, and he still has to face Angela," Bob added.

"No problem, Bob. I'm heading home. It *has* been a really long day."

I drove back to Georgetown, going over in my head what had happened at the precinct. It was so surreal staring at the guy who changed the course of American history, and even weirder that he had stared right back at me.

Parking in Georgetown was always a pain. The streets are narrow and not really designed for automobile traffic. Yet there was a rhythm to the parking. Once you got to know your neighbor's car and parking schedule, it all somehow meshed. One of my neighbors worked at George Washington University Hospital and left about 10 o'clock every evening. So on many nights, we just traded places. Tonight was no exception. I parked right outside the gate of my small garden. I could hear the phone ringing as I put the key into the lock. Hoping it was Jim, I dropped my camera equipment on the table next to the door and just made it to the phone before the machine picked up.

"Hello?" I said just a bit too loud.

"Hi, it's me," Jim answered.

"Hi, I just got back. Got another shot at the police station."

"That's great, Kate. You're really something. I only just got in. Had a couple of short meetings and then headed home. Angela is nowhere to be found. She must be with her father. They're probably packing Baldwin's bags for his move tomorrow."

I laughed. "God, that's probably too close to the truth to be funny."

"I'll come over tomorrow and bring you breakfast. What time do you have to be in the office?"

"I will have to go in about 8 o'clock. I'll call at about 7:30. Hopefully, I can go right from here to my assignment." I paused. "Jim, come over as early as you can."

"Sounds like a promising idea. Don't get out of bed too early. I like to wake you up."

"I've always enjoyed breakfast in bed." I imagined the smile on his face. "I'll be waiting." Hanging up the phone, the stress of the last thirty-six hours hit me all at once. I climbed my spiral staircase, dumped my clothes on a chair, and was in bed in a matter of minutes. I turned on the TV for the news but fell asleep almost the moment my head hit the pillow.

I woke up a few hours later to the sounds of an old movie. I rolled over, hit the off button on the remote and was asleep again in seconds. The next thing I heard was a key opening my front door.

I had a key under a flowerpot that Jim used. I was still half asleep when I heard his footsteps on the metal staircase. By the time he slid into bed, he had managed to lose his clothes. He moved in behind me, hugging me to his body.

"Hmm ... you sure are nice and warm," he whispered in my ear.

"Your feet are freezing." I laughed.

He took that opportunity to wrap his legs around me, making sure he found a comfortable place for his feet.

"Very romantic." I turned around to face him, burying my face in his neck.

He started to move his lips from the back of my neck and up to my ear when the phone rang.

"Damn nice timing," he mumbled.

I crawled over him to reach the phone.

"Hello." I had the phone in one hand, while the other one tried to stop Jim from tickling me. I slapped his hands away, balancing the phone and trying to sound professional.

"Kate, this is Scott."

"Hi Scott, what's up?"

"Kate, this is a weird, sick world we live in." Scott sounded serious. I sat up in bed and motioned Jim to quit playing around. I must have looked very serious, because he stopped and looked at me.

"What's going on?" I asked.

"Sometime after you saw Hoskins last night—"

"Hoskins?" I interrupted.

"That's the shooter's name. Oscar Hoskins. Anyway, sometime in the middle of the night, the guy was found dead in his cell."

"*What*?" My blood chilled. Jim made a face, and I held up my hand to tell him to wait.

"Can you believe it?" Scott asked.

"No, I can't. How could that happen? Where were the cops? Wasn't he being watched?"

Now, Jim was listening to me, trying to figure out what was going on.

"There is a press conference at the FBI at 9:00 this morning. Be there and then get back to the office as soon as possible. What is this country coming to?" he asked, not really expecting an answer.

"Okay, I'll be there." I hung up the phone, sank down in bed, and pulled the covers up to my chin.

"What happened?" Jim looked over at me.

"Are you ready for this? The shooter is dead."

He sat straight up in bed.

"They found him in his cell, dead."

"How?" Jim asked with a blank look on his face.

"I forgot to ask." I climbed out of bed. "I've got to be at the FBI for a press briefing. I'd better get into the shower. I'm not sure why the press thing is at the FBI. I should have asked."

"This is surreal. The bottom line is, we have a new president who is at least a bit weird and the most right-wing politician to ever live at the White House. Add to that, the guy who got him there is dead." He just shook his head. "If someone killed him, do you think there's an accomplice out there?"

"Jim, I really don't want to think about that right now. I have to focus on work."

The FBI building was on Pennsylvania Avenue between the Hill and the White House. On any day, at any time, there is plenty of traffic. Luckily, they had some parking set up for the press, so I could park next to the building. The press room was packed. We all stood around chatting, trying to get any kind of information, but mostly simply curious about how something like this could happen. We wondered whose head was on the chopping block for such a massive screw up.

The Director of the Bureau came into the room, avoiding eye contact.

"Ladies and gentlemen, could I have your attention? I have a short statement to make, and then I'll try and answer some questions," he paused. "After moving the alleged assassin, Oscar Hoskins, to the general holding area, he was given something to eat and given a pillow and blanket. Shortly after 2 a.m. he was found unresponsive in his cell. As you all may or may not know, we are upgrading that part of the building, and our surveillance cameras have been out of service for the past three months."

We all just sat there in silence. This guy had to be kidding. After catching this guy stone cold guilty, they let this happen. Finding out why it happened, and who was behind it, was going to be tough.

"Are there any questions?" the Director asked, looking extremely uncomfortable. Everyone snapped back to reality, and hands popped up all over the room. All the questions came back to the same thing, *how could this happen*?

The Director came up with the same answer. "We're still working on it, right now we just don't know."

After going around and around on this, the people in the press corps gave up. They were an unhappy and cynical group looking for answers they weren't going to get today, or maybe ever. My part in this little drama was really minimal. I tried to get several shots of the Director. The one that would end up in the newspaper was a picture of a guy looking like a school kid just caught cheating on a test, standing in the principal's office waiting for his punishment.

Chapter Twenty

Over the next few days, the press waited for information from any part of the government that was willing to talk. That, and anything the new President did, was all over the news. Baldwin was doing a good job trying to seem normal. He looked and sounded very Presidential. He kept most of Scheffen's appointments in place which seemed to comfort the country.

The next important thing would be to select the Vice President. The House of Representatives really had nothing to do with who would be nominated to fill the Vice President's slot, so Jim wasn't particularly busy. The President would nominate someone, and then both Houses of Congress would vote. That changed a bit when the short list of nominations leaked to the press, with one of the main contenders being the senior senator from South Carolina. The senator was a bit older than Baldwin, and he was more middle of the road. Robert Abercrombie had been in the Senate for three terms. He came from an old southern family with an impeccable pedigree, which included a degree from The Citadel. Jim's father also graduated from The Citadel. They were several years apart, but they saw each other socially. Because Jim was part of the South Carolina delegation, he was contacted several times for comments concerning the possible new Vice President.

Everyone always complains about news leaks, but most of the time the loudest complaints come from the leakers themselves. No better way of checking whether something will "fly" with the public than to put it out there and see what the reactions are. In the case of Abercrombie, no one seemed to have a bad thing to say about him. The Senate ended up approving his appointment with a unanimous voice vote.

Political life and my life calmed down. Supposedly, the FBI was trying to find out where the shooter came from. So far, the assassin had been a ghost. When the police had been clearing the building after the shooting, they had found one of the caterers shoved in a broom closet. He had been bludgeoned to death, and his jacket and shoes had been removed by the assassin to disguise himself. The public was content with the newly minted administration. The shock had not worn off, but life in the Capital moved on. Our democracy survived, at least for the time being.

The colleges around the city were a few weeks from final exams and graduation. My university was right in the city, just a couple of blocks from the White House. After classes, you could find dozens of students sunbathing on the grounds of the Washington Monument and on the Eclipse. Driving to an assignment, I cut down Wisconsin Avenue all the way to the Whitehurst Freeway ending up on K St. I turned on 23rd Ave. and made a left on Constitution Avenue. It was just a few blocks from the Eclipse behind the White House. Washington is a beautiful city any time of the year, but spring is really special. The azaleas were in bloom, and all the parks were freshly mown. Kids were taking advantage of the mild weather, with a couple of pick-up softball games. Close to the ballfield there was a group of scouts flying kites. I was stopped in traffic just staring at the kids and watching their kites floating in the breeze, when the cars behind me started tapping on their horns.

One of the National Park Police on horseback ambled up to the side of my car and suggested that the middle of the avenue was not a parking lot, and perhaps I'd like to move along. I assured him I understood the concept and wished him a good day. I could still see the kids with their kites as I continued toward my job at the National Archives.

The whole time I was shooting my job I couldn't get the kites out of my head. My assignment wasn't a happy one. The Archives had put together a display of the assassinated President and the new President's transition. The photos were supplied by newspapers all over the country, with quite a few from *The Post*. My contribution was the shot of the assassin. The picture I took at the police station, when they were moving him, was prominently displayed. I stood there staring at the shooter and remembered the moment I had taken the shot and the look he had in his eyes. It was unremarkable, except for the fact that he was responsible for changing the direction of America. This show would open officially the next morning, so my next stop was the office to process my film for tomorrow morning's edition. Scott was at his desk when I got back.

"Hey, as soon as you run your film, I've got a little project for you," Scott called out.

"Okay. Give me about twenty minutes," I answered, as I pushed through the darkroom door. After dropping my photos off to the copy desk, I grabbed a bag of chips and a Coke from the machine and took a seat next to Scott.

"So, what's up? What do you need?" I asked, enjoying my treats.

"Do you remember the shots of the girls flying the kites? Scott asked.

"Sure, that was my sorority, last fall. Why?"

"They called from Indiana or somewhere. Anyway, they want copies of the pictures you took for their national magazine." Scott tossed an envelope on his desk.

"No problem. I just have to locate the negatives."

All the photo negatives at the newspaper are filed and cataloged. Everything is kept for at least seven years, just in case. When a roll of film comes out of its little metal canister, it's a strip about three feet long. After the film has been processed it is cut into six-inch strips, put in a transparent glassine envelope, and labeled with the date, photographer, and a few words of description. Realistically, only a few shots will be used from any roll of film, but the whole roll is saved. I was still new at this and kept a folder with a lot of my work in the photo desk. The picture I needed was a keeper. It had run on the front page, and I was quite proud of it. I had kept the entire front page, so the date was right there: **September 23rd.** There were about two dozen envelopes in the file cabinet with that date. I used a red marker to label my negatives, so I found them almost immediately.

The darkroom was empty since the morning issue was already running. You could feel the whole building vibrate when the presses were rolling. I laid the negatives out on the light table. Seeing them, the entire day came flooding back. I leaned forward and remembered. I had snapped a couple of frames of the teenage boys who were eyeing my car, while I picked up my laundry. On the end of the roll were the pictures of the kite.

Then I paused, staring at the strips of negatives. My mouth went dry, and a cold sweat broke out on my forehead. The frames that stopped me in my tracks were the five in between. I had totally forgotten about the shots of Baldwin. The senator was parked in front of a closed-up house in Georgetown which was totally out of place. At that time, the thought of him ever being President wasn't an issue, but here we were. I printed all the frames for the sorority. It only amounted to a half dozen prints, and I was sure they would appreciate them. Once the prints were dry, I walked them out to Scott.

"Hey Scott, where do you want these?" I dropped them on his desk, barely listening to him. My mind was consumed with the strip of negatives I left on the light table.

"That was fast. Thanks. Listen, will you dump the chemicals before you leave tonight?" Scott asked, shuffling papers around his desk.

"Sure. I've got a couple more prints to make ... nothing important," I added walking back into the darkroom. I called back over my shoulder, "Hey Scott, I'm gonna take tomorrow off."

"Okay. Hopefully, it'll be a slow news day," Scott added. "You've earned it, Kate. Somehow, we never get time to chat, but I really appreciate the effort you've put in. Amazing shots. Keep up the good work." Scott turned back to what he was doing.

I was moved by the compliment. "Thanks, Scott." I paused before pushing my way through the darkroom door. Any other time, I would be reveling in Scott's words. Now, all I could think about were the negatives waiting for me on the light box. I returned the kite negatives to the envelope and took the strip with Baldwin over to the enlarger. Printing negatives becomes automatic. You don't even really look at the subject of the photo. You make sure the image is in focus and exposed properly. Then you wait until the photo is out of the developer to see exactly what you've got.

Once all four prints were off the drying drum, I took time to take a close look. I had spread the four eight-by-ten photos on a worktable and pulled up a stool. I took the magnifying loupe and studied each photo. They were sharp as a tack, and every detail jumped off the paper. Images were flashing through my head. First, Baldwin and how smarmy he was when we met in Charleston. But that quickly faded away. The photos I'd taken of the shooter when he was first brought in to the police station and then the next day when they were moving him, were playing repeatedly in my head. It was chilling at the time, as we stared at each other. Now, all the feelings came flooding back. He was so calm, it almost felt as if he were looking right through me. The gravity of what I had captured was beginning to dawn on me. I must have sat there staring at the images for what seemed like an hour. When I finally came out of my trance, I reached for the phone and dialed Jim's office.

"Jim, what are you doing?" I asked without saying hello.

"Hi, what's wrong? You sound weird," Jim paused. "What's going on?" He was alarmed.

"I'm fine ... I think. I've just come across something that you need to see. Remember when I caught Baldwin in Georgetown?" I asked, not waiting for an answer. "Well, I just came across the negatives and printed them. Jim, I'm not exactly sure what I've got, but you need to look at them. Can you come down to the paper?"

"Now? I was going to stop and pick up some stuff for dinner. I was just about to leave."

"Forget dinner. I've been sitting here staring at these pictures, not knowing what to do. I really need you to see them."

He didn't hesitate. "I'm on my way."

"I'll leave your name at the desk at 13th and K and have one of the guards bring you up to the darkroom."

"Okay, I should be there in about twenty minutes."

After calling down to the security desk, I quickly made more prints of the negatives. This time I cropped the negatives enlarging the images of the two men meeting at the door of the Georgetown house. As soon as they were in the stop bath, I hustled out to the photo desk to get my folder of clippings. I found what I needed and had everything ready for Jim to look at. I felt like the little dog that chased the car. Once he actually caught it, the pup had no idea what to do next.

"Kate?" Hank, the weekend security guy called out.

"Yeah ... in here," I answered from inside the darkroom door. "Thanks, Hank."

Hank gave me a little wave and jumped back on the elevator before the door closed. I motioned Jim into the darkroom and once we were alone, I grabbed him and held on tight.

"Hey, what's going on?" Jim asked, holding me close. "You're shaking."

"Sit down here and let me show you." I pointed to the table and stool I'd set up. I picked up the first set of pictures I had printed and handed them to Jim, letting him look at all of them before I commented.

"Baldwin looks uncomfortable. Who's the other guy?" Jim asked.

"Take a look at this second set of photos. They're the same shots only blown up so you can see the guy with Baldwin better." I put the photos on the table and moved in close, leaning on Jim's arm. When he didn't seem to be making the connection, I reached across the table for my photo file and pulled the clipping of a *Post* front page. I laid it out next to one of the close-ups of Baldwin and ran my hand over it, smoothing the folded newsprint.

"Jim, look at the guy with Baldwin. I hope I'm nuts," I said, staring down at the table.

Jim didn't say anything for several seconds then turned and looked at me. "It's the same guy." His face lost its color.

"I'd like to say no, but I think it is." I sat beside him, and we stared at my photos, the ones taken of the then senator from California standing with a man who would assassinate the President of the United States.

"This is huge," I said, staring at Jim.

"This is dangerous," he said.

"I'm gonna go get the negatives of the shooter and make some more prints."

Jim said nothing. He was lost in his own thoughts, as he continued staring at the photos.

"I'd like to see if I have any better angles, and I think we'll need to have more copies no matter what." I picked up the newsprint clipping and tucked it back in my envelope. "A photo-on- photo paper will be a lot clearer than the newsprint we have here. There shouldn't be anyone coming in, but let's cover these up just in case," I said, reaching over to flip over the photos.

It only took a few minutes to find the right negatives and get the prints made. Jim was still sitting on the stool waiting for me, deep in thought. I printed the photos so the heads of the individuals in the shots were the same size so that would make the comparison easier to analyze. I quickly printed the close-ups of the headshots and brought them back to the table. "Okay, here we go. Look at these two shots," I said, laying out the new close-up shot of Baldwin and the man I believed assassinated the President. "Look at the guy's eyebrow, the small diagonal scar. The small mark also showed on the shot I'd taken when the police moved him to the federal lockup."

"This is not good. How on earth are we going to deal with this?" Jim asked, shaking his head and staring at the two photos. Jim gathered up all the photos and put them in an envelope. "There are so many ramifications to this, I can't even get my head around it. Do you have any idea how dangerous these photos are?"

I didn't answer.

He looked at his watch. "It's almost 10 p.m. Let's get out of here."

"I'm taking all this stuff with me. This is the only proof of … "

Jim grabbed my arm. "Don't even say it aloud. From now on, we must believe someone is listening."

I nodded in understanding.

We quickly got to my car and drove to Georgetown. Somehow, everything seemed different, more ominous. My friendly neighborhood seemed shrouded in shadows. Jim dropped his briefcase and the envelope of photos on the dining room table.

"Okay, let's try and make a plan." Jim sat at the table spreading the photos out before him.

"Well, the good news is, no one knows these pictures exist except the two of us." I tried to smile.

"That is the salient point. How deep does this go? There are so many questions. How did the shooter end up dead? Who can we trust with this, the FBI? Potentially, we could just take these to them and wash our hands of the whole thing." Jim pondered.

"This may well be the biggest story *ever*." I stood there shaking my head. "Baldwin was dealing with the guy who would go on to shoot the President. This is nuts. How long was he planning this scenario? He was only a senator when these pictures were taken." I sat down at the table next to Jim.

"Several things had to fall into place, including the mess with Peru. You could argue if that didn't happen, Scheffen and Baldwin never would have been elected. God this is unbelievable. When he was put on the ticket … that put everything into motion."

"You're right. A lot of things had to fall into place, but the bottom line is, Baldwin contacted the assassin well before that guy killed the President. *And … we are* the only two people who know this," I added, tapping the pictures. "Seems we have time on our side as long as we're the only ones who know these exist."

We sat at the dining room table just throwing out unconnected thoughts.

"I think we should put a set of these pictures somewhere safe, out of reach," Jim said. "I'll get a safely deposit box at the bank tomorrow. I can take care of that on my way to my office."

"Good idea. I'll take the negatives with me and get the extra prints made. I'm keeping the negatives with me until we have a total plan. It's too dangerous to leave them at the office. I have to get in early and get it all done before anyone else gets there. I forgot to dump the chemicals, so I have a reason to go in," I said.

"God, it's past eleven o'clock. Let's go to bed and sleep on this. We have the beginnings of a plan," Jim added, not sounding very confident.

Before going upstairs, I checked the lock on the front door and looked out at the street. My paranoia was getting the best of me. Every shadow seemed menacing. I shivered and checked the door lock again.

Chapter Twenty-One

Both of us tossed and turned most of the night, but we were sound asleep when the alarm went off. I rolled toward the side table to shut it off and remembered everything we were facing.

Jim turned to look at me, still half asleep. "How'd you sleep?" He asked.

"Seems like I was awake most of the night, but of course I was dead to the world when the alarm went off," I answered.

"We'd better get moving." Jim kissed me on the top of my head.

I rolled to the edge of the bed, grabbed my robe, and headed to the bathroom.

"I'll go first." I looked back over my shoulder and gave Jim a smile. He reached for the TV remote.

"Hey, I've been thinking that we should get out of town," Jim said.

"Now? Seems like we have a lot on our plate," I replied, looking over my shoulder.

"I need to get down to Charleston. I had planned to go next week. I've been asked to speak at the Gibbes Art Museum. This had been planned a couple of months ago." Jim sighed. "What do you think? I know it's out of left field, but it might be good to get down to the beach house, away from the city, and try to figure out what we're going to do."

"I have a bunch of comp time I have to take, or I'll lose it. I'll need to run it by Scott," I answered, thinking out loud.

"I can leave at about noon. I just have to get to my office and double check my schedule. While we're down there, I think we should get a safety deposit box to stash another set of the photos."

"Why there?" I asked.

"I'm thinking we are going to need to have some insurance, and if we need to have access to the photos, Doug can be there for us. I trust Doug."

"Jim, I'm not sure about that." I shook my head.

"Hear me out. I'm not saying tell him what's in the safety deposit box, but if for some reason we are unable to ..."

"Now you're scaring me," I interrupted.

"Katie, think about it. We have proof that Henry Baldwin had something to do with the assassination of the President. We both think Baldwin is politically dangerous, and who knows what he is capable of ... Murder?"

"Okay, we've got a lot to consider," I said, shaking my head. "What have we gotten ourselves into?" I closed the bathroom door and leaned against the sink while the water warmed up in the shower.

After dressing and downing a quick cup of coffee, I drove Jim to the Hill stopping at the Riggs bank.

"When you get the safety deposit box, add Mary's name on the paperwork." I handed him a piece of paper with her name and address.

"Are you sure that's a good idea?" He took the information and tucked it in his pocket.

"Mary's a complete straight arrow. Hopefully, we will never have to let her know what's happening. This is just a fail-safe." I shrugged.

Jim went from the bank to his office. I drove to the paper, got some additional photos printed, and tidied up the darkroom before Scott got in. I was sitting down at his desk writing him a note as Stan stepped out of the elevator and gave me a wave.

"Hi kid, what are you up to?"

"Hi Stan. I'm going to take a week off and was just leaving a note for Scott. I've got a bunch of overtime. I must use it or lose it."

"Have a good time." Stan waved and went into the darkroom.

"Thanks, not sure about a good time," I mumbled.

I drove back to my apartment and threw some clothes into a suitcase. This trip was going to be a lot different from my last one. I loved the beach house, but this was going to be stressful to say the least. I picked Jim up near his office, and we were on our way. We were both overwhelmed with what we were facing and avoided talking about it.

"Jim, have you talked to Angela lately?" I asked. "With what we know about Baldwin, she could get caught in the middle."

"Not in a couple of days. Her Dad will go to the Hill to get confirmed for his ambassador post in about a week. I'll have to go to that."

"Is she going with them to Paris?"

"I haven't been keeping track of her. I wonder if Baldwin is giving her the cold shoulder. I have not wanted to ask, and she certainly isn't keeping me in the loop."

"It might be smart to find out what's going on. If she goes to France that would at least separate her from the President. And you for that matter. However we deal with what we have on Baldwin, Angela will be an ocean away."

"I was hoping to have a talk with her after the election. It just didn't happen. Now, with this shit storm, I haven't a clue how to deal with her. I have no idea what's been going on with Angela and Baldwin, if anything. And I can't really ask her. With what we know about Baldwin, I'd be glad to have her in France. No matter what, Angela cannot be given any of the information we have. My hope is he has stepped away from her." He shook his head. "Angela and her father were seduced by the vision of being close to real power. I'd bet my life they have nothing to do with Baldwin's plot. Alex, being Chair of the Republican Party in South Carolina, made him a target of Baldwin, and they fell for it. Everything now is totally different."

We both withdrew into our own thoughts. With what we were facing and the possible consequences, Angela was just a footnote. A secret isn't a secret once you tell someone. Multiply that by ten when it comes to anything in Washington. If we made a wrong decision, it could be fatal.

"Jim, I'm still not sure about sharing with Doug."

"I've known Doug my whole life. When my dad died, Doug stepped in; he has been my go-to."

"That's great, but he is totally separated from Washington."

"Actually, that's the whole point. He can be our *in case of emergency, break glass.*"

"That's a two-edged sword. His knowing could put him in danger," I added.

We settled in for the long drive, barely talking. It felt good to be leaving Washington, but we were taking the proof of President Baldwin's complicity in the assassination, that elevated him to the Presidency, with us. So much to think about ... so many decisions, ones that would rock the country.

Chapter Twenty-Two

We pulled up the driveway with the dark silhouette of the cottage in front of us. It should have looked inviting, but tonight was different. The happy memories were just that. The present was unsettled and ominous. We walked from room to room, opening the windows. There had always been a nice breeze off the ocean, and tonight was no different. It only took a few minutes to cool off the rooms and fill them with the sound of the surf. The eerie cries of an owl added to the somber note of our feelings.

"I'm going to walk to Doug's to tell him we're here," Jim said.

"I'll put the food away and unpack our clothes," I answered. "Why don't you ask Doug to come over tomorrow for supper?"

Jim waved as he walked out the screen door. After the stress of the last twenty-four hours and the long drive, I unpacked and was in bed in a matter of minutes. I rolled to my left side, hugging a pillow to my stomach, and nodded off.

Sometime later, Jim slid in behind me, pulling me into a hug, and we were asleep in a matter of minutes. We slept late and spent the rest of the day killing time until our supper with Doug. I sat on the deck reading or pretending to read. I kept going over everything in my mind. Thinking about telling someone what we knew about the assassination and what that would mean made me queasy. Jim was working on a speech he would give at the Gibbes Museum. Ever since my discovery, our everyday lives had been put on hold. We couldn't really move forward. We walked like zombies throughout the day.

"I'm gonna make the salad." I reached over and touched Jim's arm.

"Okay, what time is it?"

"Doug should be here in about a half hour. It's 5:30," I said. I cut up the lettuce, tomatoes, cucumbers, and onions and put them in the fridge.

Jim came in to help. He put a large pot on the stove to get the linguine started while I set the table. This was all so surreal. I was guessing Doug would lose his appetite as soon as we started telling our story.

"Jim, I wonder if we should eat first. Once we talk to Doug, none of us are going to be hungry."

"Ha. I think you're right. Let's eat as soon as he gets here."

Doug was right on time, with a bag of shrimp in hand. I thanked him and headed for the kitchen while Jim handed him a beer.

"Thanks for coming, Doug. Have a seat while I go work on the shrimp," Jim said turning toward the kitchen.

I wasn't really a cook, so I was happy to see him take over. He sautéed the shrimp in butter and garlic while the linguine sat in the strainer ready to be added. I brought the salad out to the table with a couple of dressing choices.

Doug sat quietly watching all this domesticity with a bemused expression.

"Okay, I think we're ready to go. Doug, come sit down," Jim said carrying the large frying pan and trivet for the table.

"Wow, that smells amazing." I said.

The three of us settled in, passing the salad bowl around and scooping the shrimp linguine onto our plates. Jim and I sat there pretending to enjoy our meal and making small talk about the weather and other innocent chitchat.

"This is really good, and I certainly enjoy your company, but what's up?" Doug asked.

"Doug, I'm not exactly sure where to start." Jim looked at me and pulled his chair a little closer to the table.

"Damn, are you pregnant?" Doug looked at me.

"Yikes, *no!*" I said, shaking my head.

"Now wouldn't that be something?" Jim added with a laugh. "But no."

"Okay, that was my shot. Someone start talking," Doug added.

Jim got up and walked into the bedroom to retrieve the envelope that held my photos. I cleaned the dishes off the table.

"Doug, before we begin, I want you to know these pictures could be dangerous to see."

"Dangerous? How?" he asked.

"Dangerous as in seeing them can put your life in danger."

Doug's face grew solemn. "You obviously called me over to show them to me, so I figure you feel it's important I see them. I trust you, Jim." He lifted his hand. "Show them to me."

***

Doug looked as if he were going to be sick. "I'm speechless. I do not know what to say."

"That's our problem. We've known about this for a few days and we're not sure what to do next," Jim said.

Doug just sat there, not moving nor speaking. He slid the pictures around the table, picking them up studying each image.

"It's hard to believe, but here it is in black and white." He looked around. "You guys, or should I say we, have to figure out what to do, how to deal with this."

"Let me tell you what we've done so far, which isn't much. Katie has made several copies of these," Jim added. "We've secured the photo negatives. We have the photos showing Baldwin in George-town with us now, and we have an extra set in a safety deposit box in DC."

"You all must have been thinking about your next step. Your lives could be in danger. I appreciate you trusting me, but it's way over my head."

"That's why we need you, Doug. You're one of the only people we can truly trust if something happens to us. We even thought about going to the FBI, but they had the shooter, and mysteriously he died the first night he was in federal custody. That was at best a huge screw-up or at worst a conspiracy," I said.

"Definitely smells like a cover-up. They had the guy cold and a day later he's dead," Jim added. "That ended any chance of finding out who he was working for."

"Did you consider just giving the pictures to the newspaper and let them figure it out?" Doug asked, looking at me.

"Yes, and that is still a possibility. Since the paper is considered to lean Democratic, they, whoever the conspirators are, might be able to discredit Katie and *The Post* and bury it," Jim said.

I rubbed my forehead to fend off a headache. "The country has gone through a lot over a brief period of time. First, there was a major change in administration. Things seemed to be running smoothly, and then out of the blue the new President gets blown away." I sighed heavily. "These photographs are going to really shake things to the core."

"Is there anyone trying to find out who the assassin is and where he came from?" Doug asked.

"I really don't know where the FBI are with the investigation. I will need to check on that when we get back to DC," Jim pondered. "I'm sure they'd like to see these pictures."

"So right now, just to be clear, the three of us know that the President of the United States had something to do with having his predecessor killed, and we're the only people who can blow the whistle on him?" Doug looked at Jim and to me.

The three of us sat there blankly studying the surface of the dining table not knowing what to do or say next.

"Okay, let's try and think outside the box. First, what is the result we want? Is our goal to punish Baldwin and send him to prison? What does that do to the country as we know it?" I asked.

Doug and Jim sat there considering what I said but didn't have a reply.

"What if Baldwin could be convinced to step down ..." Jim was almost talking to himself.

"What are you thinking?" I asked.

"How about a little friendly blackmail? If he knows that there is proof out there of what he participated in, and it could be dumped on him, maybe he can be convinced to take an early retirement. It's something to consider." Jim shrugged. "Think about it."

"Ha ... who's going waltz into the Oval Office and suggest he resign?" I asked.

"That is probably the last step, but hear me out. If he is convinced he's got nowhere to go, and the alternative is a messy impeachment, who knows," Jim said shaking his head.

"So, let's take this to the next step. It means Abercrombie would take over the presidency. How close is he with Baldwin?" I asked Jim.

Doug hadn't said a word for a while. He looked around the table, tapping the photos with his finger.

"I've known Abercrombie for over thirty years. He's a good man. I cannot believe he had anything to do with all this." Doug looked at both of us.

I gave him a surprised look.

"I agree. He was a family friend, and philosophically he has nothing in common with Baldwin. Remember he got approved by a voice vote, with no negative votes," Jim added.

"Wow, let's see, do we want to contact the one guy who would have the most to gain with our information? This sounds nuts," I said, shaking my head.

"Right now, we're the only people that know what happened. Once we make contact with other people, the danger really increases. If we make the wrong decision, we're screwed big time. Unless we can come up with something else, Abercrombie is it." Jim shrugged.

"I think I need a beer, does anyone want to join me?" Doug and I both nodded, and Jim got up and walked to the kitchen returning with three long necks. The three of us sat there silently. We all came out of our funk at the same moment.

"Okay, hear me out. We contact Abercrombie, but we do it outside of DC. Since we know him, we can talk to him, maybe here.

Also, without any of his staff. This has to be face-to-face just the four of us." Jim said.

"How are we going to make that work?" I asked.

"Doug, would you feel comfortable contacting Abercrombie?" Jim asked.

"We swap Christmas cards, and I get a card from him on my birthday, but I really don't know what he would say if I reached out to him," Doug pondered.

"I can certainly call him. We talked when he was being pushed for the Vice Presidenet spot. He and my dad were close. I'll have my office reach out to his office and see how his schedule looks." Jim got up and walked out on the deck with the phone. The phone's cord was just long enough to reach the table on our deck.

"Doug, I'm both sorry to have dumped all this on you and at the same time so relieved having someone to talk to." I smiled at Doug.

"Kate, I am still in shock. I hope I'm going to give you good advice. This is very scary. I'm fairly sure I won't get much sleep until we get this thing worked out." Doug shrugged.

We both jumped when the screen door slammed as Jim returned.

"Sorry. I just got off the phone with his office. Turns out Abercrombie is going to be in Charleston next Monday. Unbelievably, his wife is on the Board of Directors of the Gibbes Museum. He's coming down to support her." Jim grabbed his beer and joined us at the dining room table.

"Are you going to contact him and try to get him to meet without his staff involved or his wife? How do we deal with her? That might be tough," I said.

"Humm, I might be able to help with that," Doug said with a wry smile.

"Don't keep us guessing. What are you thinking?" Jim asked, looking from me to Doug.

"Well, I went to school with his wife, Jenni, and I think she would like to hear from an old friend," Doug smiled.

"Doug, you dog you. Did you date her?" Jim asked.

Doug just smiled. "I'll see if I can find her parent's phone number. I think they still live in Greenville. Seems like you have to get to the Vice President and organize his visit," Doug added looking at Jim. "I'm going to head back to my house and try and get my head around all of this. I'll try and get hold of Jenni Abercrombie tomorrow." Doug got up, leaving his half-finished beer on the table. "Thanks for dinner. I'm not sure whether a 'Thank you' is appropriate for the rest of the evening." Doug waved as he pushed through the screen door.

"Goodnight Doug. Talk to you tomorrow," Jim said, walking over to me. "I'm going to reach out to Abercrombie and see if he might be willing to say a few words at the event. I could introduce him." Jim was thinking aloud. "The hard part is going to be getting him alone. We have to have enough time to share our story and enough time for him to absorb it."

Jim gave me a commiserating look. We were trusting that Abercrombie had nothing to do with the assassination. If he did, we would be in deep shit or even worse.

"Hey, how about taking a walk on the beach?" Jim looked over at me. Our meeting with Doug had one effect. We were both physically and emotionally spent. We stood on either side of the table looking at the mess we made, and decided cleaning up could wait until we got back. We walked down the path, enjoying the smells and sounds of the ocean. People were still out enjoying the sunset. We watched an older man swimming with his two puppies, while a group of little tykes were doing their best to catch ghost crabs. It was all so normal ... so safe.

"Katie, right now we are in a good place. Only the three of us know the truth about Baldwin. That's going to change, and we're going to lose control." He stepped in front of me, holding my hands against his chest. "I'm worried. I wonder if it would be a good idea if you took a step back."

I pulled my hands free. "Jim, you must be kidding. I'm the reason we're in this. *Me.* Those are *my* photos in there, and I plan to stick with this to its conclusion. Once we get Abercrombie involved, we have given up a lot of our leverage. This is my story and likely the most important story of my career. You have to understand that."

"Katie, I can't stand the thought that something could happen to you. But I understand how important your career is to you. It's who you are. Having found you, I want to keep you safe. Katie, I love you. I had no idea what that actually meant until you walked into my life and gave it meaning." Jim stepped close and took me in his arms. "We are in this together ... forever. I want to spend every minute of my life with you."

"Hopefully, we'll be sitting on this beach when we're old and grey." I held on tight and reached up to give him a serious kiss. A kiss that sent the message that our love was forever.

We walked back to the beach house hand in hand. We both knew we had taken a huge step toward our future. This would be the first night in a long time that I really slept. No tossing and turning.

Chapter Twenty-Three

I awoke with an uncomfortable feeling we had left something out of the mix. After all, I had taken the pictures while working for *The Post*. Technically, the photos belonged to them. Mrs. Graham had supported me during my first adventure, which meant she at least knew who I was. If we were going to tell anyone at the paper, it had to be at the very top. Anywhere below the top could open the flood gates. After all, we were sitting on the story of the century.

I could hear Jim moving around the cottage and the screen door bang. Everything we talked about last night came flooding back, and there was no way to avoid it. I swung my legs over the side of the bed and took a moment, stretching my arms over my head. I walked over to the window. I could hear Jim talking on the phone but couldn't make out what he was saying. I jumped in the shower and quickly dressed for the day. Jim was still on the phone, so I quietly moved into the kitchen to pour myself a glass of milk. By the time I finished and washed my glass, he was off the phone and sitting on the deck stairs staring at the ocean.

"Good morning," I called out through the screen door.

"Hi, I've been on the phone with the Vice President."

"And, what did he say?" I asked, walking over to sit next to him.

"He seemed happy to hear from me, and we chatted about all sorts of stuff. The really good news is, he is coming down and will be available to chat after the event at the Gibbes Museum."

"Well, that's positive at least. How do we get him to see us alone?" I asked.

"I invited him out to the beach." Jim grinned.

"No! And he said yes?" I laughed. "Really?"

"It turns out that Jenni got a call from an old friend down here earlier this morning," Jim said, grinning from ear to ear. "*And* she would love to spend some time at the beach."

"Ha, isn't that something?"

I slid my arm around Jim's waist, and he leaned into me giving me a big hug.

"We're on." Jim looked very pleased with himself.

"Look at those clouds moving in." I pointed. "We're going to get some rain."

"When I was a kid, I would sit here and watch the storms roll in. I always thought it was funny how people on the beach, in their swimsuits, would scurry off as soon as the first raindrops hit," he said.

"How about taking a walk? We should be able to get back before the rain hits."

"Sounds good." Jim jumped up and pulled me to my feet.

The dark line of clouds was bearing down on us. We picked up our pace, but we were losing the race. We walked with the wind at our backs, and soon the rain was beating down on us. We tried to move faster, trying to outrun the rain, but soon it was obvious we had lost the race. We looked at each other, slowed down to a normal walk, and began to laugh. Jim took my hand and started humming "Singing in the Rain."

I laughed aloud. "I don't think I can get any wetter."

"We're almost there. Another hundred yards."

We quickly walked toward the beach house and were startled by a loud clap of thunder which came from right over our shoulders. We both jumped, looked at each other, and began jogging. With the cottage in sight, we picked up the pace and so did the rain. By the time we reached the deck, our clothes were soaked through, and our feet and legs were caked with sand. We used the hose near the back door to try and get rid of the sand. Jim sprayed off his feet and legs and then turned the hose on me.

"Yikes, that's cold," I yelped.

"I feel like my T-shirt is glued to me," Jim said. He tossed the hose aside and stepped close to me. "Can you help me get this off?"

"Sure, lean over, I'd love to undress you," I smiled at him, grabbed the bottom edge of his tee, and peeled it over his head.

"Thanks. My turn." He grabbed my T-shirt as I leaned over and put my arms over my head. It was a bit of a tug of war to get my long sleeve shirt over my head and off my arms.

"I couldn't be any wetter if I were in the shower," he said.

"Now that sounds like a plan," I said while stripping off my shorts, quickly moving through the door, crossing the living room, and moving into the bathroom. I pulled the shower knobs on and pushed the lever all the way toward hot. I tossed my underwear on the floor and wrapped myself in a nice fluffy beach towel, reaching in to check the water, which felt nice and steamy. I dropped the towel and stepped into the shower.

I stood under the hot water. All the stress from the past week seemed to drain from my body. There were so many issues pulling me in different directions. Everything seemed so earthshakingly serious. My relationship with Jim was rock solid. *But what was our future to be?* We were in the middle of what could be a meltdown of the government as we know it. Our little love story seemed so small. I had been so sure of our relationship there had been no need to push Jim.

"Hey, want me to scrub your back?" I could hear the smile in his voice.

"Sure, thought you'd never ask," I smiled.

He joined me, ducking his head under the flow of water. I handed him the soap and cuddled into his body by putting my arms around his neck. Jim took the soap and rubbed it in circles across my shoulders and down my back. We had been under so much pressure for the past week, this moment was like popping a champagne cork. We rocked against each other, enjoying the moment.

"Humm, I've got a really good idea," I mumbled into his ear. I turned the water off.

"Oh yeah, what would you be thinking?" Jim kissed my ear working his way down my neck.

I climbed out of the shower. "There's a lovely soft, warm bed waiting. Care to join me?" I asked. I grabbed a towel to dry off my hair a bit and then finger-combed it. I jumped under the covers.

Jim was only a few steps behind me. He pulled back the covers, taking a few seconds to enjoy the view, before joining me.

Chapter Twenty-Four

The sun was just about to disappear as I opened my eyes. We had both slipped into a deep sleep after making love. I had no idea how long we'd slept. I rolled over and focused on the alarm clock on the desk. Turns out we'd been out for almost four hours. Trying to be quiet, I got out of bed, grabbed a pair of sweats and a T-shirt. I didn't want to disturb Jim.

"Hi. I didn't hear you get up. How long have you been standing there?" I asked.

"Just a couple of minutes. Wow, I feel great, and I'm starving," he said, walking over to me and putting his arms around my waist.

"God, I love you," I smiled and pushed back to look into his eyes.

"My time with you has brought meaning and purpose to my life. I can't imagine living without you. What we're facing scares the hell out of me. All I can think of is keeping you safe."

The phone rang in the living room. Jim sighed, gave me a quick kiss, and turned to go answer it. I stood there watching him, knowing that our love was forever and that this beach house would be the center of our universe.

His chief of staff, Bob, was calling to check in. He hadn't been in touch for a couple of days, so Jim sat down with a pad and pen to catch up on district business. Jim was in a broad-ranging conversation that took about half an hour. I set the table, opened two beers, and walked over to Jim, putting one down on the table for him. He gave me a smile and mouthed that he was almost done. I smiled back and walked out onto the deck to give him some privacy. He finally hung up and followed me.

"I've got to make one more call. Give me about five more minutes. Apparently, Angela had a meltdown with Bob. She couldn't get me on the phone and blamed it on him. He told her I was in Charleston which really set her off." Jim cringed.

"Oh God, I haven't given her a thought."

"Let me try and call her. It will be short." Jim said. It seemed Angela was doing most of the talking and really wasn't interested in hearing, what Jim had to say. I was sure it was going to be an interesting meal. I could hear Jim abruptly hang up the phone and walk toward the kitchen.

I waited for him to start the conversation.

"Do you want the good news or the bad news?"

"That's a tough one." I pondered. "Let's go with the bad news first. What did Angela have to say?"

"How'd you guess?" Jim gave me a pained smile. "Well, where do I start?"

"How bad is it? Is she coming to Charleston? God, I hope not." I added.

"Well, I'm not sure. She's both annoyed that I am here, and probably more annoyed that she didn't know that I was here."

"How long has it been since you talked to her?"

"I haven't had any contact since you called me to see the photos. I know her dad is scheduled to be up on the Hill for his confirmation hearing. I really haven't given them a thought since we made our, what do I call it ... discovery?"

"The confirmation should go quickly, and hopefully Angela will be going with her parents to France," I said, lifting my crossed fingers.

"I don't know about that, *but* she is thinking of coming down here for the event at the Gibbes. She's in Columbia now, so she's only a couple of hours away."

My body froze. "You don't think she would come out here?"

"That's something that can't happen." Jim said. "All the years I've known Angela, she has only been here once and made it clear that she didn't plan on ever coming back. I don't think that has changed."

"What if she does?" I sat there wondering how awful it could be.

"She won't." Jim interrupted my thoughts by shaking his head. "I'm sorry. I've been a coward. It's time for me to find a backbone and end my relationship with her. God knows it has been a charade for years," he said.

"Jim, as much as I want your marriage to end, for this subterfuge to end, and this cheating to end, now is definitely not the time to rock the boat. I don't think I can handle confronting both the President and Angela right now."

We both sat studying our plates for a minute or two.

"Katie, I know I've been unfair to you. I've been selfish. This needs to stop, and we need to take the next step."

"I agree. Just to be able to go out and not worry that someone is going to see us would be nice. But *now* is not the time." I smiled. "I've hoped Angela would make the move, but I guess things haven't progressed with Baldwin."

"I didn't think they would. Now with what we know about the President, I really hope she's planning to go with her parents to France," he said. "Who knows how this is going to turn out. I'd rather have her halfway around the world than playing footsie with Baldwin."

"Okay, I think we've covered the bad news. What's the good news?" I asked.

"Right. Well, the Vice President is arriving at the Gibbes just before the event and he doesn't want to be part of the formal program. He will just sit there and support his wife. I'll be able to say hello before the event, but that's about it. Afterward, I'll drive back here with them. He will have his Secret Service protection, but no one else will be coming out to the beach."

"That might be awkward. What do we do with the agents?" I asked.

"They would just stay outside. I think that would be normal. I'm more worried about getting Jenni out of the way," Jim said. "Doug seemed pretty sure he could take care of her. I'd better get in touch with him and see what he has in mind. The event should be over by 5:00 or 5:30. By the time they get out here, it would be a nice time to take a walk on the beach. I think that's Doug's plan." He got up from the table and went over to the phone to call Doug.

"Hey Doug, my office has been in touch with Abercrombie's office. The event at the Gibbes will be over by 5:30, so we should be back on the island before 6:30." Jim paused, listening to Doug. From the smile on his face, I assumed Doug was confident with his plan. "So, Doug will be over here in plenty of time to meet us when we get back from downtown. He seems to think he can take Jenni to the beach with him. A slam dunk."

As the sun had set on the marsh, I wondered how tomorrow would change our world forever.

***

The next morning my little mockingbird did his job again and got me up with the sun. Jim was still asleep, which made it a perfect time to do a little rearranging. I slipped out of bed and grabbed some clothes on my way to the bathroom. I had second thoughts about cleaning. *Too noisy.* I decided to run over to the local shop and pick up some flowers and a few things for breakfast.

It was the perfect day for putting the top down on my Mustang and cruising down Palm Blvd. to the local supermarket, the Red and White. Outside the front of the store, there were large terracotta pots planted with geraniums. Four would do the job. They would make the beach house look like someone actually lived there. I also picked up a box of Krispy Kreme donuts. Maybe Jim wouldn't notice the plants, but he certainly would appreciate the donuts. By the time I got back, he was up and busy. He had moved a bunch of old fishing gear out of the living room. I smiled when I saw what he was up to.

"Thank you. I bought you a present," I said, handing him the box of Krispy Kremes.

"Hey you, fantastic! Remember the most important meal of the day is breakfast." He smiled as he reached for the box.

"I picked up some flowers. Could you help me get them out of the car?" We walked to the back of my car. I unlocked the trunk and stepped aside so Jim could help me unload.

"You only got four plants. I would have expected at least double that," he turned and smiled.

"Oh, is that a challenge? I can go pick up some more," I laughed.

"No, I think we're good." Jim grabbed two of the potted plants, taking them around to the back deck and, grinning as he turned the corner to the deck. I took the grocery bags into the house, dumping them on the kitchen counter.

We ate lunch in a tense silence, checking the time every fifteen minutes until it was time to get dressed to go to Charleston. Jim had to wear a jacket and tie. Since I was just part of the audience, linen slacks and a dressy T-shirt would work. I would shoot the event just to keep busy.

The plan was to drive to the event in my car, and then afterward, Jim would accompany the Vice President and his wife out to the beach. I just had to get back here to the beach before the Vice President.

We couldn't sit still any longer and ended up leaving the island in plenty of time. Jim had wanted to be there a good hour before the event started. Unless we had a flat tire, we would be there about two hours early now. I certainly wasn't going to argue with him.

The Gibbes Museum was on Meeting Street, the main traffic artery through Charleston. I'd been in Charleston only once, so Jim was the navigator. There was on-street parking, and we were lucky to find a spot on the same block as the museum. So, we were way too early.

"That was easy. Now what?" I asked, trying not to gloat.

"I guess we're here in plenty of time." Jim had a sheepish look on his face. "Did you see the church we just passed?"

"The brick one with the green roof?"

"It's not your typical colonial looking church. The sanctuary is circular so there's no place for the devil to hide, or so they say. The church is called Circular Congregational," Jim said, with a serious look. "It has a really old cemetery right behind it. Let's go take a look."

We walked back up Meeting Street and luckily the church property was open. Jim held the gate open, and it was like stepping into another world. The azaleas were in bloom. We walked down a narrow cobblestone path surrounded by a blaze of color: red, pink, and white flowering bushes. Besides the azaleas, there were vines with tiny white star-like flowers with a sweet perfume.

"What a wonderful smell." I closed my eyes and inhaled.

"Yeah, it's nice. I think it's called confederate jasmine."

"Really? It seems like a lot of stuff down here is tied to the Civil War," I teased.

"Folks down here are fiercely independent. They still call it the 'War of Northern Aggression.'" Jim smiled. "It will take time for them to realize and accept the civil rights movement as being good for everyone."

"Perhaps this isn't the time to have *that* political discussion." I smiled.

We strolled through the cemetery, and I managed to take some shots of the 18th Century gravestones. The area was packed tight. There were family plots separated with low brick walls. The age of the monuments was obvious by how weathered they were. Some of the letterings were barely readable; eroded by wind and time.

"There is supposed to be a gravestone here that says, **I told you I was sick**, but I've never been able to find it." Jim laughed. He checked his watch and decided it was time. He needed to make contact with the museum people.

I decided to stay at the churchyard a bit longer. We walked back up the path holding hands. We were both nervous as hell about the next few hours, and holding hands gave me a feeling that together we couldn't fail. After a quick furtive kiss, Jim was off across the street and into the museum.

I sat on the church steps and watched people stroll into the museum. A group of well- dressed women were about to enter. They didn't look like tourists, so I assumed they were part of the Gibbes event. It was time to get moving. As I crossed the street, I grabbed my Post ID which I kept in my camera bag. The badge was clipped to a lanyard that I wore around my neck. I was sure my ID would get me into the event. I smiled at the ladies sitting behind the check-in desk. They handed me a program and directed me to the rotunda. It was supposed to start at 4:00 p.m. After a short greeting from the Director of the Gibbes, Jim was next on deck to praise the museum and open the new exhibit. That was to be followed by the actual opening of the new show with some cocktails and nibbles. I could have cared less about the whole thing.

I was unusually nervous, apprehensive, and felt like I was going to throw up. There was a bit of commotion as the Vice President and his wife arrived. *Thank God.* At least everything was falling into place. I stood off to the side and watched Jim walk over, welcoming them to Charleston.

The local press was rushing about snapping everything in sight. About ten steps behind the Vice President, a woman dressed in a vivid red dress and oversized sunglasses swept into the room. My heart skipped a beat, and beads of sweat popped out on my forehead. Just what we needed. She couldn't be part of the conversation with the Vice President.

"Oh crap," I mumbled. *There she was. Angela in all her glory.*

Jim was concentrating on the Vice President and his wife so was about to be blindsided. As he was speaking to the Abercrombie's, he made eye contact with me. The concerned look on my face stopped him in his tracks. I nodded over toward Angela, and Jim followed my line of sight. I had to give him credit, he didn't miss a beat. He finished his conversation, stepped behind the Vice President, and greeted her. She presented her cheek for a kiss and Jim obliged. She was giving him a 1000-watt smile and dragging him toward the Vice President. She greeted the Vice President and his wife and ensconced herself next to Mrs. Abercrombie as the program was about to start.

Finally, everyone took their seats. As Jim took his seat behind the podium, he gave me a discreet nod. I tried not to react but couldn't help giving him a sympathetic smile. The head of Gibbes stepped up to the podium and welcomed the folks to the opening. It only took minutes, but it seemed to never end. Jim was introduced to a polite applause. I took a few shots, just to look like I belonged. Jim stepped to the mic and praised the museum and the city for their support of the Arts. Next, he gave a nod to the Vice President and his wife. They received a nice round of applause.

It felt as if my head were going to explode. I couldn't wait for this to end and to get back to the island. *How the hell was Jim going to deal with Angela?* I was deep in my own thoughts when I looked up. Everyone applauded and got to their feet. They moved into the new exhibit and to the bars that had been set up. I stood there frozen, not sure which way to move. I wanted to quickly leave, but then again, I desperately wanted to see what was going to happen with

Angela. The Vice President and his wife were holding court with the local dignitaries while Angela was chatting with some of the staff of the museum. Jim was talking with a group of people while also keeping an eye on me. I took a tour around the room pretending to be checking out the new exhibit. As I was making my way out of the Rotunda, Jim stepped up to introduce himself to me. Even extending his hand for a handshake.

"Hi, my name is Jim Rayford." He feigned a discreet smile.

"Ah, nice to meet you. What the hell are you going to do?" I added, smiling back at him while still holding on to his hand. "I'm going to get out of here and get back to the beach." I kept smiling. We were so involved in our conversation we didn't notice Angela coming our way.

"Jim, I need to talk to you," Angela said, ignoring my existence. Unfortunately, that didn't last for long. She turned toward me and gave me a condescending look from head to toe.

I turned toward her and introduced myself.

"Mrs. Rayford, nice to see you again. Kate Miller with *The Washington Post*. We met during the primary campaign." I offered her my hand.

She looked at my hand and limply took it, but only for a moment.

"Oh yes, of course. Could you excuse us? I need to speak with my husband."

I had been totally dismissed, which was a relief. I couldn't get out of there fast enough.

"Congressman Rayford, nice seeing you again." I smiled politely and made my getaway. I couldn't help myself; I turned to see what was happening. Jim had Angela by the elbow, moving her to a quiet part of the gallery. He seemed to be doing all the talking, which I took to be a positive sign.

I managed to drive back to the island on autopilot, not noticing my surroundings. When I arrived at the house, I could see Doug walking up the beach path. I pulled into the yard, way over to one side to make room for the Vice President's entourage.

"Hi Doug," I called out, walking around the house. "Jim should be leaving the museum in about fifteen minutes. Fingers crossed he isn't held up."

"I called Jenni yesterday. She is really looking forward to seeing me," Doug smiled. "And to 'walking barefoot in the sea,' to quote her."

"Doug, Angela was at the museum."

"What the hell. How did that happen?" Doug asked, looking a bit panicked.

"She found out about the program and just showed up. I have no idea how Jim is handling it. If she is in the car with the Vice President, my head is going to explode."

"How is this going to work?" Doug asked.

I shrugged. We sat on the back deck watching a line of brown pelicans fly by. They seemed so calm and beautiful.

"So, besides Angela showing up, how did the opening go?" He laughed.

"I really have no idea. Fine I guess." I shook my head and laughed. "I wasn't really paying attention. I couldn't take my eyes off Angela. I just wanted to get out of there and get back here. How about a beer?" I handed Doug a beer.

We both sat back down on the deck and waited for what seemed like an eternity.

Chapter Twenty-Five

There was the sound of crunching gravel in the driveway. *They were here.* Doug and I sat on the deck staring at each other.

"Okay, let's get this show on the road." Doug exhaled and pulled himself out of his chair. He motioned for me to step ahead of him, always a gentleman.

We walked through the house and out the front door. The Secret Service detail was out of the car first, checking out the area. I know they have a job to do, but besides Doug and me, there were only a couple of mockingbirds and a gecko lurking around the beach house.

Jim stepped out of the car, giving me a smile as he offered a hand to Jenni Abercrombie. The Vice President stepped out of the other side of the car. Doug and I didn't hesitate; we walked toward Jim and our guests.

"Jenni, it's great to see you!" Doug crossed in front of me to give her a hug. "Mr. Vice President, it's great to see you too," Doug said, turning to shake hands with Abercrombie.

"Doug, it's Robert. Great to see you. It's been too long," the Vice President answered, patting Doug on the back.

Jim introduced me to the Abercrombies and asked if the Secret Service needed to go into the house first. The Vice President shot that down, suggesting they might want to take a look at the ocean, pointing at the path on the side of the house. They nodded at the Vice President and walked up the front steps and right into the house.

"Okay ... that works," I whispered to Jim. "What happened with Angela?"

"I'll tell you later ... everything's okay, for now at least," he whispered in my ear. "Well folks, let's move inside." Jim smiled and pointed at the front door.

We all walked into the beach house behind the Secret Service agents.

Jenni walked straight through to the back deck, stopped, closed her eyes, and took a deep breath.

"Yes, it's wonderful, isn't it? How long has it been since you've been at the beach?" I asked.

"Oh, since last fall! We used to have a summer home down here. The kids loved it, and so did I. Robert needed to spend more time in Washington, so we sold it. With Robert's change in job, I think it was a good decision. We are so busy, traveling all the time. I don't think I'd be able to spend much time here at all."

Doug walked up to us holding a pair of my flip flops in one hand.

"Well, what do you think? How about a sunset walk on the beach?" Doug smiled.

"That sounds wonderful. I assume these belong to you ... I can't imagine you wearing them, Doug," Jenni said, pointing at the flip flops.

"Yes, they're mine." I could feel the color rise on my cheeks.

"I sort of borrowed them," Doug looked at me with a sheepish smile on his face.

"Well thank you." She looked at me. "I think I'd better use the restroom before we go." Jenni started to walk back inside.

"Of course. It's just inside the door past the kitchen," I said. I looked at Doug and shook my head.

"Take a deep breath." Doug looked at me. "I'm going to walk down toward the inlet. Hopefully, there will be a nice sunset. There's a bench down at the empty house. We can sit there for a while."

Jenni pushed through the screen door and clapped her hands. "I'm ready to go—Doug, lead the way." Jenni smiled at me, giving me a sympathetic pat on the arm. They set off down the path, over the dune, and out of sight. I turned and walked back into the house. Jim was sitting at the dining room table chatting with the Vice President.

"Can I get you gentlemen a drink ... a beer, wine, or a soda?" I asked.

"Robert, what would you like?" Jim asked.

"Thanks, but I'm good. Let's get down to it. I appreciate Jenni enjoying the beach, but I'm not out there with her." Robert looked over the rims of his glasses at Jim. "Exactly why am I here?"

"Right. Katie, would you get your envelope and join us at the table?" Jim asked.

I walked into the bedroom and took my envelope from the desk, sighed a deep breath, straightened my shoulders, and walked back to the table. Jim pulled out a chair for me and gave me an encouraging smile.

"Well sir, I was *The Post* photographer who got the shot—sorry bad word, *photo*—of the guy who assassinated the President. I was at the precinct when the PD brought him into the station. He walked right by me. About ten months before that terrible day, I was in Georgetown, picking up my laundry." I smiled, trying not to look nervous. "While I was waiting, Senator Baldwin pulled up, parked across the street, and went into the yard of a rather rundown house. It was completely out of place for him."

I looked up, and the Vice President was looking at me, speechless so Jim jumped in, "Katie thought something seemed off, so she started snapping off pictures of the scene."

I continued, "The senator walked up to the front door, and it opened just as he was about to knock. The man answering the door shook hands with the senator. They both looked around, like they were checking if someone had seen them. That struck me as odd, so I photographed them."

"Katie got busy and forgot all about those photos," said Jim.

"Right. Last week, while I was looking for another picture, I came across them." I opened the envelope and put the first pictures of the assassin on the table.

Abercrombie reached over to get a better look. Next, I pulled out the pictures from Georgetown and put them next to the other shots.

Jim said, "Robert let me cut to the chase. The guy with Baldwin is the guy who shot the President."

Abercrombie stiffened. "How can that be?" He picked up the photos and brought them closer. He sat silently studying them, and then he looked at me with questioning eyes.

"Look at the scar. It's the same guy." I tapped the photo with my finger.

He lowered the photos slowly. I sat back in my chair, exhausted from the retelling, while the photos lingered between us, and waited for Abercrombie to speak. Silent moments passed, and then he cleared his throat.

He lowered the photos slowly. "Katie, I think I could use that beer now," he said.

Jim and I had both been sitting on the edge of our seats. I took a deep breath and got up to get beers for all of us.

"This is ... shocking. I don't know what to say." Abercrombie stared at the photos.

We sat there quietly, giving him time to digest what the photos implied.

"I wondered what you wanted to talk about. This certainly wasn't it." Abercrombie sat still with a grimace on his face, pointing at my photos. "Why did you bring this to *me*?" He looked at each of us.

"That is a good question, sir," I said. "Both Jim and Doug have great respect for you, and frankly, we are at our wits end about what to do with this."

"Shouldn't the FBI be an obvious choice?" He looked at Jim.

"That was our first thought," Jim replied. "But with what happened to the shooter after he was moved to federal custody, we thought that could be dangerous."

"Who else knows about this?" he asked.

"We're it and Doug," Jim said, looking around the table.

"I've been thinking about something." I looked at Jim. "I took these pictures as an employee of *The Washington Post*. They don't belong to me. They belong to *The Post*." I looked to Jim for a response but couldn't read what he was thinking. "This has all developed in a couple of days," I added.

"We've talked about it and need advice. That's why we're looking to you." Jim said.

"God damn it, man! You have evidence that Baldwin was involved in the murder of President Scheffen. This is going to knock the country on its ass. We're just getting back to normal, and the administration is doing a good job. How could this happen?" The Vice President exploded.

Jim and I understood what he was feeling. We just looked at each other.

"Robert," said Jim, "right now, there are only four people who know about this. As soon as more people are told, the danger goes sky high," Jim paused, then added, "And you'll be the next president."

I could hear noises coming from the back deck. Doug and Jenni were coming up the stairs. From the chatting and laughing, I could tell they were having a wonderful time. That was about to end.

"We're back," Jenni called out as she walked across the deck and came through the screen door. Doug was right behind her. Jim and the Vice President stood up as they came in. The Vice President walked over and greeted his wife with a kiss on the cheek.

"My, how nice. Did you miss me?" Jenni looked at us and then back to her husband. "What's wrong? You all look like ..."

"Honey, sit down. Jim and Kate have just been telling me quite a story."

Jenni's smile fell at her husband's tone, and she took a seat. Her eyes were bright and alert.

Abercrombie spoke again. "They have shown me some information that is disturbing. Frankly, I can't really get my mind around it."

Jim and I looked at each other, not knowing exactly what to say. Neither of us had thought about discussing this with his wife. He noticed us looking at each other.

"Jenni is my closest adviser. There is nothing that I don't share with her, including this." He wasn't asking us, he was telling us. "Katie, could you please explain what these photos represent?"

***

I finished and watched Jenni take it all in, comparing the pictures I had set on the table.

"Damn it, I told you that man was trouble," she said, looking at her husband.

Jim, Doug, and I were speechless.

"I didn't want you to take the Vice Presidency. Now this. My God, this is a disaster," she added, tossing the photos on the table.

"You know I couldn't turn down the Vice Presidency. When you are asked to serve, you serve." He sounded defensive.

Jim looked at the Vice President. "This is dangerous information."

Jenni lifted her hands. "Ha, I think that's an understatement."

"Mrs. Abercrombie, what you also should know is that I believe *The Post* has to be brought into this."

"Won't the paper want to make a big story out of this?"

"I hear what you are saying, but Mrs. Graham is a very smart woman, and I trust her. As I said, these photos belong to *The Post*. And this is possibly the story of the Century."

"Doug, anyone, want a beer or maybe wine?" Jim asked, cutting through the tension.

Jenni was the first to raise her hand. "Wine please."

I was really beginning to like her. Jim opened a bottle of red and brought it and a couple of beers to the table. No one was making small talk. Everyone settled on their choice of drink, waiting for someone else to speak.

"Where do we go from here?" Doug piped up, breaking the silence.

"Doug and I have a lot of confidence in you, Mr. Vice President," Jim said looking at the Vice President and his wife.

"I'm not so sure this is the right thing to do." I shrugged.

"Ha, I appreciate your skepticism. After all, I have the most to gain, don't I?" Abercrombie added.

"We're in uncharted territory here," Jim added.

"How to handle this? What is our goal? What is our end game? Put Baldwin in jail? One thing for sure, he must be removed," the Vice President added soberly.

"Robert, we had a thought. What if we confronted Baldwin with what we have and convinced him to resign," Jim asked.

"Do you really think he would resign? The man is a rooster. He won't give up the Presidency without a fight," Jenni added. She looked at each of us to see our reaction.

"That's the concern. Since we know he was willing to kill the President, we can assume he is not going to capitulate easily. I think there is strength in numbers. If we back him into a corner, we'd better be damn sure he can't get out of that corner," Jim said.

"This brings us back to Mrs. Graham," I said. "I should have shown these photos to her straight away. Jim and I plan to return to DC in the morning."

"Right," said Abercrombie. "I know Katherine Graham. She's cool under pressure and knows a lot of players. We'll be flying back tonight too, and I will reach out to Katherine tomorrow afternoon. Hopefully, that will give you a chance to contact her before I do," he added.

"You should be able to get through to me or Jenni anytime of the day or night. You all could fly back to DC with us tonight." The Vice President reached into his wallet. "Jim, let me give you my private direct line, also our home phone." He pulled out several of his cards, picked up a pen, and wrote his private numbers on the back of each card. He then slid the cards to the three of us.

"Thanks, Robert, but we drove down, and Katie definitely needs her car when we're back in Washington."

The Vice President and his wife gave us a questioning look. I froze waiting for an uncomfortable question.

"Jim ... don't you have a car?" Jenni asked.

Jim and I both laughed out loud. *That* was not the question we were waiting for.

"What? Isn't it odd? Everyone has a car, don't they?" Jenni smiled.

"Sorry, we're not laughing at you. I have never had a car in Washington. I worked it out, and it's cheaper for me to take cabs and buses around town, instead of keeping a car," Jim said. "And Kate has a car," Jenni smiled at us. I could feel the heat rise to my face, and I became very interested in the label on my bottle of beer.

"Katie and I have been together for almost a year," Jim said. "I know there are things I have to do in my personal life, but right now is not the time. Trust me, I will make everything right as soon as this nightmare's over."

"Right." —the Vice President clapped his hands— "I think we are done for tonight. I have a lot to digest. I'm sure I'll be able to get in touch with Katherine. I'll wait until later tomorrow afternoon. Hopefully, you can contact her first. If not, I'm going to try and meet with her at my residence as soon as possible. You all should be available ... Tuesday?"

"Yes, we'll be back tomorrow late afternoon. I'll call you when we get back in town," Jim said.

Jenni was still looking at the photos. Hoping against hope that the pictures weren't conclusive. I moved next to her.

"It's really unbelievable, isn't it," I said, sitting down.

"Yes, it is. Our lives are going to be turned upside down for a while, I'm afraid," Jenni said. "How long have you been with *The Post*?"

"It's been about a year," I answered.

"You seem very young to be on staff. *And* I don't think I've ever run into a woman photographer." She smiled approvingly. "Very exciting."

"I don't really consider myself a trailblazer, but female press photographers are rare."

"It's been very nice to meet you." Jenni's gaze swept the room. "I love this little beach house. You're a very lucky young woman." Jenni reached across the table and squeezed my hand. "Although I wish we met under other circumstances. I'm not sure how this is going to work out," she said, shaking her head.

The Vice President called to Jenni. It was time to leave. We all moved out the front door and walked toward the car. There was a lot of handshaking and the Vice President reached over to give me a hug. He told me everything was going to be all right. I smiled at him, but I wasn't so sure.

The Secret Service agents jumped out of the car and opened the doors for Jenni and the Vice President. Doug, Jim, and I stood in the driveway and waved goodbye as they backed out. We turned to go back into the house.

"Doug, do you want to come back in and have a nightcap?" Jim asked.

"No thanks, Jim. I think I've had enough for one night. I'm exhausted. One thing though, I was really surprised how Jenni reacted to this whole thing. I always thought she was the quiet little lady. She didn't hold her tongue, did she?"

"I thought it was great. And it really made everyone sort of relax." I laughed.

I gave Doug a hug and a kiss on the cheek, and Jim gave him a firm handshake.

"We're going to leave early in the morning, so I'll say goodbye for now. Oh, by the way, could you come over and take our new potted plants to your house? Maybe you can keep them alive for Katie until we get back down here." Jim laughed.

I gave him a friendly punch in the arm. Doug turned and walked around the house to the beach path toward his home.

"I think it's time to tell me what happened with Angela." I looked over at Jim as we walked back into the house.

"Let's go sit on the back deck." We walked through the house to the deck and sat on the stairs leading to the beach.

"I was shocked to see Angela walking up to me at the Gibbes. No, that's an understatement. I couldn't believe my eyes. The look on your face was scary."

"I know. You looked amazingly calm. I wanted to run for the door. What did you say to her? I was half expecting her to be in the car with you."

"Well, her plan was to spend the evening with the Vice President. I think she thought we would be going out to dinner in Charleston. I told her she shouldn't have come, and there was no dinner to be had." He laughed briefly, then his smile fell, and he looked at me with a serious expression.

"Katie, I told her that I was sick and tired of watching her chase the President, and we needed to sit down and decide how we were going to move forward. She started to deny everything, and I told her that *I* had moved on."

I sucked in my breath. Jim took my hand and gently pressed it to his lips.

"With that, she stomped out. It's not over, but she knows there is no future. As soon as we're past all this; I'm going to Columbia and will ask her for a divorce. It'll still be a mess, I'm sure, but it's in the open. God, I'm glad it's over." He threw his arm around my shoulder and pulled me close.

We sat and watched to moon slip out from behind a cloud.

"God, I love this place ... and you." I took Jim's face in my hands and kissed him.

Chapter Twenty-Six

We were up at six and on the road by 6:30 a.m. Jim decided to do the driving. I was fine with that and fell asleep before we hit the interstate. We stopped along the way for lunch, and I called my office. Scott picked up the phone on the first ring.

"Hi Scott, how are things going?" I asked, fiddling with the phone cord.

"Fine ... are you back?"

"Not quite. I'll be back in town this afternoon."

"Okay, how about coming in at noon tomorrow. I've got the morning covered. I could use you to cover the afternoon."

"Okay, see you then. Scott, could you transfer me to the opera-tor?"

"Got it, see you tomorrow." Scott hung up.

I waited for the main operator to pick up. She was happy to put me through to the executive offices, and she clicked off hoping I was going to have a great day. I thanked her and hoped we all would have a great day.

"Good afternoon, how may I help you?" Mrs. Graham's office answered.

"Hi. This is Kate Miller from the photo desk. Would it be possible to speak with Mrs. Graham?" I asked. "It's urgent."

"I'll put you through to her secretary." I waited for her to pick up, looking at all the ads on the phone booth walls. If I needed a chiropractor or a lawyer, I was all set.

"Mrs. Graham's office, how can I help you?"

"I'd like to speak to Mrs. Graham, please. This is Kate Miller from the photo desk."

"I'm afraid that is not possible. Mrs. Graham has gone for the day, but she will be in the office tomorrow. I'll be happy to leave her a message that you called and would like to speak with her."

"That will have to work. Please tell her it is very important that I talk to her as soon as possible. Thank you so much." I gave her my number at home, plus my extension in the darkroom. I hadn't had any contact with her since my adventure in Tehran, and if I didn't hear from her in the morning, I would go up to her office. I waved at Jim as I walked back to the car.

We made it back to Georgetown just in time to "enjoy" the afternoon rush.

We parked near my apartment and carried our bags to the garden gate. We'd only been away a few days, but it seemed like a lifetime. The mail was on the floor inside the door. Jim stepped over it and dragged our bags up the spiral stairs to the bedroom, while I checked to see if there were any messages. The red light on the message machine was blinking. I grabbed a pad and pencil and pushed the play button.

Three of them were from Jim's office. His chief of staff seemed a bit concerned. All three messages wanted Jim to call as soon as we got in. The last message was from Mrs. Graham. She seemed surprised to hear from me. She left her number and expected a call. Jim came down the stairs and flopped down on the loveseat across from the fireplace.

"Did Graham call?" He asked.

"Yes."

"Call her," he said and sidled closer.

I dialed her number and listened as the phone rang ... eight, nine, ten times. I was about to hang up when Mrs. Graham's voice came on the line.

"Yes?"

I straightened up and cleared my throat. "Hello Mrs. Graham, this is Kate Miller from the paper. Thank you for calling me back."

"Well Kate, I was surprised by your call. Then, I talked to the Vice President this afternoon. Kate, I'm disappointed you didn't come to me first."

"I'm sorry, at that moment it seemed like the right decision. The Vice President was going to be at the same event as Jim ... Congressman Rayford. When we were discussing everything, I made it clear that what I had was the property of *The Post*."

"Yes. Who else knows about this?"

"Including the Abercrombies, there are only five of us who know."

"Well," Mrs. Graham said, taking a breath. "You must have made quite an impression with Robert. He spent a fair amount of time defending your actions. And also, Representative Rayford's."

"Mrs. Graham, I don't know what to say."

"I'm meeting with the Vice President and Mrs. Abercrombie tomorrow at 8:00 a.m. at their residence. Do I have to call Scott Flesch to get you there?"

"I'll be there." I said without hesitation.

"Good. Kate, this is more than a bit disturbing. I'm not sure how well I'm going to sleep tonight."

"Mrs. Graham, I am so sorry I didn't come to you first. You were great to me after my incident in Tehran."

"What's done is done. Let's see where we go from here. See you tomorrow morning."

"Yes ma'am. See you tomorrow." I hung up and sat there staring at the phone. I looked over at Jim.

He was slumped down on the sofa, gently snoring.

"Hey you, I'm off the phone. You'd better call Bob and see what's happening."

He sat up blinking awake. "How was your call?"

"She had already talked to the Vice President, and she made me feel like a jerk for not going to her first. She seems very unsettled about the whole situation. We have to be at the Vice President's residence at 8:00 a.m."

Jim got up off the sofa and stretched as I went over to the front door to pick up the mail and then sat down at the dining room table. He called Bob and spent the next twenty minutes discussing office business. Nothing sounded too urgent. The House wasn't in session, so he really didn't need to be in the office. He hung up, promising to try and get in tomorrow afternoon. Hopefully that would work out.

"Come over here." He patted the sofa. "I bought you a present." He looked pleased with himself.

"Really? When on earth did you have time to do that?" I sat next to him.

"I'm not really that clever. I saw this at the Gibbes and thought it was perfect." Jim took a small box out of his cargo shorts and handed it to me.

I opened it, folding back the tissue. There was a gold chain. Nestled underneath the chain was a gold sea turtle. I pulled the chain out of the box, allowing the sea turtle to swing free. The turtle was hanging on the chain by her front flipper.

"It's beautiful. I love it," I said, dabbing a tear from my eye. "I love it there, I think I could live there forever."

"Me too. That little house is ours forever. I promise."

Chapter Twenty-Seven

The Vice President's residence was on the grounds of the U.S. Naval Observatory. It was not far from Georgetown and was along Embassy Row on Massachusetts Avenue. I had done a photo shoot at the Observatory but had never been to the residence. As we turned in, there was a gatehouse occupied by two young sailors. One came out to ask us what our business was this morning. We answered, and I gave him my driver's license. He walked away, then came back with a clipboard and asked for Jim's identification. After taking a moment to check off our names, he handed me my license and gave us a pass to display once we parked. It also had directions to the residence. About a half mile up the road, a very stately French provincial building, complete with several turrets, came into view. There was a Lincoln already parked, which I assumed belonged to

Mrs. Graham. I checked my watch. *God forbid we might be late for this meeting.*

By the time we got to the front door, Jenni was standing there to greet us. After a hug and a peck on the cheek for both of us, she ushered us into the library, just to the left of the foyer. Mrs. Graham and the Vice President were seated around a game table, each with a cup of coffee in front of them. The Vice President stood as we walked into the room and came over to greet us. That included a strong handshake for Jim and a handshake, combined with a hug, for me.

"Jim, I'd like to introduce you to Mrs. Graham. Katherine. Representative Jim Rayford, First District in South Carolina."

"Mrs. Graham, it's an honor to meet you." Jim said, reaching out to shake her hand.

"Of course, you already know Katie," the Vice President smiled at me.

"Good morning, Mrs. Graham." I was on the opposite side of the table, so it would have been awkward to shake hands.

"We do seem to meet under the most unusual circumstances. What say we get right to the point of our meeting," she said.

The Vice President clapped his hands. "Right, let's get to it. Jim, Jenni, Katie, how about taking a seat."

The five of us were seated at a game table with an envelope filled with all of our futures. We weren't there for a game of cards. The game we were about to play was a much bigger one, with enormous stakes. Everyone was looking at me to begin.

I went through my story again, explaining the "who, what, and where," but I still didn't understand the "why." I stressed more of the technical photographic parts of the story, which were new to the Vice President and Jenni. While I was talking, Mrs. Graham was shuffling through the photos.

"Kate, you sure are a magnet for the big news stories, aren't you?" Mrs. Graham looked around the table. "I'm sure you all remember *The Post's* big story last year. It even won us a Pulitzer," she said, looking directly at me.

"Why, yes of course. The pictures of the murder of the oil minister in Iran. Katie were those your pictures?" The Vice President asked with astonishment.

"Yes sir, they were my shots," I said. "I was in the right place at the right time."

"Maybe after all this is over you can tell me the whole story." He smiled.

"It would be an honor, sir."

Jenni stood up looking at each of us. "Katherine, I know this is a lot to take in. Why don't we have some breakfast, and you can have time to mull this over?" Jenni walked to the door and led the way to the dining room.

"What a beautiful room. And the garden is fantastic," I added.

"This is a wonderful house. Not that long ago, the Vice President was on his own as to where he lived. Finally, Congress acted and organized this space. It was the residence of the commander of the Naval Observatory. It really makes a lot of sense. Trying to secure a house, say in Georgetown, really was expensive and totally disrupted the neighborhood with all the necessary security."

The Vice President stepped next to his wife. "FDR's Vice President, John Nance Garner, once said 'the Vice Presidency wasn't worth a bucket of warm spit.' He might have appreciated the job more if he'd gotten to live here." The Vice President laughed.

There was a buffet laid out on the sideboard with all the brunch goodies you could imagine. Jenni joined us once she was sure everyone was settled. The story I had told wasn't new to the four of us, so we still had an appetite. Mrs. Graham, on the other hand, just pushed her food around the plate. After about five minutes, Mrs. Graham was the first to speak.

"You folks must have some thoughts about this." She looked around the room. "I'd like to hear them."

"Katherine, I've thought of nothing else since we left Charleston," the Vice President said.

"This is more than overwhelming," Mrs. Graham continued. "The Republicans winning the White House wasn't my idea of a good time, but Scheffen was a decent man. I can't say I felt that way about Baldwin," Mrs. Graham added.

Abercrombie nodded his head. "Winning the White House was a good thing. Of course, that's a lifelong Republican talking. It was a tragedy when Scheffen was killed. He was so young and showed so much promise," the Vice President added. "Baldwin is another story. He's reactionary and far too right wing for me. He sees communists under every rock."

Graham said, "One good thing. Scheffen's cabinet is intact."

"That might change," said Abercrombie. "Over the past few weeks, there have been whispers that the President is going to make drastic changes to State, Defense, the AG, and that is just the beginning. Not that I've been included in any of these discussions," he laughed. "I wasn't Baldwin's choice."

"We have to move before he dismantles the cabinet," Graham said.

I was just an observer. I was listening to two real power brokers discussing the future of our country, me, a twenty-one-year-old and just out of college. Jenni had also been quiet. She moved around the table making sure we had refills of our drinks. Everyone had abandoned their food, and although it was bright and sunny outside, it was becoming gloomy in the Vice President's dining room.

Jim spoke up. "We have proof that Baldwin was involved in the assassination, and we're the only ones that have this information. What's our path forward? With this news about the cabinet, I don't think we have the luxury of time on our side."

"I agree," Mrs. Graham added.

"Mrs. Graham, we discussed going to the FBI. At first glance, that seemed like the obvious move. But because of what happened to the shooter, we just don't trust that there won't be a leak. His death might just be a coincidence, but I don't think we can take that chance, since they haven't released the way he died in custody," Jim said.

The Vice President shook his head in agreement. We were tap dancing around the edges of our challenge.

"If what we have runs in our paper" —I looked over at Mrs. Graham— "certainly every news outlet in the world will pick it up. Does that do it? Can we just step aside and watch the country go crazy?"

"As much as I'd like to see this across the front page above the fold, I'm sure Baldwin could weasel out of it. He'd attack the messenger. He *will* attack the validity of the photos and the photographer," Graham said, looking at me. "If it's true that the Attorney General is on the way out, that is not good news for us." She looked around the room.

"Robert, how well do you know the Attorney General?" Mrs. Graham asked.

"Scheffen kept him on when the new administration came in. I remember when we confirmed him. It was an overwhelming vote. It was definitely bipartisan," Abercrombie said.

"I've only met him a few times. He doesn't attend many social events," Graham responded.

"He has several kids and seems to be a dedicated family man. As I recall, he's not very political. He is a career government lawyer and has been in the Department of Justice for many years," Abercrombie added.

Jim joined the conversation. "That sounds promising. I hate to sound panicked but, could we get him over here? Now."

Everyone looked shocked.

He looked around the table. "Is there anything more important than this in any of our lives right now?"

"Fair enough. Let me get on the phone and see if he'd like to meet for lunch today," said Abercrombie.

We looked at each other and then over at Jenni. She shrugged and started clearing our plates. That brought a laugh from all of us. Mrs. Graham got up to help her. Jim and I decided to get a bit of fresh air and walked into the garden through the dining room's French doors.

After walking a couple minutes lost in our thoughts, I broke the silence. "God, where is this going?" I leaned into him.

"I feel better than I did last week. Mrs. Graham is pretty impressive and a little scary." Jim smiled. "I can't imagine how you felt when you had to present your pictures from Tehran to her."

"Right, I was terrified on the one hand and cocky as hell on the other," I said with a light laugh. "I was too green to even understand how important Mrs. Graham was. She's a 'takes no prisoners' type of person, and I didn't have enough common sense to be scared stiff."

"I'm glad she's on our side. Let's go back in," Jim said.

As we turned to go, we could see the Vice President was back in the dining room.

"Well good news folks. Attorney General O'Brien, although he sounded a bit leery, is on his way over," Abercrombie said.

"Can I get anyone something to drink? Katherine, another coffee?" Jenni asked, looking around.

The day had already been stressful, and it was about to get much worse.

Chapter Twenty-Eight

After half an hour of chit chat, we heard a car pull up to the front door. Jenni stepped out of the room to greet the Attorney General while we all sat around the table waiting for the other shoe to drop. The Vice President introduced everyone and offered Attorney General O'Brien a seat at the table. This really wasn't time for any small talk, and after a moment or two, the Vice President gave me a nod and again it was time to tell my story. Once I had finished, I spread the photos in front of him. He picked them up and studied the two close ups of the shooter. He finally put them on the table, looked around, and then directly at me.

"Miss Miller, I don't mean to doubt you, but I will need to see the negatives from these photos."

"Really? You think Katie made this up?" Jim leaned forward on the edge of his chair, pointing at the photo of Baldwin. "I was with her when she realized what was on her film. I watched her make this print." He picked up the print, showed it to O'Brien, and then tossed it on the table.

I reached over and put my hand on Jim's arm, trying to calm him down. Everyone sitting around the table looked from Jim to O'Brien.

Mrs. Graham spoke. "I know this photographer, and the photos are genuine."

"Sir, my guess is you are in shock as are all of us. With a little time to think, you will come to the same conclusion we have. President Baldwin was responsible for the killing of President Scheffen." I leaned back in my chair, and a sense of calm came over me. I'd presented my case, and now it was out of my hands. All the decisions would be made by the people around this table. I could go back to being an observer ... a photographer. "I'll be happy to show you the original negatives and the rest of the roll of film which will verify my story. Believe me, I would've loved for this to have never happened." I added.

"Nothing personal. I must investigate this as I would any evidence." O'Brien looked around the room.

"Mr. Attorney General, we will make the negatives available to you, but you must understand this is a unique situation. I have total confidence in Kate. She is not political; she is a journalist. She has been doing great work for *The Post*, and I'm sure this is the last place she would want to be." Mrs. Graham looked at me. She looked around the table and then back at O'Brien. "This is an emergency. This situation has to be solved ... soon."

"I understand—"

Mrs. Graham raised her hand to stop the Attorney General from saying another word. "Mr. O'Brien, I know this is a lot to digest, but here are the facts as I see them. Baldwin arranged to have the President of the United States assassinated. He didn't get involved in this crime just because he likes sitting in the Oval Office." She raised her voice. "He has an agenda. So far, it is not evident. But that is only a matter of time. The Vice President has told us that there is talk that the President is about to make changes in the Cabinet. Major changes."

Jim reached across the table and offered an apology to O'Brien. He, in turn, reached out to Jim and they shook hands.

"This is uncharted territory for me. The thought that I would arrest and prosecute the President is beyond comprehension," he said, looking down at the photos.

"I think we all feel the same way," the Vice President sympathized with O'Brien. "But this is where we are. We have been discussing this over the past few days and have several thoughts." Graham took a deep breath. "We all have our points of view. I'd like to see these pictures on the front page of my newspaper, but after some soul searching, I'm not sure that is the best direction for the country."

"The country has been through a huge trauma. Losing a young President was like a gut punch. And then dragging the country through an extended impeachment or having the President accused of murder would throw our whole democracy for a loop. I'm not sure how the country would ..." Abercrombie's shrugged his voice trailing off.

"It's not our duty to worry about how the country will take the truth. Our duty is to deliver the truth," said Mrs. Graham.

Jim and I were deferring to the real power in the room. I certainly had my opinions, but now was the time to be quiet and listen to Mrs. Graham and the Vice President.

Time was slipping by. I was supposed to be at the office at noon and unless I left immediately, I would be late. I leaned in close to Mrs. Graham and explained my situation. I also mentioned that to get me to leave, they would have to drag me kicking and screaming. Luckily, she agreed that I should stay.

I left the room, quickly called Scott, and told him that I was with her. That solved the problem.

"Katie ... everything okay?" Jim whispered.

"Yep, no problem, have I missed anything?" I asked.

The Attorney General was examining each of the photos, and everyone else was watching him.

"I'm a lawyer, and I always think in terms of the law." The Attorney General leaned back in his chair. "So, you all have had some thoughts. You brought me out here." He gave us a questioning look.

"I'll start the conversation," Jim said. "Some of the moves are obvious. One. Give all we know to the press and let the chips fall where they may." He counted on his fingers. "Two. Give the information to the Congress and let them move for impeachment. Or three. Give it to the Justice Department and let them indict the President."

"Each one is a possibility, yet none of them seem like the way to go. Any of the three might allow him to weasel out. What is our goal? I can't imagine sending the President to prison. My God, it's all unthinkable," the Vice President said.

"Mr. O'Brien, we have a very short time frame here. Baldwin has to be removed. If we follow all the rules, it could become a messy political debacle. We know that Baldwin was involved. He is dangerous and, in my opinion, cannot continue in the office." Mrs. Graham looked O'Brien straight in the eye.

"I hear you ma'am. We've established the problem. But you haven't given me a solution."

"No one seems to want to say it out loud, so here we go. We should confront the President with what we have. He then has a choice. He can resign and retire back to California, or he can spend every hour of his term trying to avoid being impeached, removed from office, and possibly put in jail," Jim said. "If we can convince him those are his two choices, I think he'll take the easy way out."

I took a deep breath. So, there it was out on the table. It was like the air had been sucked out of the room. Everyone sagged back into their chairs, not really knowing what came next.

"So, you think he's just going to fold?" the Attorney General asked, with an incredulous look on his face. "He is a tough cookie. He will have to feel he has no way out."

Looking at Mrs. Graham, he asked if there were more sets of the photos. We assured him there were several more sets that had been tucked away for safe keeping, and that Mrs. Graham would also have additional sets as soon as this meeting ended.

Mrs. Graham said, "We need a stronger stance, a time bomb. The President must believe if he doesn't accept our offer, we will release this information to papers all over the country, as well as to the Congress."

"If we wait until you and other cabinet secretaries are removed, this will be impossible. We need you to have your legal clout. We've got to scare the shit out of him," Jim "eloquently" added.

"Every Wednesday I have a breakfast meeting with the President," the Vice President looked around the table thinking out loud.

"Tomorrow? This is nuts," the Attorney General sputtered.

"I don't think we have any choice. If you're fired or forced to resign, how could we continue? For weeks now, my aides have been hearing whispers about big changes in the cabinet. I have total trust in you. Who knows who he will nominate to replace you," the Vice President said.

It was one thing to sit around a table and discuss the evidence, but it was shocking to think that in less than twenty-four hours this was going to be out in the open. O'Brien kept looking at the pictures. The rest of us sat watching him. He picked up the photos and handed them to the Vice President. He took a deep breath, looked around the table, and stopped his gaze at the Vice President.

"So how does your meeting with the President go? Who's involved?" The Attorney General asked.

"I usually go into my White House office about a half hour before the meeting."

"Is it just you and the President?"

"Usually. Sometimes his chief of staff drops in, but only if we need something."

"Do you ever bring anyone to the meeting?"

"On occasion. Remember I've only been in this job for a few months. Baldwin didn't choose me. He tolerates me, but I'm not part of his inner circle."

"So, how difficult would it be for me to accompany you? No, how difficult would it be for *all* of us to accompany you?" the Attorney General asked.

"I could bring you into the building, maybe first go to my office, and then walk over to the small dining room. It wouldn't be hard," Abercrombie answered.

After a long uncomfortable silence, the Attorney General said "I would suggest we carpool to avoid along line of cars arriving." It was like we were all sitting there holding our collective breath and we all exhaled in unison. "Okay, let's do this."

This was getting more surreal minute by minute. There we were, setting up our date for tomorrow, getting ready to threaten the President of the United States of America.

"Okay, ladies and gentlemen, it's decided. We will meet at my office at 7:30 in the morning." The Vice President stood up to signal the meeting was over.

After that proclamation, I said, "Mrs. Graham, I'm going back to the office right now to make some more prints and I'll bring them up to your office when I'm finished."

She nodded back, and we all got up from the table. Jenni made a point of giving me a big hug as we were walking out and taking me aside.

"I'm sorry for the momentary awkwardness on the island. I've never liked Angela." She offered a telling smile and walked away.

I smiled to myself. At least one problem in my life was on its way to being solved.

Now, to take on the bigger fish to fry: the President of the United States.

Chapter Twenty-Nine

I drove Jim up to his office and was back in the darkroom in an hour. Mrs. Graham had called Scott and informed him that I would be doing a very sensitive project for her. She asked that the darkroom be shut down for as long as needed for me to print the photos she needed. Scott was a bit nonplused, but Mrs. Graham didn't leave him any room for discussion. She also asked him not to question me when I came into the office.

He was glaring at me. "My God, Kate, what have you gotten yourself into?" Scott asked a bit too loudly.

"Hi Scott, I assume Mrs. Graham talked to you." I dropped my camera bag on an empty chair, pulled my envelope out of my case, and started to walk to the darkroom's revolving door.

"Really, that's all you have to say?" Scott looked pissed off.

"Scott. I've been told to keep my mouth shut." I shrugged. "Mrs. Graham has asked me to do something and to keep it totally quiet. It's all I can do."

"Go, I'll keep everybody out of the darkroom. Is an hour enough time?" he asked grudgingly.

I gave him a wave and escaped into the darkroom. I had the negatives I needed and began working. I loaded them into the film carrier and set up the enlarger and the photo paper holder. I planned on making a dozen prints of each negative. I didn't look forward to facing my fellow staff members and their inevitable questions and sarcasm. I heard the darkroom door open, which made me jump.

"Kate ... my, it's dark in here," Mrs. Graham called out to me.

"Oh, just stay where you are. I'll get some lights on," I answered.

"Well, I don't think I've ever been down here," she said, looking around.

I dragged a stool over to the enlarger I was using and suggested she might want to sit down.

"I'll bet Scott was surprised to see you," I chuckled.

"I think so. There are several men sitting there that gave me a real double take when I walked up. Perhaps I need to get around the building more. Let people see I actually exist," she said then laughed. She didn't seem to realize she was a legend, and on top of that, she was very intimidating.

"Mrs. Graham, I'm glad you came down; it gives me some cover. My fellow photographers are a grouchy group who don't like any change. They are very territorial, and it's taken a long time for them to accept me as one of the boys," I said.

"You have definitely been dropped into a macho world." A small, amused smile crossed her face. "I'm familiar with that world."

I half smiled in reply.

"I've been watching your progress and have been getting good reports from the section editors. Kate, keep up the good work."

"Thanks for the vote of confidence. I really appreciate it. I really love my job. It's like a dream come true," I added with a catch in my voice. I paused, getting back to the business at hand. I slid a piece of photo paper into the photo easel and clicked on the enlarger exposing the sheet of paper. The enlarger clicked off, and I quickly replaced the sheet with a new one, placing the exposed sheet in a covered box for safe keeping.

"Funny, all the years I've been involved with the paper, I've never seen what goes into producing the final product," she said. "It's very interesting."

"How many copies do you want? I'm working on a dozen of each shot."

"I plan to send messages to the major newspapers here and in London. They will be ready to go by courier, if needed. A dozen should do it. Please bring everything up to my office when they're ready." She paused. "Also, please bring the negatives up with you. I want to put them in a safe place."

"Yes ma'am. I will have everything for you in about a half hour."

"Good, see you then. By the way, Congressman Rayford seems very nice," she smiled and walked to the darkroom door.

I was glad the room was dark. I could feel the color rise on my cheeks. *Did nothing escape this woman's attention?*

"Okay then, I'll be waiting for you upstairs." Mrs. Graham left the darkroom.

I worked as quickly as possible and had forty-eight prints ready to go. I slipped them into a couple of envelopes, made sure everything in the darkroom was tidy, and walked out. Scott was sitting there—no surprise—but there were also four other members of the staff waiting to get into the darkroom to get their work done. For once, no one seemed to have a word to say. I just smiled and apologized for taking up some of their time.

Stan was the only one that gave me a smile and a thumbs up. I quickly moved to the elevator and didn't look back. I exhaled as the elevator door opened and pushed the **PH** button. I leaned against the wall and waited. As I stepped out of the elevator, I was immediately directed to Mrs. Graham's office.

The office was bigger than the whole photo area downstairs. Her desk was at one end of the room, backed up by a wall of large, framed photos and awards , and flanked by bookcases filled with family photos on each side. The room looked more like an office at Vogue, not a hard-hitting newspaper. At the other end of the room was a large conference table. Mrs. Graham was sitting there putting address labels on the partially filled envelopes, waiting for the photos.

"Kate, sit down. Will you help me put your photos in these envelopes?" She pointed at a chair next to her.

I was impressed that she was doing the work, not including any of her aides. But given the top-secret status of the project, I understood. I joined her at the table and began sorting my pictures into four piles. I couldn't see all the address labels, but what I could see was impressive: *New York Times*, *Chicago Tribune*, *Boston Globe*, *Miami Herald*, and *Los Angeles Times* to name a few. We worked quickly and with little conversation.

"How are you going to decide when to send these out?" I asked.

"That's a good question. I'm really unsure of how the President is going to react. He's bound to try and deny any complicity." Mrs. Graham continued sealing the envelopes.

"I'm giving these to someone I totally trust with instructions to have them couriered to each paper, if they can't contact me."

"Oh my God ... now you're scaring me." I stared at the pile of envelopes.

"Really, *now* you're scared?" She laughed.

"I guess it's all getting too real."

"Kate, you have done your part. You really don't have to go to-morrow."

"Oh my God. There is no way I'm going to miss that show."

"Remember, this is going to have the same result as your first adventure. If we're successful, no one is going to know what we did."

"So, what's new?"

We both leaned back in our chairs and laughed.

"But I'll know," I said with my pride showing.

With the job done, I excused myself. Mrs. Graham walked me to her office door. We agreed that we both hoped the day after tomorrow was going to be a new day in the United States. She caught me off guard by giving me a hug as I turned to leave.

I stopped on my way to the elevator and stopped to use the phone. I hadn't talked to Jim in hours, and I wanted to check in. He was in a meeting, but Bob assured me he could interrupt the meeting, as he put me on hold. It only took a couple of moments for Jim to pick up the phone.

"Hi there. How are you doing?" he asked.

"Better now that I'm talking to you," I smiled to myself.

"I've had a couple of meetings today, but if you ask me what they were about I couldn't tell you," Jim laughed.

"I'm outside Mrs. Graham's office. I helped her pack up the pictures along with some sort of letters. She's got a dozen news organizations that she is ready to send them to. Jim, she scared the hell out of me saying they would be released if somehow she couldn't be reached after our meeting with the President."

"Katie, there are no guarantees, but we decided this was something we had to do. We had no choice. We started the snowball tumbling down the hill. It's getting bigger and bigger on its way down. It started with just us, and now we've got some really powerful people on our side."

"I know, Mrs. Graham suggested that I don't have to go tomorrow."

"What did you say to that?"

I could hear the smile in his voice. He knew me so well.

"I asked her if she was kidding. There is no way I was going to miss this. I wish I could photograph the whole event."

"Funny you should say that. You may never be able to publish the pictures, but I bought you a present. Your Nikon's are so bulky, I thought you'd like a camera you could shove in your pocket," he said, feeling very pleased with himself.

"Really, how great is that? I'm speechless. With everything going on around us, thank you. I'll come get you. It should take me about fifteen minutes to get there. I'll park outside on South Capitol."

"See you soon ... love you." Jim clicked off the call.

Traffic up to the Hill was really heavy, and by the time I got to Jim's office building, he was standing on the curb reading a small booklet. I gave him a friendly honk and pulled over to the curb. He jumped in, and we were on our way back to Georgetown.

"So, do you want your new camera now? Or we could wait until we get home?"

"Can't wait to see it, but since I'm driving, maybe we should wait," I said. "I hate to ask, but how did you decide what to get?"

"Well, the guy at the store was really helpful. He's a retired photographer, and he recommended this," pulling a Leica out of his jacket pocket.

"Oh my God, you bought me a Leica?" I had to hit the brake hard to avoid hitting the car in front of me. "That's the Stradivarius of cameras!"

"They had a used one, but it comes with a year warranty," Jim said sounding quite pleased with himself.

"It's a different kind of photography. I can't wait to try it out."

"You'd better practice tonight, so you can use it tomorrow."

"I can't wait to get my hands on it ... and you, actually!" I laughed out loud.

"I've got an idea. How about not thinking or talking about tomorrow for a couple of hours?" Jim looked very serious.

"We can try," I replied.

We drove to Georgetown in silence.

I spent the rest of the evening playing with my new toy, a rangefinder 35mm Leica. My Nikons were single lens reflex cameras. This was a rangefinder, which meant you were looking through an eye piece which framed out the photo, but it wasn't exact. Everything else was basically the same, setting the shutter speed, "f" stops, and focus. One nice feature of this type of camera was that it was very quiet. I could shoot photos and not alert the subject. That could really come in handy tomorrow.

"It's already late. We have to be up in about six hours," I said, sitting down next to him.

"Are you ready for tomorrow?"

"Not really. I really don't have a clue what the President is going to do. How much can we strong-arm the President of the United States?"

"We'll know pretty soon." Jim leaned into me and took my hand. For better or worse, we were in this together.

Chapter Thirty

The alarm went off at 6:00 a.m. It was not as pleasant as my friendly mockingbird on the Isle of Palms. *God, I wished we were back at the beach.* I rolled over to hit the off button and turned back to cuddle Jim.

"Hey," I whispered. "It's time."

"I wish we could just stay in bed," he said, rolling on top of me. It did seem like an attractive idea, but the thought of the Vice President knocking on the front door brought me back to reality.

"I tell you what, how about meeting right here as soon as possible after this morning's meeting. Clothes optional."

I gave him a kiss as he rolled off me and sat on the side of the bed.

"That sounds like a real plan. If you see me smiling while we're at the White House, you'll know what I'm thinking." Jim made his way to the bathroom. He finished dressing and was downstairs making coffee when the phone rang.

Bob was on the line and seemed stressed out. I called down to Jim to pick up the phone. I could hear him raise his voice but couldn't really figure out what was being discussed. By the time I finished dressing, the sky visible from my bedroom window was turning pink. In less than half an hour we would be on our way to change the future of the country. It was more than disconcerting to consider what we were facing. I did one last check in the mirror and was ready to face the day. Jim was still on the phone as I made my way down the spiral staircase. He was doing more listening than talking. I held my hands up, and he just rolled his eyes.

"Listen, Angela, I have to go. I'll be in meetings all day, and I'm not sure if tomorrow looks any better. I'll call you when I can, and I think we'd better get together and talk. I'll come down to South Carolina. No, don't come up here. Listen, I really have to go ... Bye."

Jim hung up the phone and leaned against the wall. "She couldn't reach me so, she called Bob at home. That's why he called me. I'm going to see her as soon as possible and see if I can convince her that we both need to move on. To end our relationship. Our marriage."

"Wow, do you think you have enough on your plate right now?" I asked, shaking my head.

"No matter what, it's time I end this so we can move on with *our* lives." He smiled.

I knew Jim was committed to our relationship, but it was nice to hear him say it.

"I think we'd better get ready to leave. I have a feeling the Vice President will be early."

I walked into the dining room and checked to see if there was a car parked outside my gate. Sure enough, there was a government black Suburban. We hustled out of the house. One of the Secret Service guys opened the car door for us, and we joined the Vice President in the back seat. I leaned back and listened to Jim and the

Vice President talk. It only took a few minutes, and we were pulling up to the entrance of the West Wing.

The Vice President rated a parking space right next to the door. The Secret Service jumped out of the vehicle and opened the car doors for us. With the Vice President in the lead, we moved through the West Wing entrance and right to the security desk. He introduced us to the security people, who gave us clip-on visitors' tags. After a quick look through my bag, we were cleared. As we were getting our passes, the President's press secretary came through the door and saw me. She walked directly my way. The Vice President and Jim had already left the security desk, so unfortunately, I was cornered with no way to avoid talking to her.

"Kate, hi. Did I miss something? I don't have the press down for anything in The Oval today?"

Jim and the Vice President had stopped at the door leading into the West Wing, turning to see why I had stopped.

"Hi, how are you doing?" I asked, trying to look completely nonchalant. "Actually, I'm here for a meeting with the Vice President and a South Carolina congressman. Not sure what my angle is yet, but at least he's cute." I smiled and gave Jim a wave.

"You've got me there; he *is* easy to look at." She also gave Jim a wave, who half lifted his hand to wave back at us.

I quickly said goodbye and joined my fellow conspirators.

"What the hell was all that about?" Jim whispered to me.

"She asked why I was here. I had to improvise. There's nothing on the President's schedule today for a photo op." *Little does she know.*

The Vice President had several offices. His main office was in the Executive Office Building, next door to the White House. Since the Vice President is the President of the Senate, he also had an office right off the Senate chamber. We walked through the entrance lobby and hallway to his third office in the White House.

I had been in the Oval Office many times, but I'd never been to this office. Funny thing, it was set up similar to the Oval, only it was a rectangle. There was a large desk was at one end, a fireplace at the other, with facing sofas in the middle. Jim used the phone on the Vice President's desk. Mrs. Graham and the Attorney General had arrived and were sitting on the sofas in the middle of the room. The Vice President had been leaning on his desk with his arms crossed. I walked over to stand by Jim. He put his arm around my shoulder and we waited. The morning meeting was supposed to start at 8:00a.m. and the Vice President hoped to enter the dining room after the President had already started his breakfast.

"It's time," the Vice President said, looking around the room.

The consensus was that the Attorney General would do the talking. I would be happy to stand in the corner and try to blend into the wallpaper. The Vice President led the way. We headed to a small dining room just off the Oval Office. We walked down the hall toward the Oval and stopped at the last door before the turn. There weren't many people walking around, but you could hear phones ringing in the distance. I took my camera out of my pocket and took a few shots, one of the Vice President with his hand on the door handle. Jim looked surprised but then gave me a sly smile. The Vice President pushed the door open and stepped into the room.

Chapter Thirty-One

"Robert, I was just about to call your office," the President said. "I don't remember you mentioning you were bringing guests today." The President looked at us surprised. "Mrs. Graham, how nice to see you. My, we've got quite a crowd. Vinnie, don't we have a meeting coming up? Please, everyone come in."

"Good morning, Mr. President," *Vinnie*, the Attorney General, said.

"Well, I think we may need some more food. Robert, would you call down to the mess and have them send up more?" the President looked over to the Vice President.

"Mr. President, we are not here for breakfast." Mrs. Graham took a seat at the table. "The Attorney General has something you need to look at."

The Attorney General stepped up to the table, opened the envelope he was carrying, and spread the photos on the table in front of him. At first, the President had just a blank look on his face and was about to make some sort of friendly remark. But then he looked down at the photos on the table. He hesitated and looked back up at the Attorney General.

"What is this?" the President asked.

"Well, Mr. President, we have a problem. Please take some time and look at all of the pictures."

I held my breath. I couldn't miss this moment. I quietly took the camera out of my pocket and held it against my stomach, pointing it directly at the President. I loved how quiet it was but didn't want to press my luck. I took about five frames and then held it by my side, behind Jim.

"Well Vincent, what exactly do you think you have here?" The President looked up at the Attorney General.

"What we have here, Mr. President, is you meeting with the man who would go on to assassinate President Scheffen," Mrs. Graham cut to the chase.

The President paused and the color drained from his face. He shuffled through the photos, clearly stalling and planning what he was going to say.

"Where on earth did you get these pictures? This one is obviously a fake. I've never met this man." He pointed at my shot of the two of them taken in Georgetown.

I could feel sweat beading up on my forehead. I was about to become the center of attention.

"The photo is real and has not been doctored," the Attorney General said, tapping the photo in front of the President. I was waiting for the next logical question. I knew it would include me. I think Jim figured the same thing because he reached down to hold my hand.

"I'm telling you; I've never seen this guy. My God, you're accusing me of being involved in murder. I'm the President of the United States," He said, raising his voice.

"You may be President, but you are not above the law." The Attorney General tapped the photo again to make his point.

"Who took these pictures?" He looked around the room. He seemed to be stalling. He was cornered.

"Mr. President, unfortunately for you, a photographer that works for my paper, and who coincidentally was across the street from the house where you met with your associate."

"Listen, I know your newspaper is opposed to my agenda, but this is absurd," he sputtered.

"No, it is not absurd, it is a crime, and you are responsible for the death of a wonderful man." Mrs. Graham looked the President straight in the eye.

"I'm telling you this is a fake," the President pounded on the table. I wasn't really planning on speaking, but I realized I had to defend my photos and hopefully take some of the wind out of his sail.

"Sir, I took these pictures."

Everyone in the room turned and looked at me. Stepping up could put a target on my back, but hiding behind the paper was not an option. If this didn't go the way we planned, everyone in the room would be in trouble. I was in good company.

"Who the hell are you?" The President gave me a dismissive look then paused. "I'm good at remembering a pretty face. Didn't we meet during the campaign?"

"My name is Kate Miller. Yes, we met during the campaign. I'm a staff photographer for *The Post*. Unfortunately for you, I was in Georgetown and photographed you meeting and shaking hands with Oscar Hoskins ... the guy who shot President Scheffen. I can prove that the picture has not been doctored." *There it was. I'd told the President who was to blame for his predicament. How far might he go to punish me? Would I ever be able to put this behind me, or would I hope Baldwin were to drown himself in scotch?*

"I'm not going to stand for this. I'll have you arrested. My security people are right next door," he blustered.

"Let's cut to the chase. We have a proposal for you. We are willing to keep this just between us and allow you to resign from the presidency," the Attorney General said.

"Vincent, this picture doesn't prove anything. You are trying to blackmail the President of the United States. I won't stand for it."

"Blackmail is such an ugly word. We are giving you a choice: resigning or facing a very ugly impeachment and possibly jail." Mrs. Graham gave him a polite smile.

"This is ridiculous. I'll have you removed from here."

"Let me help you out." The Attorney General walked out of the dining room and returned with the head of the Secret Service and Director of the FBI.

We all looked around at each other. This was not part of the plan. You could see the President's body language change. He looked deflated and old.

"Henry, we know this picture is real and so do you. If it were my choice, I'd spend every waking hour impeaching you, have you found guilty in the Senate, and then have you found guilty of complicity in the assassination of President Scheffen and sent to jail. I'd work to see you never live as a free man again," the Vice President said.

"But Robert—"

The Vice President continued, "I have been convinced by these people," he said, pointing to each of us, "that it would be better for the country if you just resigned and quietly disappeared. You can go back to California and play golf or whatever you do."

"I need time to think about all this." He stared at the pictures and then up at me.

"You son of a bitch, your time has run out." Mrs. Graham stared at the President. "You aren't listening. We aren't *asking* you to resign; we are *telling* you if you don't resign right now, today, this morning, these photos will be in the hands of every major newspaper in the country, as well as the Speaker of the House and the Majority Leader of the Senate."

"Keep in mind the pictures are real, and the FBI will continue to investigate the assassination. With this new evidence, they might just find out, for example, how the shooter was paid, and we still don't know how he died," The Attorney General added, looking over to the Director of the FBI who nodded.

The door to the room opened, and one of the President's secretaries poked her head in. Before she could get a word out, Baldwin screamed at her to get out. I guess we had achieved our goal as Jim said, "to scare the shit out of him."

"Just so you understand, we are not leaving here until this is finished," Mrs. Graham said. "I took the liberty, with the help of the Vice President, to write up a very sincere resignation letter. You are resigning because of your health. Take a look at it; it's very good. You'll leave this building with the thanks and good will of the country." Mrs. Graham handed him the envelope that contained the resignation letter.

"I really don't see that you have a choice. Nice pension and a life in California, or a possible life in prison after being impeached. Your choice. There really isn't any doubt about which way you should go," Mrs. Graham said.

The country had survived the assassination of a middle of the road Republican and the super right wing neanderthal who took his place. So many things were at stake ... civil rights, our future in Vietnam. There was talk of replacing the cabinet. The fact that the assassin was dead might be a way for him to avoid being found guilty ... my photos ended that possibility.

The Vice President leaned against one of the chairs. Baldwin was a defeated man, nothing like the cocky campaigner I covered during the primaries. We all stood there watching to see what he was going to do next. By then, he was slumped over with his elbow on the table and his head in his hand. He pulled out the resignation letter, actually two copies, and looked over at the Vice President.

"Well, what a nice touch, official White House stationery," he said, his voice dripping with sarcasm.

"I've tried to anticipate every detail, to make this as painless and smooth as possible. I have Air Force Two waiting at Andrews, ready to take you to California. I have also arranged for a helicopter to take you directly from the back lawn as soon as we're done. Your belongings can be packed up and shipped tomorrow. How can I put this, Henry? Sign and you're out of here. Don't sign, and all hell is going to break loose." The Vice President was in complete control.

The Attorney General pushed the resignation letter closer to the President. "Mr. President, I want this to be very clear. If you ever tell anyone what has transpired here today, we will unload this information and bury you. If you decide to have a beer and a chat with your golf buddies or have a bit of 'pillow talk' with your latest roll in the hay, we will bury you. Once this is done, it is for all time, no going back," the Attorney General said.

The Vice President put his hand on the President's shoulder and picked up the resignation letter. "Henry, I think it would be appropriate for you to sign this in the Oval Office. After you have finished, I think we should call in your staff and tell them your intention."

We all moved toward the door of the dining room. The President pushed his chair away from the table and stood. He looked a bit unstable. I hoped that was an understatement. He knew he was cornered and was pragmatic. Moving back to California sounded far better than fighting impeachment.

It was only a few steps, and we were in the Oval Office. To think of all the history that had happened in that room, and now this. The only redeeming thought was Vice President Abercrombie was a good man and would do a good job. From the first moment I was introduced to him, I felt his warmth and sincerity. He'd spent years serving the people of South Carolina and now the rest of the country was going to have the honor of knowing him.

The Vice President walked over to the President's desk, put the resignation letter down, and reached for a pen. Baldwin slowly walked across the room and sat down at the desk. As he looked around the room, I could see hatred in his eyes when I clicked off a couple of shots. The desk was in front of three floor to ceiling windows. But, from my point of view, the light made for lousy photos. I tried to get over to the side of the room. I wanted to get a good image with good definition. Light from behind the President would leave his face in shadow, as well as the resignation letter. Everyone else seemed to understand their place in this scenario.

They moved in behind the President's chair and waited for him to pick up the pen. Baldwim looked around the room and saw me take his photo. He frowned.

"Well, young lady, I'll always remember you."

That sent a chill up my spine.

Jim stayed with me. I shot a few frames and waited for Baldwin to sign away his future. I had mixed emotions. I was happy to see Baldwin go, but I hated the fact that he would never be punished for what he'd done. Losing power was definitely a punishment for an ego like his. I never really thought about it, but one of the attractive things about being a photographer was how you were usually an observer, not a participant.

"Well, Henry, let's get this show on the road. I can hear the Marine helicopter landing on the South Lawn."

"Abercrombie, you son of a bitch, I never liked you. I never would have picked you as my running mate."

The Vice President picked up the pen and shoved it into Baldwin's hand, while I put my camera to my eye. Baldwin was looking around the room. He was realizing that his Presidency and his power were both gone. I clicked off a few shots, watching Baldwin sign the document.

"Are we crystal clear on what's going to happen now?" the Vice President asked.

"I'll keep my mouth shut and hope you fail miserably at this job. Tell you what, I'm walking out this door," he pointed at the door to the Rose Garden, "and I'm getting on that helicopter. I'm out of here. You'll get your chance to *play* President."

Baldwin pushed back from the desk and walked out of the Oval Office without looking back. He quickly walked across the lawn and climbed the stairs into Marine Two. I moved to the door and got a couple of shots, including one of the helicopters in the air with the Washington Monument in the background. I couldn't help but think about the pictures I took at the beginning of this ordeal.

I turned and clicked off another shot; everyone was standing by the window, looking outside, stunned.

"Well, doesn't that beat all?" The Vice President looked around the room. "I have a feeling all hell *is* going to break loose." He moved quickly to the telephone and called his aide. A press briefing was set up.

It was really impressive to see Abercrombie take over the situation. He asked Mrs. Graham, Jim, and I to leave. The Secret Service chief was sent to rearrange his staff and inform them of the changes. That had to be done immediately.

"I have to inform the Congress and the Court of what has transpired. I think the swearing in will be tomorrow at my residence. I hope you all will be there," he looked at the three of us.

We smiled and said we would be honored to attend.

"Ah, this just occurred to me. We got a ride here, maybe we can call a cab?" I asked.

"Katie, I think we can arrange a ride back to Georgetown." The Vice President walked over to me and gave me a hug. "See you tomorrow."

"Thank you, sir, I look forward to it."

The Secret Service gave the three of us a ride. We swung by *The Post* first to drop off Mrs. Graham. Jim and I were next. The weird thing was, we weren't happy or sad about what we'd just experienced. We were numb and rode all the way back to Georgetown in silence.

Mrs. Graham had asked me to cover the swearing in and was going to talk to editorial about an opinion piece. I was happy to hear that. I couldn't imagine attending the swearing in and not shooting the event.

Chapter Thirty-Two

The answering machine was blinking with messages when we walked into my apartment. I pressed the playback button and sat down to listen. First up was Scott from my office. Obviously, Mrs. Graham had talked to him. I was to be at the Naval Observatory by 11 a.m. the next day. The swearing in would be at noon. The second call was from Jenni Abercrombie. She was inviting us to join them for brunch at 10 a.m. tomorrow.

"How about I call Mary and get her off the hook. Then the phone's all yours." I smiled at Jim.

He pulled me to my feet, and we held each other tight and just stood there. We'd been running on nerves and adrenaline for days, and now it was like the air was being let out of the balloon.

"I'll call Doug and then the office. Turn on the TV. When the news gets out, all the channels will carry it."

The TV was upstairs in the bedroom, so I climbed the spiral stairs, clicked it on, and quickly made a trip to the bathroom. I could hear the announcer breaking into their normal programming for a report from the White House.

"Jim, there's a report coming on from the White House," I called downstairs.

He hustled up and flopped down beside me on the bed.

The announcer and a crowd of reporters were waiting for someone to come into the press room. The commentator was relaying the fact that the President had been seen walking across the south lawn of the White House and leaving in a Marine helicopter. That wasn't really unusual. What was odd and newsworthy? He was alone. We sat on the bed waiting for the news to blow the top off the story. The door to the left of the podium opened and the Vice President came through the door with some prepared remarks and what looked like the President's resignation. We waited to hear how he was going to present all this. He looked great, very dignified ... presidential.

He told the assembled news outlets that the President felt that his ongoing medical challenges were preventing him from carrying out his duties to the country. With that as his guiding principle, he was resigning from his office and would be returning to California immediately. Abercrombie announced that he would be sworn in at noon tomorrow and that all government functions were working. He said it was a sad moment for the country, and he would pray for President Baldwin's speedy recovery. We would pull together and move this great country forward.

"God, he sounds great. Really on top of his game." Jim leaned back and clasped his hands behind his head.

"Is this over? I wasn't sure Baldwin would leave without a fight," I asked.

"I'm not sure it will *ever* be over. I don't trust Baldwin. He's such a vindictive SOB, but it's out of our hands. Thank God." Jim smiled.

"I'd better call my office. I'm surprised Bob hadn't tried to call." Jim got on the phone with his chief of staff, and from what I could hear, everyone was bouncing off the walls. Bob seemed to be doing all the talking with Jim getting a few words in occasionally. After a while, Jim finally hung up, looking a bit frustrated.

"Everyone at the office is bonkers. I told them I would not be in until after the swearing in tomorrow. Angela called *again* this morning, just before I talked to Bob, totally unhinged. I need to call her now, before she has a total meltdown." He shrugged.

Jim walked downstairs to make the call, which allowed me to continue watching TV. The Vice President fielded a lot of questions. The answers were the same, even though the words changed a bit. The President resigned. Everything was running fine. Everything else will have to wait until later. I turned the TV off and waited for Jim to get off the phone with Angela. I could hear his side of the conversation. Angela had been chasing Baldwin for over a year, and at least in the early days, Baldwin enjoyed being chased. I really didn't want to eavesdrop, but I couldn't wait to hear what he had to say. I stretched out on the bed, and the last forty-eight hours caught up with me. I dozed off. The next thing I heard was Jim whispering in my ear.

"Hey, no fair taking a nap without me."

"Hmmm. I guess I nodded off. How long have I been asleep?"

"I'm not sure. I just got off the phone."

"How did that go? What did she say about Baldwin?"

"She was shocked, of course. But she said she hadn't seen him in several months, which was a surprise to me. Of course, we have never discussed her crush on Baldwin. Her father was trying to call him, but so far, no luck. I suggested that her father get in touch with Abercrombie since he is going to be a US Ambassador."

I hesitated. "That sounds like a good idea."

"Katie, I need to talk with her face-to-face. I have to end it for good. I'm going down to Columbia."

"When would you go, and how long would you stay?" *So, it was time.* I was glad I hadn't pushed. I trusted our relationship, but I didn't want him to feel pushed. It had to come from him.

"As soon as possible. After all that's happened, I want us to live like normal people, go out, and have friends over for dinner. I want you to come up to The Hill and be introduced to my colleagues." He leaned over and kissed me. "Let's go over to Martin's and just sit there and listen at the bar. I bet the conversations are amazing."

"Okay, but only if we go to my office so I can look at the film I took this morning. Please?"

"Sure, I really want to see what you've got too." He planted another couple of kisses on my neck and ear.

We both got off the bed and made our way downstairs, locked the front door, and walked out of my garden gate. It was surreal. We had gone through such pressure, and no one would ever know. Kids were playing Frisbee in the street, and moms were pushing strollers, chatting with friends. We just turned the American government on its head, and no one knew. We walked hand in hand to Martin's. Not that I really liked the place, but Jim was right; the chitchat around the bar was bound to be interesting. The bar was packed, so we ended up at a table close to the kitchen.

While we waited for service, we listened to the conversations at the bar. It was about 50/50. Whether they liked Baldwin or not, they were shocked at the suddenness of the news. I could get behind that. Almost universally, no one knew much about the soon-to-be President Abercrombie. At least no one had negative things to say, either. Our food arrived, and we shared our burger and shrimp.

Everything tasted wonderful. It was like a weight had been lifted from our shoulders, and we were almost giddy. The beers helped that along.

We finished, paid the bill and were on our way to my office. The strange thing was that everything seemed so normal. The photo desk and surrounding editors' desks were empty. That would change in a few minutes. Jim followed me into the darkroom, sat down, and grabbed a photography magazine while I went into the film room and loaded my film. About twenty minutes later, I was looking at my negatives. I had laid them on a light table which allowed me to check each frame. Using a loupe, which magnified each image, I could see they were correctly exposed and all seemed in focus. Usually, I wouldn't worry about this, but I was unsure, using a new camera. I had images, and they looked good. I cut the film into six-inch strips. My plan was to make a couple of eight-by-ten contact prints for Mrs. Graham. To do that, all the negatives were lined up, pressed against the photo paper by a sheet of glass. After the paper was exposed and developed, she would have all the images in one place along with the negatives.

How the pictures would be used was completely up to Mrs. Graham. I was happy that they were acceptable, but I really couldn't wait to get rid of them. I didn't know if they would ever see the light of day, but *I'd* never forget each one of those images. *It all worked out so smoothly; almost too smoothly?* I shuddered to think of how it could have turned out. I exposed a couple of sheets of photo paper and processed them. I could hear them pop off the print dryer. I brought them over to Jim with my magnifying loupe. He carefully studied each frame.

"Katie, these really look good. The look on Baldwin's face is perfect. I like the one with him walking to the helicopter." Jim turned his head and smiled at me.

By the time we got back to my apartment, it was dark. Jim drove us back, and I nodded off. He reached over and gently touched my cheek with the back of his hand.

"Hey ... we're home. I think you've run out of gas."

"I think you're right. I haven't gotten a good night's sleep since this all started."

Chapter Thirty-Three

We were dressed and out the door right on time the next morning. We would get to the Naval Observatory in plenty of time. On the last trip, we were nervous as hell. On this trip, we were honored to attend a real piece of history. Robert Abercrombie, of South Carolina, was being sworn in as President of the United States. We parked in front of the Vice President residence beside Mrs. Graham's Lincoln. As we stepped out of my car, we were greeted by some young military types. They weren't in any uniform that I had ever seen. Jim greeted the young men as they saluted us and offered to carry my camera bag.

"Katie, let me introduce you to these young men. They are cadets from The Citadel. Robert's a graduate of The Citadel, and it's impressive that he could get these guys up here for the ceremony."

The door opened, and to our surprise, Doug stepped out to greet us. He quickly walked up with his arms extended to give us a huge bear hug.

"God it's great to see you. How did all *this* work out?" Jim asked, pointing to the cadets.

"Ha, can you believe it? I got a ride with the cadets. Jenni organized this." Doug smiled.

The three of us walked arm in arm toward the front door. The soon-to-be first lady was there to greet us. More hugs all around and a kiss on the cheek for me.

"Robert said you all did a really great job yesterday. I'm so thankful it worked out smoothly." Jenni wiped a tear from her cheek. "I was very worried. Vinnie also did a brilliant job, didn't he? Imagine having the FBI and Secret Service right there and ready to go. Amazing, I think that sealed the deal."

"You're absolutely right. That move came out of left field, and you could see Baldwin literally deflate," I said.

"Well let's put all this behind us." She patted my arm.

We walked into the residence and into the dining room. Once again, there was a beautiful buffet set up.

The cadets were digging in, and we were happy to join them. Jim worked his way around the table, introducing himself to each of the cadets. Several of them lived in his district. I filled my plate and joined Doug at the far end of the table. Doug was telling me about how Jenni called him and insisted he make the trip here today. Jim joined us with a huge plate of food. Doug and I both did a double take.

"Jimmy, doesn't she feed you?" Doug gave me a friendly poke in the ribs.

"Ha, neither of us has had any kind of appetite for the last week. I feel like it's a holiday, and this food looks great."

The soon-to-be President and Mrs. Graham entered the room and came directly over to us. She put her hand on Jim's shoulder, and the Vice President took the seat next to me, leaning over to give me a kiss on the cheek. He pointed over at the cadets.

"Jenni organized the Cadets. Isn't it wonderful? You know The Citadel is my alma mater. I love everything about that time of my life. Things were certainly simpler then," he mused.

"I was so surprised to see Doug. It's perfect," I said.

The Vice President excused himself after he thanked us for coming and for being patriotic Americans. I looked over at Jim. I think we were both a bit embarrassed by the attention.

"I've got to get ready. See you after." I smiled.

Jim leaned over and gave me a kiss on the cheek. The garden had been set up for the ceremony with folding chairs and a bunch of flags set up as a backdrop. Most of the Cabinet were in attendance as well as a congressional delegation from South Carolina. Jim would be sitting with that group. I had retrieved my camera bag and was all set to go. The Chief Justice of the Supreme Court took his place, and the Vice President and Jenni took their spot facing the Chief Justice. Jenni held the family Bible; the Vice President placed his hand on it and repeated the oath of office—ending in "So help me God." Everyone applauded, and there it was—Baldwin was history, and Robert Abercrombie was officially the President.

My next step was to get my pictures processed and ready for the next issue of *The Post*. There was a spread of food and champagne set up in the garden. *Damn, Jenni was a super hostess.* After putting my camera in my shoulder bag, I retrieved the envelope with the contact prints of Baldwin leaving the White House and the Presidency. Mrs. Graham was walking toward me.

"Mrs. Graham, what a beautiful morning." I smiled.

"Yes, it is." She smiled back.

"Here are the photos and negatives from yesterday," I said, handing her the envelope. "I wanted to give them to you directly."

"Thank you. I will tuck these away in a very safe place. Who knows? Someday it may be appropriate to publish them." She smiled and pointed at my camera bag. "I assume you are heading to the office with today's very important story."

"Yes ma'am, I've got a deadline to make." As I turned to leave, I could see Jim and Doug enjoying the moment. I gave them a wave and put my hand to my ear like I was holding a telephone.

Jim gave me a wave and Doug blew me a kiss. I waved again and turned to leave.

The newsroom was jumping. Reporters were working on every angle. Where was Baldwin? Who was this new President? What would an Abercrombie Presidency look like? I hustled through and into the darkroom. Stan was the only one working. I loaded my film and got the timer set before talking to him.

"Hey Stan, nice shots at the White House yesterday."

"Thanks, Katie, how did it go today?" he asked.

"Fine, actually easy." The timer went off in the film room. "Let me go finish." I moved away from Stan and finished fixing and washing my film. Once I checked to see if the film looked good and printable I relaxed. There was a downside to doing my job. If something went wrong with your film, there was no way to fix it. You were out of luck. I took my dried film to an enlarger and loaded it into a film carrier.

I knew what the "bread and butter shot" was going to be. *That was easy.* I needed a picture of the new President with his hand on the Bible. That shot worked out well. The Chief Justice and Abercrombie were looking at each other, but the best part was the loving look in Jenni's eyes as she watched her husband be sworn in and thrown into the hardest job in the world. I finished printing my photos and got them to the copy desk. I was walking out and heard the darkroom phone ring. Stan called my name and quickly walked back. The phone receiver was lying on the light box.

"Hi, this is Kate Miller," I answered.

"Hi, it's me. How are you doing?" Jim asked.

"Fine, I'm done. What are you doing?" I pulled up a stool.

"We're still with the President and Jenni. Katie, I'm going to hitch a ride back to South Carolina with the cadets and Doug."

I wasn't ready for that. "Oh?"

"Katie, it's time. I've got to finish it with Angela."

I was silent. I knew this was coming, but I was still surprised it was so soon.

"I thought we'd talk about when you'd go, not just jump in." I sounded a bit pitiful.

"I know, but the time is right. I can fly down with them and rent a car in Charleston and see Angela tomorrow. If she is going to France with her parents, I want to get this done. I know it feels sudden, like I'm abandoning you, but I don't want to let this to just hang there and her be off to Europe. Once it's done, we can move on, from everything. I'll call you when I get to the beach house. I'll stay there tonight and drive to Columbia tomorrow." He paused. "Listen, they're calling me. I think they are getting ready to go. I love you."

"Will you call me tonight?"

Jim agreed. Neither of us hung up the phone. Finally, we both laughed and hung up in unison.

Chapter Thirty-Four

I drove home in a daze. I felt deflated. We had been so tightly wound for the past week and now nothing. I'm not sure if I was depressed or just exhausted. I had no assignments for the next day, which was good and bad. If I was working, at least I wouldn't be able to dwell on feeling sorry for myself. I drifted through the rest of the afternoon, paid a few outstanding bills, and then took on the laundry. Since Jim had basically moved in, his clothes were mixed in with mine.

I picked up one of his button-down shirts, and I could smell his aftershave. I berated myself for being such a wimp and stuffed the laundry into a bag. I threw the bag over my shoulder and walked the block and half to Mr. Chow's. Everywhere I looked, there were memories of the past year. The telephone booth on the corner, Jim had called me from there after dropping me off after our date. That night was the beginning of our relationship. I smiled, thinking about how he called and with—I guess—a little encouragement from me, he came running back to my apartment and into my life. Mr. Chow greeted me as always and this time asked me what I thought of the new President. While he was writing up my ticket, I stared out the window at the house that started it all. The yard had been cleaned up a bit, and there was a **For Sale** sign on the door. I wondered if anyone had checked into who had rented or was staying in that house when I took my photo of Baldwin and the assassin. Something to think about.

Mr. Chow handed me my receipt and told me everything would be ready in three days. He gave me a knowing smile. I blushed. He must have noticed the boxer shorts. I walked back to my apartment, enjoying how normal everything seemed. Jim and I had been spending so much time together that I really didn't know what to do with so much free time. I could hear music coming from some of the windows and patios. The summer humidity hadn't settled in yet and neither had the mosquitos. As I was opening my gate, I could hear my phone ringing. I quickly got the door unlocked and lunged for the phone, picking it up before the call went to the answering machine.

"Hello," I said, sounding winded.

"Hi, it's me." It was great to hear Jim's voice.

"Hi you. Where are you?" I smiled.

"I'm at the beach house. Doug and I just got back. What have you been doing?"

"Nothing very exciting. Paying bills and getting the laundry organized. I hope you like your boxers lightly starched."

"Hmmm, I'm not sure about that," he laughed. "Hey, I miss you. Somehow, it doesn't seem right being here without you."

"Have you decided exactly what you're going to do?"

"Doug is going to lend me his car, and I plan on driving up to Columbia tomorrow morning. I called her a few minutes ago, and she assured me she would be home. So here we go. Having Doug's car will give me a reason to not stay too long." He tried to sound positive.

"It's weird. Everything seems so ordinary, almost boring. When I walked back from the laundry, people were grilling hot dogs and drinking beer. If they only knew."

"I know. At least everything is out of our hands and hopefully, after tomorrow, we can get back to normal."

"Do you know what you're going to say?"

"I'm not sure. It all depends on what she has to say. I hope it goes well. I just don't know. She can be explosive sometimes. It's going to be disturbing no matter how it goes. I'll admit it's gonna be a relief one way or another."

"Call me as soon as you get back. Will her parents be there?"

"I think they're there. I didn't ask. They're leaving for France in about two weeks. Hey, Doug is cooking some fish over at his place. I'd better get off the phone. I said I'd come over as soon as I finished talking to you."

"Okay, I'm beat. I think I'll open a bottle of wine and take a long hot bath. That should put me to bed early."

"Well, that really should be my job—to put you to bed."

"And you're so good at your job." I laughed.

"Good night, I wish I were there to scrub your back." he laughed.

"Call me when you can. Take care," I half whispered into the phone.

"I will. I love you." Jim hung up the phone.

After tossing and turning, I finally fell into a deep, dreamless sleep. It was past 8:30 in the morning before sunlight came through my window. I lay there for a while wondering what I was doing. I stayed in bed and counted the minutes waiting for a phone call.

When the call didn't come, I threw some clothes into a suitcase, got dressed, and was on my way to the Isle of Palms. Depending on the traffic, I figured I should be at the beach by 6:30 p.m. at the latest. I enjoyed driving, and I was pretty sure my press pass would get me out of any speeding tickets. The weather was clear and the traffic light. I managed to cruise down Interstate 95 in record time. I made two stops then took the turn off to I-26. I was happy to see the road signs signaling Charleston. By 6:00 p.m. I was crossing the Breach Inlet and arrived on the Isle of Palms.

I pulled in front of our beach house, next to Doug's car. All the tension in my shoulders and back disappeared at the first whiff of sea air. Peeking in the front windows and around the back, Jim was nowhere to be found. *Of course, the door was unlocked.* I smiled and walked into the house. Jim was sitting on the deck steps watching a line of pelicans flying just inches above the water's surface. I quietly walked up behind him and whispered, "I wonder how they do that?" as I sat down next to him on the steps.

"What, how did you get here?" Jim's face revealed his shock and joy at seeing me. He threw his arm around my shoulder and pulled me against his body. With his other hand, he took my hand and pulled me until I was on his lap.

"Hey, did you miss me then?" I grinned.

"Damn, are you nuts? When did you leave DC? I hate it when you speed."

"Ha, you're funny." I put my arms around Jim's neck and kissed his forehead, his nose, and ended on his lips.

"I didn't want you to be alone. I'm sure today was tough and talking to you on the phone wasn't good enough."

"God, I'm happy you're here. Today was awful ... just awful."

I got up off Jim's lap and pulled him up. "Let's take a walk on the beach. There's the bench down toward the inlet, the one Doug used last week." I smiled encouragingly.

We walked hand in hand toward the southwest end of the island. The light at sunset was a photographer's dream. The sky shifted from pink to gold, lending the earth and sky a warm glow. Nowhere does the sun set with more panache than in the low country of South Carolina. We strolled to the bench then sat quietly, holding hands, watching the sky's colors deepen from gold to lavender and finally dark cobalt blue. *Was Jim waiting for Twilight to tell me about how his day went?*

"Look!" Breathlessly, I pointed to my left. A full moon was just breaking the horizon. It seemed to set the stage for a memorable night.

"Beautiful."

I could tell from his tone that his mind was preoccupied. I waited.

Jim squeezed my hand, then began to speak. "It was awful ... just so uncomfortable."

There were no words I could add, so I just listened.

"I got there about 10 o'clock and didn't leave until after 4. That was six long hours. I'm not sure what I expected. I was trying to keep everything calm, but she was just going nuts. She asked if I wanted a coffee when I arrived, like nothing was wrong. It was surreal. I haven't seen her, one on one, in at least six months. She acted like I'd just gone to the corner store to pick up a bottle of milk and was back. It was weird." Jim leaned back and just sat there silently.

"I'm sorry it was so hard for you. I was hoping she'd throw *you* to the curb."

"Me too. No such luck." He laughed. "I told her I wanted a divorce. I told her we'd been separated for years."

"What did she say?"

"Well, that's an interesting question. At first, she seemed surprised. Then she asked if it was because of her 'relationship' with Baldwin. Can you believe it? I asked her exactly what her relationship was. Then the fairy tale began. She said they were just friends and nothing happened."

"Really? That's not what it looked like when they were in Charleston. But really, Jim, aren't we being a bit hypocritical?" I asked.

"Yeah, for sure. I asked her why we stayed married. She asked me the same question." He laughed. "We danced around the subject for a while, so I finally put it all out there. I suggested she get a lawyer, and that if she didn't file for divorce, I would. Suddenly, she acted shocked, like we'd been a happy married couple. I told her the easiest way would be to use the same lawyer. She balked at that. Like we had all sorts of assets to split." Jim was getting more and more frustrated recounting what went on.

"When I moved to DC, she moved back to her parent's farm. We don't own any property. Hell, I don't even own a car. I told her to make me the bad guy. We've always had a joint checking account, and I've never questioned how she spent the money. You know she's never had a paying job in her life? She's an only child, and her parents totally spoiled her. 'Want a new horse?' 'Sure, honey, whatever you want.'" Jim was beginning to sound mad.

"Jim, were you thinking you could get away without admitting that you are in a relationship?"

"Well, actually that horse is out of the barn. I told her I was moving on with my life, and she needed to do the same. She took that to mean that I had met someone, and that's when the conversation went off the rails. She then understood why she could never get a hold of me, and she accused me of being unfaithful. I kept repeating myself and left it saying that I would wait for two weeks for her to choose a lawyer, which I would pay for. I also told her that you can't get blood from a stone, and she'd better be realistic." He sighed and shook his head. "It went on and on. I didn't handle it as well as I'd hoped."

"Jim, I don't know what to say." *What could I say?* My thoughts were whirling. I was both sorry for what he was going through and happy that the lie we were living would soon be over.

Jim continued, "I'm going to call a friend of mine tomorrow morning and get some advice. We were in law school together, and he's a divorce lawyer in Columbia. There's a lot more to tell, but let's leave it for now." He put out his hand. "Let's walk back."

Jim pulled me to my feet, and we strolled back toward the beach house, watching the moon rise in the night sky. I was feeling every mile of my nine-hour drive along with the added stress of Jim's conversation with Angela. I was asleep on my feet. We'd left before the sun had gone down and now the house was totally dark. As we climbed up the deck stairs, the only light I could see was the flashing light on the answering machine. I cringed, wondering who was calling Jim.

"Oh no, I don't like that," Jim said, pointing at the little red light.

I walked through the door first and went directly to the kitchen.

"Do you want a drink?" I grabbed the last two beers in the fridge.

Jim grabbed a pencil and paper and pushed the replay button on the answering machine. The first call was from his office. Bob must have called before Jim had gotten back from Columbia, and I guessed he didn't see the light flashing when he'd gotten in.

"God damn it." Jim threw his notepad on the table. "Bob called. My bank contacted him because they were concerned. A check made out to cash was presented just before the bank closed today that would have emptied my account."

"No ... Angela?" I asked.

"Of course. Thank God, the bank put a hold on the check and told her it could be processed tomorrow after they had contacted me. Tomorrow, I'm going to stop the direct deposit of my paycheck. A pretty stupid move on her part. If she had written a smaller check, I would never have noticed. I guess my hope for an amicable divorce is out the window."

"Ya think?" I rolled my eyes.

Chapter Thirty-Five

We were heading back to Washington the next morning after a short walk on the beach. The beach was beautiful and peaceful. A group of shorebirds were feeding along the water's edge. They moved in unison with the incoming waves and stayed just ahead of us, just out of reach.

"We'd better get going. I wish we could stay. I feel guilty that you drove down yesterday and now we're driving back."

"I'm glad I drove down and that you weren't alone last night."

"Me too. Did I say thank you?" Jim put his arm around my shoulder and kissed me.

"Tell you what, I'll do all the driving. *But* let's give ourselves one more day at the beach before going back ... what do you think?" He smiled.

"Now that sounds like a plan. I've got to call my office and tell them I'm not coming in today. I've got comp time, so hopefully it won't be a big deal."

"I've got to make a couple of calls also. You go first, and I'll make the bed and tidy up."

I got through to Scott right away with no problem. He hates having comp time on the books and was happy to have me use it.

The bank suspended all activities on Jim's account until he could get in there to close it. He made one more call to Angela to explain that the checking account was on hold, and she couldn't write any checks. Unfortunately, or maybe fortunately, Angela's dad picked up the phone. He was unhappy with Jim, but he was calm and civil. Jim explained the checking account and about wanting to keep the divorce civil and fair. Alex made noises like he understood, but after all, it was his daughter, his only child.

"Alex, I'm giving her half of everything we have together, everything. If she fights this, I'll have to rethink my civility."

What I pieced together, from what Jim had told me earlier and the side of the conversation I could overhear, was Jim was convincing Angela's dad to get things rolling. Alex's nomination to be ambassador to France had passed, so he was planning to leave South Carolina within the month. Jim gave him the name of the lawyer in Columbia and tried to convince him it made no sense to have two lawyers. Jim was willing to be the bad guy, so Angela could hold her head high at the country club and have all the sympathy of her friends. He told Alex he was going to give Angela half of his checking account and half of his retirement account and that he didn't want anything from her and that Angela was a beautiful woman. He was sure once she was free, the good old boys in Columbia would be beating down her door. Jim was going to file if she didn't, and it would be far easier if she took the lead on this. If Jim were to file, everything about her relationship with Baldwin would be out there for everyone to see.

She really hadn't been very discreet. There were dozens of photos showing her with Baldwin. No matter what did or didn't happen, it would have a negative effect on her whole family. Her father would be spending a lot of time defending her decisions, instead of being the Ambassador to France.

Jim was losing patience with his father-in-law and repeated that he wanted it over with and would have the paperwork shipped over by Fed Ex. Jim thanked him for all he'd done for him and said he hoped they could continue to work together.

Hopefully the old saying, "time heals all wounds" would work for them. Jim hung up and looked around the sweet little beach house and over to me. He was slumped down on the sofa. I walked over and sat next to him.

Jim sighed. "Alex didn't know what to say, and that he always thought of me as the son he never had. Angela had made some bad choices in the last few years, and he knew about them but didn't stop her. He did say 'consider it done' at least. It was amazing actually. He apologized for what had happened, said he had stars in his eyes when he got involved with Baldwin, and that it was one thing to support him politically, but he allowed Baldwin to come on to Angela, and he did nothing to stop it."

He seemed exhausted and done with the subject.

"So ... I have a good idea." I took his hand.

"Yeah ... I could use one now," he said, giving me a weak smile.

"Remember when we were in Charleston? What do you think about getting some of those great smelling plants to put all around the house?"

"Confederate Jasmine?" Jim smiled. "That would be a great idea. The best idea I've heard all day." He laughed, slumping deeper into the sofa.

Chapter Thirty-Six

The welcoming soft cushions of the sofa were irresistible after the stress of the past weeks. We fell asleep, my head on Jim's shoulder. Hours later, the annoying ring of the phone brought us back to reality.

"Maybe we shouldn't answer it," Jim said. "No news is definitely good news."

"It could be my office. Or yours for that matter. I think we have to answer it." I said, as we sat there staring at it.

On the fourth ring, we both reached for it.

"Hello?" Jim sounded tentative. "Doug, what's going on? I managed to get everything straightened out with Angela. We should be heading back to DC tomorrow."

I sat beside him, wringing my hands. *Why was Doug calling?*

Jim straightened up and looked at me. "Right now? We're on our way!" Jim smiled as he put down the phone. He rose and pulled me up off the sofa.

"What?"

"That was Doug," he said with excitement shining in his eyes. "He thinks there is a turtle nest hatching in front of his house."

I gasped. This was the last thing I expected.

"What ... now?" I looked out the window.

We had been asleep for some time. The clouds over the ocean were turning pink from the setting sun.

"But it's not dark."

"Yep. It's really unusual for the hatchlings to emerge in daylight, but that rain shower that passed over may have cooled the sand enough to bring them out. I'm thinking it's a great chance for you to get some photos."

I beamed as realization set in.

"Right," I exclaimed as I grabbed my camera bag.

We slipped on sandals and were out the door, making our way down the path in a matter of minutes. The beach was nearly empty.

The sun was low in the western sky, creating long shadows as we made our way toward the nest. We passed a few tourist stragglers, sandy and sunburned, heading home. We quickly walked up the beach toward Doug's cottage. There was a small group of people staring at what looked like a flat patch of sand. Doug was coming down his steps and gave us a wave. We joined the group, wide-eyed and leaning over with our hands on our knees; we looked at the sand surrounded by orange tape, trying to see any trace of what was about to happen. A slight breeze blew grains of sand over any tell-tale signs of turtle activity.

"Doug, what makes you think this nest is ready to hatch?"

"Yep, I hear you. You can't see much now because the wind has covered it up, but earlier you could see a small dip in the sand. That's a sure sign the nest is hatching." He pointed to a smooth bit of sand we had been watching.

A little girl looked from Doug to me. Shaking her head in agreement, she looked so serious I couldn't help but smile at her.

"Hi sweetheart, what's your name? My name is Kate."

"Hi, I'm Vivian. My mom and dad and I are visiting from Ohio." She was so excited, she danced from one foot to the other. "There was a big dip, like someone pushed a bowl down into the sand. Really! Right there." She pointed at the sand.

"Wow, that's really exciting," I said. I enjoyed listening to this child sharing her knowledge.

"Do you know what kind of turtles these are?" I knew that loggerheads nested on Isle of Palms, but I couldn't resist her enthusiasm.

"Mr. Doug told me that the nest was laid by a loggerhead mama," she said, her eyes wide. "And guess what?"

"What?"

"There might be a hundred eggs in the nest. A hundred! I can't believe it!" She clasped her hands together close to her chest.

"That is really fantastic." I looked over at Doug, trying to hide my smile.

"Well ladies," Doug said. "We might be in for a long wait. Ya'll might as well sit down and relax."

Jim had been standing behind me enjoying my conversation with my new young friend. "It looks like we are in for a wait. I'm going back to the house to get something to sit on."

"And maybe something to nibble on." I added with a plea in my voice.

"You got it," he said. "You and Vivian can keep guard while I'm gone." He winked at me and headed back up the beach.

Vivian's parents introduced themselves, and I loved how supportive they were of their daughter's interest in the turtles. After we chatted, they set up their folding beach chairs off to the side of the nest and made themselves comfortable. They knew not to get in the way of the parade of hatchlings as they crawled to the sea. Everyone settled in for a wait, no matter how long it would take.

"So, how old are you?" I asked Vivian.

She held up her hands to show me she was nine.

"Almost," Vivian amended. Then she added, "I'm gonna be a scientist when I grow up."

"Really?" I replied. I just nodded and let her talk.

"Or a policeman."

"Policewoman," I corrected.

Vivian giggled and put her hand over her mouth. I loved how children at this age believed fiercely that they could be anything they wanted. Such imagination and courage were uplifting after all I'd been through over the past weeks. It gave me hope for the future.

"Why a policewoman and a scientist?"

Vivian's expression grew serious.

"I want to help the turtles."

"I get the scientist," I said. "But why the policewoman?"

She looked at me like I was daft. "Because of the holes on the beach," she exclaimed, lifting her hands for emphasis. "People dig deep holes in the sand. Some people even fill them with water and sit in them." She leaned closer. "Do you know what my daddy calls those deep holes?"

When I shook my head she said, "Hillbilly hot tubs." She put her hand to her mouth again and giggled.

I laughed, too. Vivian continued in all seriousness, "If a little hatchling fell into a hole, it wouldn't be able to get out of it. And it would die."

"People could get hurt, too. I have an idea. Maybe we should fill in any holes in front of the nest," I suggested.

She jumped to her feet. "Yes! Let's do it. I'll take care of that." She was off, using her hands and feet to scrap sand into every hole she could find. She came back, quite satisfied with her efforts until she realized that her footprints created a whole new group of dangers for the tiny hatchlings.

We were discussing how to solve the problem when Jim was back, loaded with two beach chairs, a couple of towels, and a cooler filled with goodies. I waved him over.

"You two look very serious. Has anything happened?" He looked at us and then at the patch of sand. "Look. Hasn't that changed?"

We scrambled closer to the nest. There was a tiny funnel shaped hole about the size of a tip of a sharpened pencil. Vivian and I were down on our hands and knees with our noses about a foot from the surface of the sand.

"I don't remember that being there. Do you?" I looked at Vivian.

Vivian shrugged, then her expression changed. "We've got to rid of my footprints!" She seemed panicked.

"What's the problem ladies?" Jim asked.

"Jim, you haven't been formally introduced to my new turtle friend. This is Vivian. She's going to be a scientist when she grows up. Or a policewoman." I smiled at Vivian.

"Hi, Vivian, so nice to meet you. My name is Jim." He waved to Vivian's parents. "So, about your footprints. How about using the bottom edge of my beach chair like a rake? You can drag it along the sand and smooth out all the footprints. Then walk back to the nest from the side. That way. everything will be smooth."

Vivian perked up and was on her feet with the folded beach chair. She dragged the chair behind her, covering up all the footprints and dips in the sand.

"Nice job," I told him.

Jim unfolded the other chair, and we settled in to watch our young friend's comical attempts to rake the beach with the edge of a lawn chair. The sun was still illuminating the clouds over the ocean, but it wouldn't be too long before we would lose the light. Vivian came back, tired but quite pleased with her job well done. She leaned down to see if there had been any progress with our nest.

"Look, there's another tiny hole!"

We hustled over to get a closer look. Sure enough, there was another little funnel-shaped hole.

"It's happening," Doug said. "But again, this could take a few hours."

"Let's sit a little closer to the nest," Jim suggested.

We moved the chairs closer to the side of the nest. Vivian went over to her parents to update them on the nest's progress. By the time she came back to sit with us, one of the holes was getting bigger. It looked as if the sand was sliding down the hole like an hourglass. We were so intent on watching the small hole we didn't notice a couple of lumps of sand which had popped up on the surface. By then, all of us were sitting around the nest staring at the sand.

"Look! The sand is moving." Vivian pointed at the nest.

A crack had formed near the little lumps, and you could see a four-inch circle of sand heaving.

I reached over, took Jim's hand, and gave it a squeeze. "This is absolutely magical. I can't believe we are sitting here witnessing this miracle. *And* it's all that we have to think about." I laughed out loud. "Seeing it all through Vivian's eyes makes it even more special."

I leaned in, and Jim kissed my cheek.

"Look, look, look," Vivian squealed. "I can see a flipper. Oh! *and* a little head. They are so cute and so tiny."

Doug had been sitting quietly until now.

"Hey sweet girl, remember they can hear you. You don't want to scare the little critters."

"Oh, I am so sorry," Vivian whispered. That brought a smile to all our faces. "How much longer do you think?"

"They're coming," Doug answered. "There's a lot of work going on down there. All the hatchlings have hatched out of the shells. They lie there for a while, waiting for the shells to straighten. And you know what? All of them are breathing. Then they all start to dig their way up to the top, and then they wait. Then, something triggers them to climb out of the nest. We don't know what that is, but it may be the cooling of the sand in the evening. Once they get started, they just keep moving. See? There they go!"

The whole surface of the nest was beginning to heave and shift. The first little hatchling swung his flippers and somehow managed to climb out of the nest. We all collectively sighed. Vivian put her hand to her mouth to cover her squeal.

"That's the scout," Doug said. "We don't know why there is a lone turtle that comes out first. It's not like he comes back and makes a report," he added, chuckling at his own joke.

We watched the lone hatchling head right toward the ocean in its determined, if comical, crawl. Suddenly, the nest heaved, and the surface was teeming with hatchlings. I was so enthralled with the scene, I almost forgot about taking any photos. I turned to grab my camera bag and to my surprise, Jim had gotten my Nikon out of the bag and handed it to me. I looked up at the sky. There was just enough light for me to get a few shots. I could not use a flash near the turtles. After checking the settings, I started to shoot. I wanted to get a shot of Vivian. The look on her face was priceless. All sorts of emotions—happy, excited, amazed, and with tears welling up—all at once. I knew I really didn't need photos to remember this moment, but I was sure Vivian would love to have some to show her friends back in Ohio. I was losing the light, but with a little extra work in the darkroom, I would have some good shots.

"How's it going? Are you getting anything good?" Jim whispered.

"No prize winners, but the look on Vivian's face is priceless. It's amazing how quickly the hatchlings move. Luckily for me they stop periodically."

We both looked toward the ocean; over a hundred three-inch hatchlings were racing to the water. They crawled and pushed each other out of the way. Instinct had taken over, and they had one goal—to make it to the safety of the sea.

We were their honor guard, walking beside the hatchlings, protecting them from squawking gulls overhead and the pincers of ghost crabs on the beach.

"It's so fantastic," I said.

"Only one in a thousand of these little guys will make it to be a mature adult."

"Don't tell me that. Those are terrible odds." I looked at Jim. "Actually, seeing how small and vulnerable they are, I guess it's not really surprising."

"Hopefully, in thirty years or so, some of the hatchlings from this beach will come back to nest in South Carolina."

"And hopefully, we will be here to see them." I smiled at the thought of being here with Jim for what seemed like a lifetime.

"Let's walk down to the water's edge." I could see the tiny hatchling tracks clearly on the freshly raked sand. As they made their way to the water, their tracks fanned out. Vivian came up next to me and gave me a big hug. I put my arm around her shoulder and kissed her on the top of her head.

"This is the most important night of my life. I will never forget it." Vivian had the most serious look on her face.

We watched in awe as the hatchlings crawled down to the water's edge and fearlessly entered the sea. Some were carried off by an outgoing wave. Others were swept up and tumbled back to shore. Instinct persevered, and they righted themselves and headed back out.

In a matter of minutes, they were all gone. All swimming toward their destiny. In the aftermath, we hugged and shared a moment of joy. I lined everyone up next to the outgoing tracks and got a couple of shots that I would send to them, so they'd have a keepsake of this special event. With no turtles on the beach, there were no worries about disturbing nature with a flash. I took a notebook out of my camera bag.

"Vivian, I'd like to send you some photos of the nest. Can you give me your address?"

"Would you?" she exclaimed. "That would be great. I'll take them to school to show them to my friends. They will be so jealous."

We said goodbye with hugs all around. Vivian was still talking as she walked off with her parents.

"I'm thinking that little girl will not be sleeping much tonight." Jim laughed. He looked at me. "And neither will you. Doug, we're leaving tomorrow morning, so I won't see you. I can't thank you enough for tonight and for everything."

"No worries. I'm glad you got to see this. Man, it never gets old."

"Thanks so much, for everything," I said, feeling suddenly teary-eyed.

"Please drive carefully," Doug said. "Kate, I'd love to see a couple of the photos you took tonight."

I hugged Doug and promised to send some shots.

As Jim opened the front door of the beach house, an envelope fell to the ground. He reached down, picked it up, and handed it to me.

"Probably someone asking for a donation for a charity down here." Doug waved goodbye.

The envelope had no markings on it. I was going to toss it on the table, but my curiosity got the better of me. I ripped it open. There was a single sheet of paper with a single typed sentence. It sent a chill through me. All it said was …**We know who you are and what you've done**. I folded it up and shoved it into the table drawer. *I'd deal with it later*. I couldn't let this ruin what was a perfect end to a stressful day. I walked back to the beach, looking for Jim. In the last glimmers of light on this fateful day, his profile was strong, determined, and yet, there was a tenderness embedded in his features. A goodness of character that had been revealed in our most dire moments. I took his hand. He turned his head, and our gazes met.

In that moment, I knew we were ready to turn the page and really start our life together.

THE BEGINNING

About the Author

Born in Chicago and raised in the Midwest, Barb Bergerf discovered her passion for photography at an early age. After earning a degree in International Affairs from George Washington University, she worked in government service before returning to Chicago, where she built a career in photojournalism, including time as a staff photographer for the Chicago Tribune.

A lifelong creative, she later founded an award-winning stained-glass studio in Northfield, Illinois, where she spent more than twenty years creating and teaching Tiffany-style stained-glass.

Now based in South Carolina's Lowcountry, she works as a photographer with organizations including the Center for Birds of Prey, the South Carolina Aquarium, and the Island Turtle Team.

Her debut novel, *Fatal Exposure*, brings together a lifetime of visual storytelling and a long-held passion for writing.

Acknowledgements

Writing is a solo endeavor, but for me, it was backed up by loyal and loving friends. They encouraged, prodded, and pushed me forward. Without their help, this book would still be a dream and not a reality.

Marion Dier, Cindy Moore, Bonnie Havrda, and Sally Murphy pushed me to get the words on paper, but the true champion of my work is Mary Alice Monroe. Her love and support have made this possible. She is a great writer, but more than that, a tough taskmaster and teacher.

A special thank you to the talented young writers at Green Ferns Publishing House. Hopefully, this is the beginning of a wonderful relationship.

www.ingramcontent.com/pod-product-compliance
Lightning Source LLC
Chambersburg PA
CBHW030428160726
47991CB00005B/1635